# SUMMERFIELD 1:

# SUMMER STORM

## BY

## LAZETTE GIFFORD

Summerfield 1: Summer Storm
A Conspiracy of Authors Publication
www.aconspiracyofauthors.com
Copyright © 2021, Lazette Gifford
ISBN: 978-1-936507-97-9
Cover Art: Copyright © 2021, Lazette Gifford


First Print Edition, April 2021

# TABLE OF CONTENTS

# CHAPTER 1

Lightning blinded me -- the flash so bright that for one heart-pounding second I thought an atomic bomb had gone off over the city. I hit the brakes at the same time thunder shook the world and wind swept through the area in a frantic gust, driving dirt and debris across sidewalks and the street. I still feared the end of the world until rain began to fall in a sudden deluge.

Just a storm after all.

Although *just* didn't approach the description for the sudden fury unleashed around me. Rain obscured the view as though a semi-sheer curtain dropped between me and the rest of the world. A moment later hail the size of marbles fell in a pinging frenzy as they dented the car and shredded leaves from nearby trees.

Despite the weather, a wave of relief rushed through me at how lucky I had gotten this morning. If I hadn't played the good son and gone out to help with some paperwork at my parents' house, I would have been walking to work in this mess.

I contemplated my luck while hail approaching the size of golf balls hit the corner of my hood. I stomped on the gas and darted for the underpass beneath the railroad crossing about two blocks away. Various sizes of hail pounded against the windshield as the car slid on the slick street. I saw a half dozen other cars far ahead, but no one nearby as I came to an ungraceful stop beneath the concrete bridge. Torrential rain and large hail pounded the world outside my little shelter, changing my view of 13th Street into a veil of running colors, swirled by a vicious, erratic wind which changed direction with each gust.

Dangerous storm. Lightning hit a tree about three blocks away, shattering pieces of a limb. The roar of sound afterwards made the car tremble and I blinked as bright patterns played across my eyes. For a moment I thought I saw odd shapes racing across the intersection a block away. I blinked: They disappeared. Good. I had enough weird in my life.

With nothing better to do, I turned on the radio. Lighting cascaded across the cloudy sky and trailed static on the stations, but I fiddled with the settings until I could hear voices.

". . . unexpected! An unusual cold inversion along the Missouri River came out of nowhere and hit the warm front and . . . chaos!" The woman sounded breathless, and static covered a few words before I could hear again. "We're getting some of the wildest readings on Doppler I've ever seen!"

Static rose over her words. I tried another setting.

". . . Lake Manawa," a man shouted, loud even over the storm and the interference. "Damnedest thing I ever saw! The sky lighted like a bomb went off!"

"There was no bomb," the DJ replied, cutting him off. Wise to quash that rumor right away. At least I hadn't been the only one who had experienced the gut-wrenching moment of fear. "This is nothing more than a very unusual storm. We have another call . . ."

". . . Angels calling out to hold tight, to hold back. This is the apocalypse . . ."

*My.* The storm had unsettled quite a few people. I fiddled with the radio, watching hail build up on the ground and looking like a fall of hard snow. The winds began to lessen, though the rain continued to fall as though someone had opened a spigot. A huge limb swept past in the growing rush of water and a pond began to grow in the depression beneath the bridge. I'd have to leave soon or risk water in the engine.

". . . Flying through the sky . . ."

Another limb wedged itself into my little sanctuary, so I eased the car forward, despite the hail. The tires slipped on the slick road and leaving even the slight depression proved difficult.

"... Adams Park," a woman said over the static. "And it's raining huge rocks!"

I glanced towards grey clouds glimpsed between the snap of my windshield wipers and fervently discounted the idea of falling rocks. The hail proved bad enough, pinging off the roof and hood with loud thumps. I fought the wheel of the car and pushed on the gas, fearing the storm would sweep me away with the rest of the debris.

And my cell phone went off; *Age of Aquarius* rang out, startling me into a breathless curse. The tune repeated twice. My boss was calling, of course. She has an incredible knack for calling at the wrong time. I pulled over to the curb and yanked on the emergency break. My hands trembled as I took out the phone.

"Julia." I tried to sound calm while hail fell harder, and a circle of cracks appeared in the middle of my windshield.

"Summerfield." She sounded distracted and I could hear the police band radio in her office squawking in the background. Things sounded lively. I switched off my radio but could barely hear her. "Where are you?"

"Not far from the office."

"Walking?"

"No. I drove out my parents' house today."

"Bless the Lady. I worried," she replied with such

sincerity I remembered one of the reasons I enjoy working for her.

She must have leaned closer to the police band radio; feedback made me yank the cell phone away from my ear with a near curse. I thought I had heard someone yelling about Valkyries this time. Damned odd weather when you can get the Angels of God and Norse Valkyries in the same storm.

"You there?" she asked.

I dared to put the phone to my ear. "Yes. I'm waiting out the storm."

"What's that odd pinging noise?"

"Hail hitting the car." I could count the insurance money with each of those dings in the hood and the new chip in the windshield glass.

"We have hail here, too," she replied.

"About six blocks away. What are the odds?"

"I don't know. I'll have to find someone who can tell me." Sometimes irony is lost on this woman though she made me smile. "I'm glad you have your car, Summerfield. Tessa gave me a reading last night and said today would be important. Hold on. I have to check something."

Tessa, the astrologer, ran a little shop about two blocks from the office of Wolton World News, where I worked. The paper covers stories on the *unusual* side. Julia frequented Tessa's place for readings and Tessa had been right predicting this one with the angels and Valkyries and falling rocks.

Julia Wolton, owner and publisher of Wolton World News had a knack for smelling out good stories for the paper, even here in Omaha which is not exactly the arcane capital of the world. People reported from several places around the world, and she had hired two local reporters to cover stories she unearthed and to rewrite material from elsewhere.

I enjoyed my job, though I wasn't certain you could call my coworker, Jacobs, a reporter. He got far too many of his stories from the bottom of a beer bottle and I spent too much time fixing the man's prose to consider him a writer of any sort. He fabricated more than he investigated, and we had to double check everything. He did answer phones, though, and sometimes we needed him in the office to catch things while Julia and I did the real work.

Someday there would be an accounting for his actions. *Karma.* I'd seen the power at work too often in the past to doubt the ongoing tally of good and bad. Jacobs' attitude and ethics inched him ever closer to a big fall. I'd try not to snicker.

The storm eased. Water, mud, bits of trees and other debris raced along the edge of the street. Stalled cars sat in the street ahead and a few people took cautious steps outside. A blue jay landed on the hood of my car, glanced around as though startled by the destruction, and took off with a raucous shout of protest.

"I've got something for you, Summerfield," Julia said, startling me. "Something came in about two minutes ago -- a report from out near Ralston, along the Big Papio Trail. Several people have spotted a huge, strange cat."

I held the phone out and stared. Angels of God, Norse Valkyries, falling rocks, storms like atom bombs going off . . . and she wanted me to go check into a lost cat story?

"Summerfield?"

"Cat?"

"The police have sent a couple squad cars already," she added, which at least made this sound a little more interesting. "They have several witnesses in the area."

"Something loose from the zoo?"

"The zoo says no. Maybe someone raising a big cat got careless. The people out there are saying this is a strange cat, though. Can you go check? Or I can wait for Jacobs to come in and send him instead."

I sometimes think she plays the Jacobs card on purpose because she knows I don't trust him to report honestly on anything. I snarled something rude under my breath.

"Summerfield?"

"Yes, fine. Where am I going?"

"The police are at the Big Papio Trail along Towl Park. Stay off the main roads. I'm hearing reports of stalled cars and accidents throughout the city. And don't go anywhere near the Interstate or Bypass. It'll be hours before they clear that mess out!"

Good warnings. I inched the car towards a driveway where I could turn around. I would have been closer if I'd stayed at my parents' place for a while longer.

"I'll see what I can find, Julia."

"Good luck. Goddess go with you."

I dropped the phone on the seat beside me and began the laborious work of going back the way I had come. I couldn't get through on 13th because of stalled cars and downed power lines. I cut through side streets, helped clear two branches, and found damaged trees all the way to the Henry Doorly Zoo. The Desert Dome looked to be intact. I hoped the botanical gardens hadn't been hit too badly.

I found less damage once I got south of the zoo. I didn't think I would have too much trouble getting to Ralston.

Where I would go looking for a big lost kitty.

The clouds moved in odd ways, and sometimes the wind gusts came so hard I had to fight the steering wheel to keep from careening off the road. Once I thought I heard voices somewhere above me; my imagination playing with me after the radio reports.

After more than an hour, I arrived at the area of the missing cat and found two police cars and big crowd. Given the weather, I would have thought they'd have better things to do. Ah, but maybe watching the Big Papio rise in its banks drew many of them out here. I could see it stood almost bank full already. Not a good sign.

I parked well back in the Towl parking lot with a half dozen other cars and dropped my cell phone under the passenger side seat for safekeeping. I hated when the thing went off in the middle of an interview. I also grabbed my press pass from the glove compartment and a camera bag from the backseat before I braved the weather and threw open the door.

I don't know how it could be so hot, humid and raining at the same time. I'm used to summer weather in the Midwest, but I paused, almost gasping this time. As I crossed the lot, the rain lessened to a drizzle, which was no help since I was already drenched. I could see trash rolling into piles near the storm drains and rivulets of rainwater rushing through the street. However, the storm hadn't hit this area as hard as some locations I had driven through.

Clouds skittered across the sky in several layers, and each chaotic mass headed in a different direction. I'd seen such movement happen with two layers before, but not four or five. I watched in amazement for a moment and then forced myself to head for work.

The cops were starting to herd some of the people away from the trail along the banks. Holding up my press pass won a couple grunts and nods until a tall, lanky cop with gray sideburns, a mustache, and a no-nonsense look stopped me. His plastic raincoat couldn't be comfortable, though at least he stayed dry.

"Summerfield?" he said looking at the press pass. The plastic made an odd crinkling noise as he moved. "I'm Officer Lenz and I'm in charge here. I have rules. Don't go down the bank to get closer to the water. It's moving pretty damned fast and the bank is slick. The cat was last seen heading south, so unless you want to chance meeting the animal by yourself, don't get out of sight."

"Did you see the cat?"

"Nah. But the first cop here did see some tracks before the rain washed them away."

"What am I looking for?"

"Huge golden-brown cat with *glowing* green eyes." He stared me straight in the face without even a glimmer of a smile.

"Right."

I headed towards the closest group of people watching the water and asked who had seen the cat. After four tries I found a nervous, anorexic woman of about thirty who must have been out jogging. Her mascara ran in lines from the corner of her eyes and her bleached blond hair hung in limp strands, clearly showing the darker roots. She'd be appalled when she realized how bad she'd looked in public.

"Yes. I saw it not long after the rain started. The cat ran right past me!" She gulped air a couple times. "The zoo -- the zoo will be held accountable for this. They should do better!"

"The zoo hasn't lost any cats. Someone near here might have illegally raised something --"

"No one in *this* neighborhood would do such a thing!"

I buried an amused grin. "Well, cats can run for quite a distance. Can you describe the animal?"

"Golden and brown, ticked fur," she said and her eyes narrowed. She held up her hands, flashing perfectly manicured fingernails which didn't look any more natural than her hair. "A long tail, too. Not short haired, but not a Persian or angora length, either. Would have made a gorgeous coat."

"Thank you." I pulled out a little notebook I always keep in my pocket and jotted notes, hoping I could keep the paper dry enough to avoid the ink running like her makeup. Glancing upward, I could darker clouds moving in, promising more trouble soon.

The woman dabbed at her eyes, got a horrified look on her face, and hurried away without saying anything more. I moved on to another group of people, but most had arrived after they saw the cops show up.

One person had seen the cat sniffing around at the edge of the trail. He gave the same general description, adding that the face had been a little flat, the eyes huge and glowing and with paws a peculiar long and narrow shape.

Julia would love the part about the glowing eyes if I could get the detail confirmed somehow. I followed the path along the edge of the Big Papio with a wary eye on the weather and the water. The winds kicked up and rain fell in a sudden burst and stopped again a moment later. The crowd thinned out and one cop car took off so I didn't think anything more would come of this.

I considered leaving. I glanced at the clouds and felt as though I stood in the heart of a hurricane, with everything swirling around in different directions. The sight could almost make a person dizzy.

"Damned impressive, ain't it?"

A short, older black man moved along the path towards me. The weather didn't bother him in the least. He squinted through raindrops on his gold-rimmed glasses and brushed water from his short, coarse hair as he watched the sky for a moment before turning back to me.

"I've never seen a storm like this," I admitted.

"Me neither. Lived here all my life and the weather can still surprise a person. Sure hope it doesn't get any colder, though. Don't want snow."

"This is summer," I pointed out.

"Yeah?"

Okay, the weather had been odd enough. I couldn't tell what might happen next, so he had a point.

"My neighbor told me you asked about the cat," he said.

"You're a reporter?"

I held out a hand. "Summerfield, from the Wolton World News."

We shook. He had calloused hands and a good grip. "Tim Dorey, from the Retired and Damned Glad of It. Wolton World News -- that's the odd paper, ain't it?"

"Yes."

"Well, this is odd enough," he admitted. "Biggest damned cat I've seen outside of a Siberian Tiger. I worked for the zoo for twenty years, and I've never seen or heard of anything to compare to this one. I'm going to call my old boss and tell him about it."

I grabbed my notebook and began to take notes not only on what he'd seen, but also who to contact at the zoo. He gave me an excellent description with the height of about four feet at the shoulders, lean, long legged and with big, oddly shaped paws. The face had been somewhat flat like a tiger, with small ears and green eyes. He didn't say glowing, but I saw the way his eyes twitched at that point.

"Has to be some kind of cross-breed," he said, shaking his head. "You can cross a lot of the big cats, you know. Lions with tigers and such. Or something mutated. I don't know. It was just the damnedest thing I'd ever seen, though. The cat saw me, too. I couldn't have outrun it."

"What happened?"

"The truth? The cat nodded his head like he was saying howdy-do and walked down to the edge of the creek bed. Well-trained. Maybe something from a circus? You know, sometimes they dye the animals and trim them up to look odd."

"Maybe," I agreed. I could tell he didn't believe such a simple answer. I did not, suddenly, want to think about such an animal loose in Omaha.

"Odd day. Damn strange storms, damn strange cats."

Tim Dorey glanced around as though he expected something else strange to turn up. "I hope things don't get worse."

Lightning flickered across the sky, several bolts darting from cloud to cloud. The wind bore down on us and rain began to pound the area in a torrent. We both glanced up and back at each other. Mr. Dorey shrugged.

"I think I'll just head back to my apartment," he said with a casual nod. "Before I provoke the Almighty into some other little show of humor. Get out of the rain before you catch a cold."

"Thanks for the information." I shook his hand once more. He appeared pensive. "You have something else?"

"Yeah. But this will sound odd."

"This is the day for it."

He laughed, brushing rain from his hair. "Okay, this is going to sound more than odd. I saw the cat there by the bank and I swear he searched for something. He'd dig a little bit at the weeds and then move on. Not hunting the way normal cats do, big or small. Cats, when they hunt, get all tight-muscled and slinky. This one acted annoyed and bothered in a . . . well, in a human way."

I glanced towards the Big Papio and measured the height of the water from the top of the banks. "Here?"

"Right there in the grass and weeds where everything is kind of flat. I don't know you should go down there, Summerfield --"

"You better get in out of the rain, Mr. Dorey," I said with a smile.

"You be careful. I don't care what anyone else thinks; I know what I seen and big cats are dangerous." He turned and walked away. He had a good point, and one to remember as I stood there in the rain. I knew I should head to the car, but I found myself staring at the flattened weeds and grass.

I had to know what might be hidden down there.

# CHAPTER 2

I slipped off the trail -- *slip* being the quite proper word -- and hurried through a covering of wildflowers. A rabbit darted away scaring the hell out of me.

I heard distant voices. They sounded as though they came from overhead and I flattened myself to the ground, expecting someone to go by on the path. No one did, so I moved towards the weeds.

The ground, already soaked, had become a slippery layer of muck. I cursed under my breath as the stream rushed by about a foot away from me. Water would soon cover this area where the cat had been hunting. I trusted Dorey told me the truth and his tale had intrigued me. He seemed a good, sane man.

Sane enough, in fact, to know better than to search the area where he'd seen the cat. No, no. I'm the one who went there in the pouring rain, with the day going dark again as thunder shook the world.

Lightning flashed in quick succession overhead and the wind gusted hard enough to make me slip. I grabbed at the wildflowers, as though they would keep me from sliding into the water. The area felt unsafe and dangerous as I moved to where the cat had been hunting. This is my job, I told myself and wondered why I didn't take a nice calm position working for the Nuclear Regulatory Committee. Good pay. Less mud. One would hope no huge mutant cats involved.

I reached the patch of weeds as a splattering of rain and small hail began to fall. I moved faster, remembering the huge stuff hitting my car earlier. I didn't want the cops searching for me, either. I had to hurry, so I scrambled around in the overgrown area, pushing aside a stand of yellow cinquefoil and wild lupine. Mud caked on my hands and knees.

The extra work proved to be worth the discomfort. As I parted the weeds, I found a paw print and it did look odd as hell with long thin pads and the claws had dug into the ground. I grabbed the camera out of the case and shot a few pictures before shoving it back in, out of the rain. If I hadn't talked to Tim Dorey, I would have believed someone had been out here dressed in a cat suit. But no one could have fooled him.

I scrambled around on my hands and knees, hoping to find something more, but the rain began to wash everything away. I didn't dare stay any longer, so I began to claw my way up the incline, still on my hands and knees. I paused halfway up and moved off to the right instead, but I couldn't decide why. I had learned to trust my instincts very early on in life, though.

I did find something odd. About halfway up the incline my fingers tangled in a small, silver chain. I pulled upward and found a round pendant about the size of a half dollar and covered in mud, dangling from the links. I held the medallion so the rain washed away the muck and I could see the outline of a dragon with emerald green eyes. I didn't recognize the odd writing. Intrigued, I turned the disk over a couple times --

I thought I heard shouting. I threw the chain over my neck, since the links appeared unbroken, and tucked the medallion into my shirt. I scrambled up to the trail and stood, brushing as much mud and plant debris from my clothing as I could.

I felt dizzy. So much so, I almost went back to my knees.

I think the wind had changed and the pressure dropped. The sky grew so dark, I half expected to see the coming of night with stars and a moon. Lighting branched from cloud to cloud and thunder shook the world. I wanted out of the storm.

I jogged along the path and found Lenz heading my way from the edge of the park. My timing had been good.

"There you are. Damn fool. Didn't you see the weather changing?"

"It came pretty fast," I complained, feeling breathless. I don't know why since I hadn't run far. Maybe he thought I had. He nodded, his plastic raincoat crinkling with sound.

"You find anything interesting out there?" Lenz asked, glancing down the path as if he expected some other fool to be out in this storm.

"One paw print right before the rain hit. Got a couple shots. And I found someone's lost necklace."

"We got a few shots, too. All of them off the bike path." He glared at me for a moment, but I said nothing. He sighed, as a father might with his wayward son, though he didn't lecture me. "Better get to your car. We're closing this area off. Not because of the cat. We're going to be bank full in about half an hour if this rain keeps up and we could have flooding afterwards. We don't want gawkers."

"I'm not a gawker," I protested but didn't argue as we headed up the incline towards the lot. "I'm a reporter."

"Tell me the difference."

"I get paid to gawk."

He gave a short cough of a laugh as we reached the edge of the lot. He even caught my arm when I started to slip. A nice guy and I hated to lie to him, even by omission. Best to move on and be glad he hadn't found me crawling around in the weeds. The rain fell in a torrent and Lenz watched the stream with a shake of his head, worried.

"Thanks for coming for me," I said. "Good luck here."

"I hope it doesn't go over the bank," he confessed. "But this isn't the worst place to be. I heard things are bad elsewhere in town."

"I drove across town from a few blocks south of Old Market. I saw some badly hit areas out there, but I think things could have been far worse considering how fast and strong the storm was."

"I didn't think anyone could get through from what I heard."

"Took some maneuvering." I glanced at the sky and frowned as the chaotic clouds began to move once more. "This is going to get worse. I need to get moving."

"True. Good luck."

Lenz waved me away and I jogged out towards edge of the lot -- and leapt back in haste as a car raced around the corner and squealed to a stop. A gutter full of rainwater splashed over me, but since I was already soaked I just sighed and stepped away.

Brian Kenwood stuck his head out the passenger side window of the black Eclipse. I tried not to snarl. Kenwood is an aging, wannabe yuppie with the kind of attitude that could make Mother Theresa want to reach over and slap him silly. He worked as a freelance reporter and sometimes we crossed paths. He'd had articles printed in a half dozen newspapers, all but one of them in Nebraska, which made him act superior and smug. I found his writing mediocre at best.

"Hey, it's the Woo Woo Reporter!" he shouted and drew not only my attention but also Lenz as well.

"Woo Woo?" Lenz asked, glaring as he came to my side.

"Wolton World News," I replied with a sigh. "Woo Woo is his nickname for it. He thinks he's funny or smart or something."

"Ah. Like he thinks driving recklessly on wet streets is

funny?" he asked, glancing at Kenwood.

"Yeah. Like that."

"You haven't fooled this good man into thinking you work for a *real* paper, have you?" Kenwood demanded, faking shock and dismay, though he came across as smug and condescending.

Lenz didn't appreciate the attitude any more than I did. He frowned as he leaned closer and stared Kenwood in the face. "He has a press pass. And you are?"

"Brian Kenwood." He waved his press pass like a flag. "I freelance for several *real* papers. Wolton World News is not a real newspaper."

"Could have fooled me since I have a subscription."

I glanced at the man, startled and he smiled. "My wife enjoys the paper. I've read some of the articles. You write interesting material, Summerfield. And you were right in the opinion piece last week. There's too damn much unusual stuff in the world to ignore, no matter what the real answer might be."

I couldn't have paid someone to do this for me. I worked very hard not to laugh in Kenwood's face.

"Thanks," I said while Kenwood muttered something beneath his breath. "Online Subscriptions doubled in the last four months, too, besides more print ones. We have almost as many overseas readers as we do here in the US. The website is getting well over two thousand hits a day on the archive stuff."

Kenwood snarled something and pulled his head into the car. Lenz leaned forward and held up a hand to stop him.

"Can you step out of the car please, Mr. Kenwood? I think we need to have a few words."

"I'm here to check out this cat story."

"Not much to see with this new rain. And we've closed the area off because of possible flooding. So you don't have anything to do but stay and talk with me."

"You let Summerfield in. You have to let me --"

"I don't have to do crap," Lenz replied and grinned quite brightly. I hadn't thought Kenwood was so stupid he would purposely annoy a cop. "However, for the record, Summerfield arrived before this new round of rain. You're just late to the show. So, let's talk about your driving, shall we?"

I left the good Officer Lenz to deal with Kenwood. I *did not* skip over to my car, though I felt the urge, despite the downpour. As soon as I got in, I began to write a few more notes on what I'd seen and heard from the others. I checked the camera, pleased to see my shots of the print came out well, even though they looked unreal. I'd have to take a print to the zoo and see if anyone there could identify the animal. I'd check some websites, too.

After I had jotted down everything I could think of, I pulled the phone out from under the seat and grimaced when I found a call had come through while I'd been out playing in the rain and splashing through mud puddles. Violet, my oldest sister, was not someone to ignore. I speed dialed her office and got the secretary who hadn't been working for Violet long. My sister is hard on the hired help.

"Can you tell Ms. Summerfield her brother returned her call, and I'll be in touch later? I'm working."

"Her brother?" she asked, sounding startled. I often hear the reaction. I have five older sisters, and they don't always mention me. "Can I give her a name?"

"She only has one brother." I laughed, enjoying the moment. "Let her know I called."

"Oh. Of course, Mr. Summerfield."

Sometimes I have way too much fun giving the secretaries a hard time since they often sound flustered by the idea of a brother in the family. I think my sisters don't mention me so they can enjoy the reaction, too.

The constant rain combined with playing in the mud had soaked my clothing and I felt a sudden chill. I kicked the heater on, holding my fingers out in front of the vent. *We would not have snow.* I could see Lenz and Kenwood standing in the rain, Brian with his hands in his pockets and his head bowed like a kid being lectured.

I smiled at the sight of Kenwood getting called to account about his childishness. Kenwood annoyed the hell out of me, pulling the 'Woo Woo' crap a few times too often. Even I thought the nickname funny the first time, but I didn't appreciate some of the insinuations. What Kenwood said might be true about Jacobs though, who I suspected invented most of his work. I did not, however. I had seen more than enough weird stuff out in the world, and I didn't mind working hard to find true stories for the paper.

The radio ran a litany of trouble throughout the city. The Interstate Bypass, Dodge, and a half dozen other high traffic roads remained impassable. I figured I could reach the Old Market by following the odd path I'd taken to get here, though.

When the hail started coming down, Kenwood and the cop both headed for their cars. I waited while Kenwood drove away, wondering if he would be in a worse mood than usual at our next meeting.

Would I be able to tell the difference?

Once Kenwood disappeared around a corner, I put my notepad in my pocket and realized the dragon necklace had disappeared. I couldn't find it in my shirt. The chain must have been broken after all and I knew it'd never find it out there in the rain and mud.

I drove away, keeping my eyes open for a big cat. I loved puzzles, which is why I enjoyed working for Wolton World News. This story was going to be fun.

And more exciting than I expected.

# CHAPTER 3

The drive to the office took longer than I expected since the last round of storms had knocked down more trees and flooding had grown worse, though nothing very dangerous. I saw broken windows on cars and buildings and counted myself lucky with my cracked windshield. It would have been hell trying to drive without that protection in this weather.

People milled about on corners and sometimes out in the street. I tried not to get annoyed and anxious as I crept forward. The radio reports returned to weather people talking about the unexpected severity of the storm and warning how the unstable mass of cold and warm fronts sat virtually on top of us.

I wanted inside a good strong building before another round hit. And besides, Julia would have tea or coffee, and maybe some warm rolls this morning. She lived upstairs from the Wolton World News office and she loved to bake. Last winter I had gained way too much weight but I never complained.

By the time I pulled into the private parking lot by the big, old building, the return of heat and humidity brought summer back in full force. I couldn't believe how fast things had changed and knew this wouldn't last for long.

As I got out of the car, I realized I couldn't feel the rhythmic pounding of the old printing press. Power out. At least Julia planned for problems so we had four days before the current issue would be late. I hoped the laptop's batteries held out for the story I wanted to write, though. I always wanted to get the first parts written while fresh in my brain.

Jacobs' old pickup sat parked in his spot. I had hoped he'd claim the weather as an excuse not to come in today, but from what I'd guessed, he found the office far better than being home with two preschoolers and a harassed wife. I felt sorry for Pam Jacobs who came to our Solstice Day dinner because Julia told Jacobs if he showed up, he had to bring his wife, too. I had the impression his job might depend on it. So we had a good party that night, with many local subscribers, the group that ran the printing press, some of the salespeople who call on us, and even UPS and FEDEX guys showing up.

The weather hadn't improved as I paused by the door to the building. Down the street, I could see the edge of the Old Market and quite a few people wandering around. Maybe they didn't know better or maybe the hotels lost power too. Sitting inside a room without the air conditioning and cable channels would have driven them mad. I wouldn't want to be out on the street if a storm broke loose, although Old Market had enough small businesses and open doors for them to get to cover.

The front door of the Wolton World News building opened to a landing with half a dozen steps to the main floor and a stairwell to the basement. Julia Wolton had moved in a somewhat outdated printing press and hired people who knew the esoteric, old-fashioned work. The print version of the paper mailed to places all over the world, while the Internet Edition had several thousand subscribers. People sent us reports from all around the world, many of which I reworked besides researching my own material.

I didn't see much of the crew who stayed in the basement and did the technical work of getting the paper out, but I could hear their voices from down the stairwell.

Julia heard me come in and she waved me enter her office to stop as I passed the door. She listened to her cell phone. Her blond hair, held back in a wide purple band to restrain the curls, still bounced whenever she nodded. She mumbled *yes* several times.

I leaned against the door frame and waited.

While the entry to the building appeared normal and sedate, with a nice potted fern in the corner and a framed cover of the first Wolton World News issue on the wall, once you got to Julia Wolton's office, you pretty much knew things weren't normal. She kept framed drawings of arcane symbols on most walls and anyone who knows Feng Shui would recognize a layout done by an expert. Incense burned by a statue of The Goddess, a figure representing the female and creative aspects of the universe. A Green Man mask hung on the opposite wall with a plant thriving below. She had Tarot cards laid out on her desk, probably trying to get a connection with the oddness today. I'd seen her do it before and she had some talent at reading the signs.

"Yes, Tessa. Thank you so much!" She flipped the cell phone closed and smiled. "Tessa says we're going to get a lot of interesting material from this storm. You have something?"

"A wonderful little mystery for us," I admitted and saw her smile grow. She never wore makeup and the lines around her eyes showed she was older than people first guessed. I told her about what I'd learned and whom I had talked to, and then showed her a picture of the paw print. She clapped her hands with delight.

"Go write. This is great work, Summerfield."

"I don't have enough for an article yet," I reminded her. "But I have interesting pieces. I'll wait and call the zoo this afternoon or maybe go out there with the picture and talk to someone. I suspect they're busy with the storm, too."

"Yes, you're right. Don't bother them yet," she agreed.

Thunder shook the window behind her and we both glanced out at the street, watching the rain splash against the cement yet again. I shook my head and felt a few drops of water slip out of my hair and run down my neck. I grimaced and tried to wipe some of the dampness away.

"Go get something warm to drink. I'll have cinnamon rolls ready in about half an hour," she said, glancing at her watch. The day grew darker outside. "I wish it would stop doing that."

I nodded agreement and headed to the room I shared as an office with the other reporter. Jacobs hadn't heard me come in. He sat with his feet on a second chair while he read a porn magazine. Okay, he looked at the pictures. I'd never seen him read anything, including his own articles.

And he'd moved things around in the room. Jacobs thought it funny, but Julia didn't. She believed in the ways of Feng Shui (and many other things as well), and Jacobs didn't quite get it. I'd noticed he didn't take women seriously in general and one as his boss didn't rate any higher than the one who married him.

The solar panels on the roof of the building had provided enough stored power for the coffee machine and a few blue lights in the walls, giving the big, long room an eerie glow. With the storms, the panels wouldn't be working today, and I hoped the power came on before things went out. I wanted my coffee to keep warm.

Jacobs lowered the magazine, as though I wouldn't have noticed. "What the hell are you doing here?" he demanded as I went past his desk.

"I work here. Which is more than I can say for you." I kicked the second chair out from under his feet and he grunted as he fell forward. I returned the chair to the spot by the wall, snagged the plant and put it back in the corner and straightened a picture by the coffee machine. He smirked when I got my coffee and I wondered how many karma points I'd lose if I accidentally spilled my cup on him. Not worth the trouble. Besides, Pam would have to clean the clothes and I wouldn't purposely make more work for her.

I went to my desk and pulled the laptop from the drawer. My notes had run a little in the rain, but I remembered everything, so I had no trouble typing the preliminary article in the half hour before Julia brought us the cinnamon rolls. My stomach growled. She made certain I had a couple and gave one to Jacobs and took the rest to her office where she would share them with anyone who came in today. The UPS and FED EX people loved to stop here, though I wondered if any of them would be on the roads today. I glanced out the high placed row of windows between us and the wall of the building next door and could see rainwater pouring from the gutter spout.

As soon as Julia left, Jacobs leaned back in his chair and pulled out the magazine.

"How about putting that away and doing some work?" I said, glancing at queue of material still waiting to be formatted.

"Hey, you aren't the Bossy." He flipped through some pages and made kissy noises.

Karma, karma, karma.

A few minutes later Julia returned. She glanced at me, and then at Jacobs who had grabbed a pen and pretended to jot something on a scrap of paper.

"Jacobs, go help the guys downstairs reset the press. Oakley couldn't get here today, and Masterson needs help so they'll be ready when the power comes back on."

"Why me? Why not Summerfield?" He sounded like a kid whining to his mother, which didn't impress Julia.

"Because Summerfield has an assignment he's working on. All you have is a tits and ass magazine. So, get moving."

He shoved his chair away and stalked out of the room. I

went back to work.

Julia brought me another roll.

Sometime around noon the power came back on. The sudden whirl of air conditioning and the flicker of lights startled me just before everything went dead once more. I heard Julia mumble out in the hall and turn the air conditioning off. The lights came back. Died. Came back. We'd gone through this with storms before.

I had almost drained the battery on the laptop, so I went to work with pen and paper, making notes on anything crossing my mind for the article. Free writing sometimes helps to expand my thoughts in fresh directions. A few minutes later, with some new angles I wanted to check out, I began calling people on my cell phone. I reached one lower echelon person at the zoo who agreed to check the paw print picture as soon as I could get one, but we still had no power. I said it would likely be tomorrow.

Unfortunately, I felt worse as the day wore on. I didn't think a cold would kick in this fast after my walk in the rain this morning. I sneezed a few times and felt wobbly when I went for coffee. I skipped lunch, though Jacobs, who got done downstairs too soon, made a big show of not missing his.

He smelled of chili, onions and beer when he returned, fifteen minutes late, none of which helped my already less than benevolent mood towards him. I made a couple more calls and with the power finally steady, I plugged in the laptop and checked websites about big cats.

Nothing fit what people had described. Odd, odd, odd. I even began checking cat costumes, cat robots, cat clothing. . . . I started wandering into sites which might interest Jacobs, but didn't help me with my work. Nothing matched up.

I sneezed and grabbed a tissue --

"Summerfield, go home," Julia said from the doorway. "You sound like hell and you look worse."

She sounded upset and perhaps guilty about sending me off on a story in this weather. I thought about arguing with her, but a glance at my watch showed little more than an hour to closing anyway. I had printed out copies of the paw print, but I could wait until tomorrow to take them to the zoo.

"Yeah, good idea." I grabbed the pictures from the printer and handed one to her at the door.

"Oh, this is wonderful!" She patted me on the shoulder. "Jacobs, make sure the website is updated before you go home."

Karma can be a real bitch if you're not careful.

I stepped outside and found the day hot and muggy, though I felt cold, which couldn't be good. Ragged pieces of leaves, shredded by the hail, littered the sidewalk, along with pieces of paper and a couple badly battered cans. I felt an odd kinship with the cans today.

I thanked God, Goddess, Karma and every other force in the universe which had set things, so I'd driven the car today. The idea of walking ten blocks home left me trembling. I hurried to the car and frowned. The Subaru's damage was worse than I had expected. I could see the dings from the hail all over the hood and roof, and a crack in the rear window as well. Even the sticker my sister Lily had slapped on the bumper as a joke -- *My other car is a Mercedes* -- had taken some damage. Damn.

Something moved in the alley between the Wolton World News building and the flea market next door. I squinted into the shadows and saw a big dog. I decided not to test if the creature was friendly or not. I got into the car and pulled out onto 10th Street.

But as I started out of the lot, I caught the glimpse of something huge as it stood up on two legs. I hit the brakes, rolled down the window and looked back, but whatever I had seen had already retreated. I thought I could hear the click of claws on the cement as the creature hurried away.

I drove around the block and checked the alley. I couldn't see anything. It must have been my imagination and the fever working overtime.

No huge mutant cats here. Definitely no huge mutant cats standing up on their back legs. No glowing green eyes, so what I saw couldn't have been real.

Yeah. Logic at its best.

I drove away and didn't look back.

# CHAPTER 4

I had to wait while hordes of tourists crossed the street near the Old Market. Quite a few glanced at the sky rather than at the quaint, cobblestone street. When I'm walking, I don't mind the tourists. I enjoy moving along with the crowds and listening to what they find interesting in the area. The fountain in the Heartland of America Park is often a favorite on hot summer days, though here in Old Market the food places usually win out over the quaint little shops. I imagined some of the people stopping at every little pub and restaurant, testing out the food.

A few blocks later I parked in the garage to my condo building and took the elevator up rather than the stairs. My apartment has a wonderful view of the Missouri River and the fountain. On good days, I go out on the balcony and watch the world. Today was *not* one of those days. I stumbled into the kitchen, dropping keys and cell phone and wallet on the counter. Then I heated water for tea in the microwave -- heresy, I know, but I wanted something in a hurry. I added some of my favorite private blend of tea, poured in honey, stirred, and went to the sofa.

I drank the cup of tea and decided bed would be better than sitting there, shivering. Bed and warm covers where I could let myself slip off into sleep. I felt exhausted. I stumbled into the room stripped to my underwear and crawled under the blankets, grateful to be still.

I didn't sleep so well.

The nightmare began almost immediately. I think I jerked awake once, grateful to be out of it -- but maybe I dreamed I was awake, because as soon as I went to sleep, I fell right back to the same spot.

I stood in the midst of a medieval battle. No, a fantasy battle. I could hear swords and the yells of men and other creatures as they fought. I directed things, which on one level scared the hell out of me since I know nothing about tactics and strategy. My dream self knew what to do, though.

People surged through the courtyard, shouting, angry, worried and afraid. Other *things* came out of the darkness and through the already destroyed gate: huge creatures, with red eyes and blood-stained mouths. I watched one catch a woman, break her neck, and bury his mouth in her chest. I could hear the crunch of bone and the tearing of flesh. I would have been ill, but the me in the dream ordered an attack.

When I raised my hands and blasted the creature, the magic felt right although I could see we wouldn't stand up to this onslaught.

"We can't hold!" I shouted. I heard cries of dismay and shock. "Get to the keep! Protect Vane!"

"There is no protection for me," someone said at my back. I spun to see a tall, thin man shaking his head with loss as he watched the continuing battle. "I must fight with you or we are all lost."

"If you are lost, sir, we lose ourselves. Go back to your chamber!"

"They have already breached my chamber. There is no safety, my friend."

Shock, horror; but I fought those emotions aside. We could not have fallen this easily! There had been treachery involved, but I didn't have time to hunt out the threads with all else falling around us.

I wouldn't give up! I spun to fight, creating my sword from the magic around me while trying to keep Vane at my back. He wouldn't stay from the battle, though. More of the clan surged in around us, and we formed a square, but the enemy broke through before we could draw on the power. Others rushed past the breached gate, swinging axes and killing everyone they saw. I couldn't tell the clan. They hid their identity from us.

I knew we couldn't hold against this unexpected onslaught, but I refused to give up the fight. We had to do something to survive.

"We have to go," I said, frantic as I tried to gather the others around me. "We have to get out of here. Retreat to one of the lesser holdings."

"There is no time," Vane replied, his voice steady. "But I will give you what help I can."

Vane began to change: his human outline melted, shifted, and grew. Huge. Gigantic. Others leapt away as the dragon took shape. I knew this meant we had little chance of winning if we needed the dragon to help us.

And we did need him. A wall of creatures of a sort I had never seen before swarmed through the gate: black, shapeless things moving in waves across the keep. These things came from the Other Side which made them dangerous and unpredictable. We were already losing against the other fae and creatures. We could not fight these as well. We used magic to drive them back, but they surged in around our spells and they swept in and killed everything they could reach.

Before I could shout a warning, they swarmed over the dragon who threw himself before them to protect the last of us. He howled and began thrashing. We all backed away, friend and foe alike. I had to help him!

Vane rose on his back legs, screamed to the sky, and threw himself amid the enemy, crushing everything he could. He battled with a fierceness I had never seen and broke a path for us to the gate. We could get clear!

The dragon fell and didn't get back up.

A great shout went up from the enemy, which spurred us to new anger, though we had lost all hope. I fought and killed everything I could, heedless of my own wounds, and reached the dragon. Vane blinked at me, the emerald green eye already half clouded. Wounds bled everywhere across his damaged silver scales.

"Get the egg," he whispered with a sound too soft from such a huge creature. "Get the egg and go . . . elsewhere."

"*We won't let you go.*"

His eyes closed; his breathing stopped. I saw a flutter of color lift from his skin, dance in the air and dart into the keep. The essence of Vane would migrate to the dragon egg and impregnate it with life so the dragon could be born again. We had to protect the egg, which I knew we couldn't do here.

"Get the egg!" I shouted. The others hadn't realized the dragon had died and a cry of despair rose around me. I sent a wave of magic at the enemy and so did a dozen others, using all we could to make a shield, though the magic wouldn't hold long. "Get the egg! Gather, everyone gather! We're going to ride the wind. We're going *outbound*!"

I heard more calls of alarm, but everyone obeyed. People came from the keep carrying something large wrapped in magic. We didn't have time to take more precautions. Damned dangerous work, to take off like this.

"Brandis, try to center us," I yelled to a man who came limping towards me. He had good, strong magic.

The shield started to flare and break. I glanced frantically around. "Protect the egg! You hold our hope of the future!"

We grabbed horses out of the magical wild. I glanced back at the dragon's body and shook my head as I put my hand to the symbol at my neck. "We will meet again, Vane. You'll remember us."

We wove magic so strong it felt like fire in the air. The

shield went down, and we dashed through the gate and out of the keep and through the wall of ancient magic which should never have been breached. Treason, I thought, but I didn't know by whom or how.

With the keep and the magic behind us, I touched the dragon medallion hanging from my neck and opened the way. In a heartbeat we went *outbound* through the ether, the world of the fae disappearing in a blur of colors and angry shouts as we left the enemy behind. The others formed into squares upon squares, those holding the egg in the middle. We traveled the netherworld for a breath and another, holding to this cold place of too bright colors where we did not truly belong. If we remained too long, we would be lost.

I brought us out *somewhere else* and skimmed along clouds stretching below us. I caught a glimpse of buildings and a river. We drew magic from the flowing water and the air tasted fresh after the stink of battle, though I felt the taint of technology all around us. We wouldn't be staying here. I put my hand on my medallion and tried to believe we would survive, regroup, and win over the enemy. The sun rose in our faces and while half-blinding, still felt warm and welcome. I could see hope in this new dawn.

"We'll follow this river for a little way, gather power, and head *outbound* once more. We need to gather strength and catch our breath!"

"Where shall we go?" Brandis asked. His long dark hair hung in snarls and he sounded worried and lost.

"Not far."

"What took down the dragon?" he asked, his eyes narrowed as he glanced back at the egg.

"I don't know, but I felt they came from the other side."

I heard shouts of anger as the rest of the clan learned the enemy had banded with such creatures --

*Magic!*

I felt a shield spring into existence before us, so sudden and strong the air turned to ice. Some of the clan tried to catch the wind and go outbound -- No telling where they went! -- but many of us remained trapped by the maelstrom of magic. The storm clouds we had ridden danced in a chaotic frenzy and lightning flashed bright, blinding us. We spun and I tried to keep track of the others, and see where the egg had gone, but the squares broke up. Dangerous --

"Hold on! Hold back!" I shouted, knowing we'd fallen into a trap.

I saw a few hundred of the enemy rushing us with weapons and magic already flying. My horse faltered. I put my hand to my chest and the dragon medallion I wore there and wished the next leader of the clan a better chance. I took it off --

I saw the javelin flying towards me and I dropped the chain as the weapon hit.

I fell, fell, the storm, the wind the rain --

Falling. . . .

I leapt up, calling out in surprise, dismay, and loss, with my hand on my chest. I expected to find blood.

No. I stood in my bedroom, not riding horses in the clouds.

I had never, *never* experienced so real a dream before. I could still feel the wind in my face, the smooth glide of a horse flying beneath me. I felt sadness at the death of the dragon and hoped the egg had survived and hadn't fallen to the enemy --

*Not real.* The battle, the dragon -- everything had been a mishmash linking the storm with the dragon medallion I had found.

I settled into bed, staring out the window where another storm raged. The remnants of the dream haunted me through the remainder of the night.

# CHAPTER 5

I awoke after dawn feeling muscle aches as though I had truly fought the damned battle. A shower helped and cleared my head. I had class later at Creighton University, but if I hurried, I could get out to the zoo first, and maybe get some answers about the pictures of the paw prints. I wanted to focus on the weirdness in the real world and drive the dream away.

After I dressed, I went out on the balcony. Everything appeared quiet and calm today, though I felt as though a storm grew in the patches of grey clouds covering some of the sky. Something lurked out there. . . .

The pictures of the cat paw print sat on the counter and I grabbed them and started for the door just as the phone rang. The ID was Rose, my second oldest sister. Rose worries more than Violet, and if I didn't answer, she might track me down. She had done so in the past.

"Morning, Rose," I said, trying to keep some lightness in my voice.

"Little brother." I heard the shuffling of papers and wondered why she had gone to her office this early. "Thought I'd check on you. The news said your end of town took a hard hit by the storms."

"I seem to have weathered them without a problem." I smiled at my own little pun, but she moaned. She never enjoyed my jokes. I wanted to get to the zoo, but if I told her, she'd ask why, and I'd tell her about the strange cat . . . and the conversation wouldn't go well afterwards. Rose didn't care much for the unexplained. So I choose the lesser of two evils. "I have to get ready for class, Rose."

"Class? You're back in class? Are you ever going to stop?"

"Stop learning? I hope not."

She did laugh this time. "What's the interest this year?"

"I'm taking a course in Terrestrial Ecology at Creighton." I glanced at the clock. "And I had better get moving. Have a good day. Let the others know I'm fine, okay? I don't want to have to field calls from the rest of the Unholy Five for the next two days."

She laughed at the old nickname for my five older sisters. "You take care. I think the weather could turn bad again today."

I thanked her and said goodbye. I called the zoo and asked for a few minutes with someone who could check a picture of a paw print from the cat loose in Omaha. Of course they'd heard about it. After a few moments on hold, the woman told me to come out right away and they might be able to get me in with someone first thing.

Good. I had a limited time frame before class. I'd never missed a single class in all my college years, and despite feeling lousy, I wouldn't skip today, either. A little walking at the zoo might help work out some of these odd aches and pains.

I refused to think about the battle and the death of the dragon.

Trying not to moan, I leaned over and picked up the newspaper outside my door, glancing at the front page on the way to the elevator. I had expected news of the storm to dominate the paper, and I was *half* right. The top half of the front page showed pictures of downed trees and talked about superficial damage. One of the police helicopters had taken an overhead shot showing traffic backed up on the Iowa side all the way to the Lake Manawa exit and north to at least 480.

Looked like a typical morning commute to me.

I glanced over the main report as the elevator sped to the garage. The zoo and gardens had both come through with minor damage, because the storm changed direction -- *magic shield, the air turning to ice* -- and most of the chaos flew right over them before hitting the city. The same held true for the Old Market and riverfront district, which took some wind and hail damage, but not much worse. Straight line winds had taken off a couple roofs elsewhere, and trees had crashed onto cars and buildings. They reported injuries from glass and hail, but nothing worse.

I turned the paper over as I reached the car and stopped in shock. The bottom half of the front page covered something more alarming than the storm. A gang war had broken out overnight: The Rojos and the Black Knights had gone at each other, with about twenty in the hospital and five dead. The police reported some brutal hand-to-hand fighting. Despite several gun's firing, they found evidence of no gunshot wounds or deaths which was something odd enough to merit notice. Odd enough, in fact, it drew my attention and I thought I might check into it . . . at a distance. The police expected the situation to get worse.

Great. They'd done more damage to their fellow humans than the storm had managed.

I glanced at the warnings to stay clear of certain areas of town because of storm damage and gang warfare. I did see a note at the bottom of the page saying a big cat might be loose in the Ralston area.

City crews were clearing downed tree limbs and other debris as I drove up 10th Street. I passed Tessa's Astrology Room, a rather sedate frontage for such a popular occult place. I didn't see anyone around, though I knew Tessa lived in the building. I drove past my workplace a block later but saw no movement there, either.

At a little before nine a dozen cars sat in the parking lot of the Henry Doorly Zoo, and by ten this place would be packed, despite the humid and hot weather. I stepped inside the glass-fronted visitor's center and they directed me to the Cat House. Two peacocks patrolled the Lion Pride statue near the zoo entrance. Both displayed as I neared, showing wide fans of gorgeous feathers. I wished I had the camera with me.

As I drew closer, they screeched so loudly someone came at a run. Seeing nothing wrong, the woman shrugged. I went past the two birds, feeling a little wary as they watched me. I'd never found peacocks frightening before but I feared these two might be psychotic.

The koi in the little pond darted about in chaotic swarms as I passed, but I didn't have time to stay and watch. I hurried past the Desert Dome and off towards the Cat House which I could see through the trees down a steep hillside. I skipped the elevator, reminding myself how I needed exercise.

The peacocks followed me all the way to the Desert Dome and stood sentinel at the stairs as I hurried down to the path. They both screamed. I hurried a little faster.

At the bottom of the curve of the hill, a huge Siberian Tiger stalked along the edge of his outdoor enclosure. As I neared, he laid his ears back and growled so ominously I retreated a few steps and hurried around to the wide entrance to the building.

"Summerfield?" A man came from the shadows and even he almost spooked me.

"Yes. Thank you for seeing me Mister --"

"Ted Thomas." We shook hands. "You have a picture?"

I pulled a printout of the envelope. He studied the photo while I watched another Siberian Tiger stalk along the huge glass window to our right. He didn't appear any happier than the one I had passed outside.

"This can't be real," Ted said shaking his head.

"I thought so as well, but I talked to a Mr. Dorey who used to work here --"

"Dorey! What did he have to say?"

A few cats began to roar. Ted glanced over his shoulder frowning and signaled me outside which proved marginally quieter.

"Don't know what's up with them. What did Dorey have to say?"

I recounted the discussion and Ted studied the picture with renewed interest. "Dorey knows his cats. Can I keep this? I want to fax a copy to others and see what they think. I'll let you know if I get any answer."

"I'd appreciate the help." I gave him my card.

"Let's go over to the jungle. We have a specialist in from New York who's studying our Clouded Leopard enclosure there. She might have some ideas."

We headed up the hill. I did my best not to gasp, but I felt as though I breathed in more water than oxygen. We were in for another miserable day when things got hotter. I intended to spend as much of the day in nice, air-conditioned rooms as possible.

The peacocks had moved on. Ted Thomas discussed some things about the picture, and I took notes: nail size and how the animal appeared to be plantigrade, which meant he walked with the sole of the foot to the ground, as humans do. Cats are often digitigrade; they step on their toes.

We found the woman inside the Lied Jungle where she appeared to be talking to a gibbon, though he disappeared as soon as we arrived. Maria Riley stood almost a head taller than me and a discreet glance showed she didn't wear heels. She reminded me of the no-nonsense sort of professors I'd seen in some Eastern colleges, though she smiled as she took the picture. We walked the path beneath overarching jungle growth, saying nothing until we reached the darker cavern.

"This can't be real." She handed it back, though I could hear a little doubt in her voice.

"Someone who worked here for years saw the animal," Ted replied. "I trust him."

But he gave me a worried glance, realizing he only had my word on what Dorey had said.

"He said he'd talk to his old boss about it. Might have had trouble getting through with all the lines down and such," I added and won a nod of relief. "I didn't see the animal. I did get this print in fresh mud yesterday after the initial storm - -"

We passed by the window with a huge python on the other side. The creature lifted his head and pressed against the glass, moving so fast he hit with a distinct thump. We all stepped aside, surprised. I'd never seen the snake move much at all.

"Must be feeding time," Ted decided as we went past. I glanced back and saw the eyes following us.

"Someone must have done this," Maria decided.

"I saw no other prints, human or other animal, anywhere near."

"Perhaps a hybrid of some sort," she suggested. "I would love to see this animal."

"If I track it down, I'll let you know," I replied. I watched while a long black monitor lizard of some sort stood and stared at me, eyes blinking. I'd never been to the zoo before official opening time. The animals acted a bit odd this early in the day.

Maria Riley gave me her card. I gave her a second copy of the picture and left heading out into the humid day. Sad when the Lied Jungle is more comfortable than the weather outside. I love to visit the jungle on cold, snowy days, though.

The zoo gate opened, the crowds already starting to

gather and mill about inside as they studied their maps. The two peacocks walked past the doors to the Exploration Station and the moment they spotted me, they displayed and yelled. I hurried out to my car.

# CHAPTER 6

I considered driving all the way to Creighton, but I enjoy the walk from my place to class, and I felt better. After all the trouble yesterday, this morning, despite the heat, proved lovely. Maybe we'd have a better day --

Four police cars screamed past me with lights flashing and sirens wailing. I watched with a sigh and headed back to the garage to put the poor, battered Subaru somewhere safe for the day. I'd have to remember to call the insurance company later.

Creighton University is not as well-known as the University of Nebraska at Omaha. The Jesuit-run college has a feel of sanctity, no doubt helped by the huge church right in the middle of the campus, an anachronistic spire in the midst of downtown Omaha's towering buildings.

I've taken classes there before, in a random, haphazard sort of way whenever something took my fancy. They'd run a special summer session on Terrestrial Ecology this year, and I'd enjoyed working with most of the students and the teacher.

I especially liked Glynis. I smiled when I saw her waiting outside the building, lounging by a maple tree. Tall, blonde, not too thin: she dressed casually but with class, and she had a smile that would warm a winter night. I grinned when I saw her, getting the same loopy feeling I always did. It was silly. It was fun. I hoped it didn't go away.

"You're almost late," she said, surprised as she frowned.

"You don't look well."

"Caught a bit of a cold." I snagged her arm in mine. "What an incredible storm yesterday!"

"You went out in the weather?  What were you doing?" she asked.

I hadn't told her about my job for Wolton World News. Glynis had her feet firmly planted in the scientific world and explaining I wrote articles about the inexplicable didn't seem wise so early in our relationship.  Maybe in a year or two?

"I went out to my parent's place," I said, half a truth at least.  "I had to sign some papers and stuff for them."

"They're still out of town?"

I nodded and escorted her into the class. We sat side-by-side.  She had her paper done and I had a couple more pages to retype.  The professor talked about the storm for a while and the impact such weather would have on the area, but the power went out about midway through the class and the room became stuffy.  The professor dismissed us early.

"If the storm had hit the nuclear generators face-on, we would all be dead," Christopher said as he followed us out. The short, stocky guy with a perpetual squint.  I don't know why he didn't get glasses or at least contacts.  "They should tear the plant down.  It's a danger to the city."

"It would take more than a hit by a storm --" I began.

"Yeah, like you know everything?" Christopher demanded.  He'd been building up to this argument for several weeks.

I waved him off and took hold of Glynis's arm as we started away.  I think her glare convinced him not to bother us anymore.

"Join me for lunch?" Glynis asked with a bright smile.

Food didn't appeal to me, though spending time with Glynis did.  So I agreed and we went to her car.  She threw books into the backseat so I could ride up front, and we drove to the Old Market, parking in a lot on the north edge. I eyed the changing weather with some worry, but we got out and walked along with the crowds as Glynis led the way to her favorite pub.

"You're too quiet today, Summerfield," she said as we sat. Then she sighed. "When are you going to tell me your name?"

"Not today," I replied and grinned. We played this game once or twice a week. She wasn't from town, but she would have found a lot of Summerfields in town and could have gotten my name from any of my cousins. Or one of my sisters.

Instead, she kept at our little game. I liked her all the more for it.

We ordered, and I chose a salad. She took pleasure in seeing people eat healthy food. Glynis took the idea of helping others make good decisions a little too seriously sometimes. I hoped she outgrew it.

Though my sisters hadn't.

"Did you hear Brandi after class?" she asked over an iced tea.

"Missed it."

"Horses. Some horses got lose in the Crossroads parking lot yesterday."

"After the storm?" I asked, feeling a little shiver at the mere idea of horses associated with the damned weather.

"More like during it. Lots of people saw them, but by the time the police got through the blocked streets, they had all disappeared. Not a prank call since several people reported them."

"Sounds odd," I agreed and somehow kept from taking out my notepad and writing notes.

"I'm sure there's a perfectly fine explanation," she said with a wave of red-lacquered fingernails. "Someone transporting them through town had a problem during the storm. He must have rounded them up by the time the police got there."

I agreed with a quick nod. A good logical explanation, so I banished the memory of riding horses from elsewhere across the storm-tossed sky.

The salads arrived, and I nibbled at mine while we talked about class, about meeting for some study time and about the weather. I would have stayed and talked to her about anything.

My cell phone rang. *Age of Aquarius.* Bad timing, as usual. I grimaced and answered.

"Julia?" I said with a frown.

"You're out of class, right?" she asked with a kind of breathlessness I knew meant she had something good.

"Yes, but --"

"Good! I have something I want you to check out. I talked of one of the people who watched Doppler radar yesterday when the storm hit, and he says some strange things happened. Can you to go over to the WOWT Station and talk to him?"

I could have said no but the idea of Jacobs messing with the story bothered me more than usual. I glanced at Glynis. She gave a little sigh of resignation. Julia had called at other times and I let her believe the work concerned my parents. Yes, I know. *Karma.* I would have to stop the half lies soon or there would be a huge backlash.

"Summerfield?" Julia said.

"When should I be there?"

"Within the next hour if you can."

"No problem. I'll talk to you when I'm done." I shoved the phone back into my pocket, already sorry I had agreed. "Glynis --"

"I know, I know." She pouted a little. Hell. I wanted to stay. "I'll take you."

"No, you stay and finish your lunch." I stood and kissed her forehead. She gave a delighted smile. "I'll see you soon."

"When are your parents coming back?"

"I wish I knew." I patted her shoulder and headed out, though I did stop long enough to pay for the meal.

It wasn't far to my apartment. I grabbed the poor, hail-pocked Subaru and drove away, wondering what roads remained closed. At a couple spots where I could see the sky, I noted huge cumulonimbus clouds on the horizon to the southwest; menacing mountains about to tumble over onto the unsuspecting city. I grabbed my cell phone and called Glynis.

"The weather looks nasty, Glyn," I said, navigating around an abandoned car at the corner of 10th and Farnham. "Thought you should know, so you can get home."

"Thanks. You be careful, too. I'll talk to you later."

I smiled and put the phone on the seat. I could see city trucks down many streets, the crews grabbing fallen limbs and feeding them into the chipper. Terrestrial Ecology had me thinking about the impact on local animals, a nice diversion from worrying about the weather or how I felt. I hate being sick.

WOWT sits somewhat atop a hill and the better view of the clouds didn't improve my mood. I hurried across the lot and into the building where the woman at the receptionist desk gave me a quick, but guarded smile. When I showed my press pass, she directed me straight to the meteorology department, down a beige hall with pictures of the current top shows and right into a large, somewhat messy room.

"Mr. Summerfield?" a man waved from a computer station, directing me around a couple tables and to his spot. He'd pulled a chair over and I sat, grateful to be off my feet. "I'm Rich Anderson, the morning computer guy here. Julia Wolton said you would show up soon." His fingers hit keys on the computer, jabbing at stuff while pictures changed on the screen. "Know anything about weather and Doppler Radar?"

"What I see on the Weather Channel and the news."

He nodded and I could tell I had impressed him with my extensive knowledge of meteorology. I did know a little more because of some of the courses I'd taken. However, I wanted him to explain things in terms I could use to tell the story to the readers. "You don't need to know much for this show. Here's what the weather at 7:43 AM yesterday morning looked like."

I studied the graphic: bands of green, indicating light rain moved over the Omaha area. The time line ran at the right hand corner of the screen, counting off the minutes, which passed quickly in this speeded up version. I would have been heading towards the office right about --

Red flashed in an almost straight line down the middle of the screen, startling me.

"Gets your attention, doesn't it?" Rich asked and paused the animation. "Never seen anything like it. Neither has anyone else."

"You were here yesterday when this happened?" I asked, starting to take notes.

"Yes. Scared the shit out of me. I thought it had to be a computer malfunction or maybe someone hacking us. I kept fiddling with the monitor until the winds hit and the calls started coming in. And by then . . . well, things had gotten even stranger."

"Stranger than this?" I waved a hand at the screen.

He nodded and keyed the simulation on once more. I watched the line of red which remained stationary from about Missouri Valley and south past Offutt Air Base. Straight, which could not be natural.

*Shield*, I thought, and shook my head, chasing the idea away once more. I leaned closer and watched as those bands of rain hit the shield -- the line of red -- and bounced away in a new chaotic swirl of greens. Spots of red began moving through the bands.

"What are those?" I asked, tapping one.

"Damned if I know. They read solid and warmer than the air around them, which is pretty much impossible. If this had been ice, it would have melted and it sure as hell wouldn't be warmer. There appear to be maybe two hundred or more. Some of them went straight down to the ground while others spread out. They sometimes moved against the prevailing wind current. And there; more just appeared."

I shook my head once more denying inner thoughts. "How big are those things?"

"I'd say most are about three to four times the size of humans."

Or humans riding on horses. "Any ideas?"

"I'd go with aliens, but maybe I've seen Close Encounters and X Files a few too many times."

"Is there any way I can get screen captures?"

"I sent a full copy of this video to your boss. You can pull pictures from it," he said and leaned back. "We have some important bigwig meteorology people showing up to study the local weather today. If I hear a reasonable explanation, I'll let you know."

"I would appreciate it. And if I come up with anything --"

"Yeah, let me know."

"Why are you giving this to us?" I asked. "You have a news department here --"

"There isn't a station manager or NOAA person in the area who isn't sharing this stuff in hopes someone, somewhere might come up with an answer. We're giving the vid out to everyone, Mr. Summerfield. Even Woo Woo News, because God knows this isn't normal."

# CHAPTER 7

I left the building with a few notes in my pocket and my head buzzing. Walking outside didn't help because the weather had turned worse in the short time I talked to Rich Anderson. Dark clouds obscured the sky, and lightening flashed, striking downward somewhere to the south. I decided standing on the hill was a bad idea, though I wasn't alone watching the sky with open dismay. No one wanted a repeat of yesterday. Something told me I had been wise to warn Glynis. I hoped she had listened to me and headed to her dorm.

I wanted to do the same. I thought I might go to my place, write the report and email the article to Julia. I sometimes work from home in the winter when it isn't worth frostbite to walk to the office and the ice or snow makes things too dangerous to drive. Julia didn't care, as long as I got the work done. I appreciated her trust more than I ever had before.

She always made Jacobs come in though. The woman wasn't a fool.

I reached the Subaru as the rain started. The cool drops against my fever-warm face felt good. I closed my eyes, welcoming anything to help lessen the heat and humidity. A breeze brushed against me and for the briefest moment, I remembered flying through the clouds. The feeling should have scared me but as long as I didn't think about the falling part --

Of course, I did think of it and had a sudden heart-thumping moment when I grabbed at the car. A glance around the area showed the others had already retreated from the storm. Wise people.

I got into the car, thinking of home and. . . .

*Age of Aquarius.*

Damn. I grabbed the cell phone and took a moment to calm myself before I snarled at Julia.

"Yeah, Julia?" I asked, trying not to sound too miserable.

"How did the talk go?" she asked.

"Oh, oddly. You watch the Doppler stuff he sent you?"

"Yes. Wonderful material. Are you done?"

"Heading home to do the notes," I replied though I feared she had something else in mind.

"I walked down to talk to Tessa," she said. That astrologer was trouble, I knew it. She sounded busy for a moment, then came back. "Tessa told me you should investigate the gang story."

"Gangs," I repeated. I really disliked this idea. "Tessa thinks we should deal with the gangs. The ones the police think are going to war and everyone should avoid."

"Well, yes." She sounded uncertain. "I did talk to a woman who lives next door to one of the Rojos who died last night. She subscribes to Wolton World News. She says if you get there before she goes to her shift job at the Hilton, she'd talk to you."

I held the phone out from me for a moment. She couldn't be serious and want to send me into a war zone to discuss gangs? What did their problems have to do with Wolton World News?

And there was *the* question. Hairs on my arms started to stand up.

"What have you heard about and I haven't?" I asked.

"You know none of the gang members died from bullet

wounds, right?"

"Yes."

"Most died of blade wounds or else. . . ." She paused and I heard her take a deep breath. "Or else something bit through their chest and ate their insides."

I froze with the key in the ignition, remembering the nightmare and the huge creatures breaking through, grabbing --

"Summerfield?" she asked, pensive this time.

"Where did you hear about it?" I forced my voice to stay calm even though my heart pounded.

"From the police department first. That's why I called her. They're sending the reports out since this wasn't something they could keep quiet anyway and they want people to be aware there might be a dangerous animal loose -- very likely the big cat. Are you all right? You don't sound well."

Thunder shook the car. I hadn't seen the lightning this time.

"I'm fine."

"Listen, I can send Jacobs instead. Really."

"Jacobs out there in gang land? He'd kick off a war just by being himself. I'll go. Where am I heading?"

She gave me an address right in the middle of the Latino neighborhood. I might have a chance of working my way through the Rojos territory without too much notice which wouldn't happen if I drove into Florence and the black community. Maybe no one would shoot me before I got out of the car.

I thought the gangs would be the real problem, but as I drew near the area, the storm damage and National Guard Patrols proved to be the first obstacles. I found the off ramps from the Kennedy Freeway blocked, so I had to make a wide circle. I wanted off the freeway as soon as I could, though, because the storm kept building, with wind gusts and an occasional splatter of rain. I didn't want to spend most of the rest of the day watching the clouds pass overhead while traffic inched forward at a rate which would make a glacier seem speedy. I'd been in those situations a few too many times.

I found an off ramp in South Omaha and cut through the Metro Community College lot, bypassing a pile of three cars piled against each other. Maybe the cars formed some sort of local art. At any rate, someone had already painted graffiti on the doors and hoods.

I found my way into the neighborhood by taking side streets and alleys. I knew coming here wasn't wise. I saw people glance my way at every corner, eyes narrowed, and hands reaching for things I didn't want to see.

Yeah, I felt nervous. But I found the house with little trouble and parked half a block away. A lot of people had gathered at the house next door to my destination. Great. Wonderful. If I had half a brain, I would not get out of the car. I'd call the woman. Yeah. Call her and talk to her by phone and. . . .

Two young people walked past the car, staring at me with dark, mistrusting eyes. I grabbed my press pass and got out to follow them, acting as though I belonged. The guy glanced back and frowned once, but I didn't get too close and no one else questioned me. At the proper house, I ducked through a little wooden trellis covered in dead vines and gave a bow of my head in recognition to the Madonna of the Bathtub. Lilac bushes, long past flowering, screened me from the group of toughs next door, but I sensed eyes on me, and knew these people prepared for trouble.

Black iron bars, a couple of them bent, covered the door and the windows on both floors of the house. Graffiti gave the front of the white house a bit of color: Rojo signs, mostly, here in the heart of their territory. I heard a dog barking in the backyard.

The young men next door talked about the trouble, and I paused long enough to listen to a few scattered words about guns, knives, and what sounded like real concern about the upcoming war. Their worries troubled me because these young toughs didn't scare easily. Gang warfare was endemic in their lives but the few words I heard made me think they treated this trouble differently.

I reached through the bars and knocked lightly on the door, afraid the others would take too much notice of me. Someone twitched back the curtain at the window, and I heard three locks release before the door opened a crack.

"Summerfield?" the woman asked, one dark eye peering out at me.

"Yes," I answered and held my press pass where she could see. She gave a quick nod and pulled the door open and undid the lock on the bars. I scurried inside, grateful to be out of the light. We both gave sighs of relief.

"Sorry," she said. "They just come, the last few minutes. I didn't expect half the gang to be outside the door when you arrive."

"No problem. I don't know your name --"

"No, you don't. Better this way." She waved me into a house with drapes pulled tight, shadows everywhere, and the scent of vanilla in the air. Three young children sat close by a television with the sound very low. They looked my way, large round eyes measuring the stranger in their house.

I had a chance to glance around while she relocked the doors and I spotted an unexpected picture on the wall. I knew the place, though I hadn't been there in more than a decade.

"Lake Coatepeque," I said, waving towards the picture. The area showed some of the lake front, and a group of people gathered together; none of them rich, all of them laughing. I thought I could recognize my hostess in the midst of the group, maybe ten years ago as well. She had seemed young, happy, and hopeful.

"You know this place?" she asked, frowning.

"Yes." And I switched to Spanish, hoping to make the discussion easier for her, and so I didn't keep secret about how I would understand if she spoke to others. "I spent about three years there with my parents. They helped set up some schools."

"Oh." Her eyes narrowed, as though she wondered if we had met. Maybe we had, a long time ago and in a different place. I hadn't expected to find a tenuous connection with someone here. Karma, perhaps, helping out. I suddenly thought this woman might have answers I should know.

She led me to the kitchen and waved me to a chair away from a window through which I could hear the people next door talking. She pulled the glass down and the curtains into place, but I could see through the gauzy fabric.

My hostess settled across from me, her hands on the table, the fingers laced. She was medium height, thin, her hair short and her makeup perfect. She already wore her work uniform, so I knew we didn't have much time.

"I came here because I got tired of Mara Salvatrucha, you know? Gangs and killing. And now, look at this. I didn't go to LA or Washington -- Mara Salvatrucha and the 18th's -- they're too strong there. I thought Omaha. Nice place -- but here is the trouble, too. I can't get away."

"And things are worse because you're from San Salvador, and not Mexico, right?"

"Oh yes, this too. But my husband is a Rojo. He's next door. He knows you were coming. It's all right. It's . . . things are bad. Things are *odd*."

No time to waste. "What's going on?"

"The Black Knights and the Rojos didn't go at each other last night," she said, leaning towards me. Her dark eyes blinked several times. "This was as close to fighting on the same side as they're ever going to get."

My turn to blink a couple times, trying to understand what she said. "Who did they fight?"

"New gang," she said. "New gang comes out of nowhere and walks around like they owned the place. Or like they didn't know no better. The Black Knights, they did some damage down here last week. The Rojos thought, since the power went out, they'd go up and make trouble in Florence. Nothing better to do. But these others come and . . . I don't know, but it got strange."

She watched me, as though judging how much to say. She seemed older than she should be. I'd seen too many women who looked that way in third world countries, where life wore them down too soon. I hated to see the same thing here in Omaha.

Somewhere not too far away a car backfired and we both jumped at the sound. I refused to think it was anything but a car needing a tune up; not while I sat here in the heart of gang territory.

"Can you tell me anything about this new gang?"

"The guys call them the Browns because most had fancy brown vests. They looked as though they'd already gone through a battle."

"And they used knives, not guns."

"Knives? Maybe. Swords is what I hear. Pablo thought they searched for someone. And they had trained bears. Weird, huh? I thought maybe Pablo made that part up, but the news reported something this afternoon. How could they train bears?"

"I don't know." I tried to fit this information into the new perspective. Tessa and Julia had been right to send me here after all. The gang war wasn't what anyone thought. Damn. We didn't need a third gang in the area. "What about the guns?"

"They didn't have any." She stared across at me, dark eyes narrowed. Tired. "And Pablo says they must have armor or something. Bullets didn't work on them. Pablo thinks maybe they're some military group, you know. Come in to wipe us all out."

It wasn't much of a jump from gang war to real war for these people. They'd lived with gangs all their lives, here and elsewhere, fighting a long war many people never noticed, even within their own cities. I felt sorry for the woman. Felt sorry for her, her children and even her gang-member husband. Sometimes survival depended on joining.

She had come to Omaha believing in something better. When had America stopped being a land of hope?

We talked for a few more minutes, touching a little on the gangs and some about the home she'd left behind. We twice heard shouts next door, and she'd start at those sounds and glance with worry towards her children, ready to grab them and hide.

I had cookies and coffee with this unnamed woman, wife of Pablo the Rojo. I won a couple laughs from her when we spoke about the weather. I'd have to leave soon and I didn't know if I wanted to stay because I enjoyed the company or because I didn't want to go out and face the gangs or the weather.

"I gotta' get the kids settled." She switched back to English as she stood. "And then get to work. It felt good, you know, to talk to someone outside the neighborhood. Even at work, we tend to stick with our own. It's stupid, I think."

"What kind of work does Pablo do?" I asked as I stood.

"Mechanic, when he can. Places around here keep closing. But he's on a hire list at some station across town. If . . . if things go well, we'll maybe move out of here. I don't know where to. I don't know if we can escape, but I think this would be nice, yes?"

Shouts rose from next door.

"Yes, I think it would be very nice."

"I'll walk you out."

"No!"

"*Sí*. Yes. I told Pablo I'd walk you out if I thought he should come to talk to you. His English isn't so good, but since you speak like a native, maybe he can tell you things. I think he'll feel better. They're all nervous. They all saw things, you know. Things not normal. We talk our way around it saying it is a new military group, trained bears, but there's been a lot of people praying at night."

She went to the living room, kissed three little heads, and started a video. *Finding Nemo*, I think. The kids laughed and clapped their hands in delight, enthralled. She smiled as she went to the window and twitched the curtain aside before she went to the door and worked the locks for us to go out.

The rain fell, though not too hard, adding to the growing mud puddles in the yard. I didn't know if I wanted to talk to any member of the gang, though I wanted answers. And I wanted to look into Pablo's face and watch when he talked about what had happened.

As I stepped from the porch to the yard, a young man came from the house next door, moving past the lilac bushes and to the porch. My hostess gave him a quick hug and whispered something. He nodded.

"You speak Spanish," he said as we stood there in the rain.

"Yes."

"Good. She tell you everything?"

"I think so. You want to walk to my car and maybe tell me the things you didn't tell her?"

They both laughed and I had the feeling they had a good marriage. Pablo gave a nod. I felt better for having an escort.

As we started out of the yard, a black Eclipse stopped in

the middle of the street, oblivious to any traffic. I recognized the car and grimaced before Kenwood opened the door and stepped out, giving the area a hardly concealed disdainful look.

"Son of a bitch. The guy thinks he owns the place," I mumbled, and drew Pablo's grim nod. "He's a reporter."

"Like you."

"No, not like me. I have manners."

Pablo grinned. "Well, maybe we'll learn him some manners before he goes."

"He's stupid, but he's more trouble than he's worth." Kenwood raised a hand to block the rain. He already looked like a drowned rat.

"That's the problem with you gringos. You worry too much about the people you don't like."

I couldn't argue the point.

"Hey! Anyone here want to see his name in the paper?" Kenwood shouted in English, putting a camera on top of the roof of the car, pointing towards the houses. He smirked. "Come on, get a little famous, huh?"

I stared at him in shock. Kenwood was more than stupid to come here with his stupid 'I'm better than anyone' attitude. He still smirked.

"You sure you want to worry about this guy?" Pablo asked with a shake of his head.

"I might change my mind," I admitted. Some of the young men next door had taken notice of Kenwood and not in a good way. My fellow reporter plainly didn't speak the lingo or have a clue about body language. If he'd understood either, he would have been in the car and halfway to Lincoln.

Kenwood glanced my way and glared. "What the hell are you doing here, Summerfield? Not the usual Woo Woo crap you chase after."

Damn I was getting tired of his attitude.

"Gringo." Pablo stepped forward and waved for me to

remain by his wife. "I think maybe you go, now. Right now."

"Hey, if you talk to him, you can talk to me. He's a reporter, you know. Not a very good one. I have credentials --"

"He's my friend," Pablo's wife replied. "You aren't nobody's friend."

"Listen, chica --" he began, his voice taking on a bit of a snarl.

He didn't get any farther. He should *never* have talked back to her or hint he might insult her. Pablo and the ones from next door moved towards the car and I expected to see guns. Kenwood noticed how being annoyed with him changed to belligerent in a single heartbeat.

"Hey, hey -- didn't mean anything," Kenwood began, but the young toughs crossed the yard and reached the sidewalk. Kenwood grabbed the camera, threw himself into the car and hit the gas. I thought he would spin out on the wet pavement. He reached the next corner, the backend fishtailing as he disappeared.

Everyone laughed but me. Pablo stepped back and slapped me on the shoulder. "Come on. Drink a beer with us. You talk the talk, Summerfield. You aren't stupid."

"No? Then what am I doing here?" I asked.

Pablo grinned, wiping rainwater from his hair. "You are looking for answers."

# CHAPTER 8

I sat on the porch next door and drank a beer with the Rojos. They told me a little about Umberto, one of the two Rojos killed up in Florence. He was dead at seventeen, and from all I could tell, no one appeared surprised. He'd always walked on the wild side.

They talked a little about the bears and more about the new gang, wondering how The Browns would affect the already strained gang relationships. I learned The Browns were Caucasian with maybe an odd accent, which led them to speculate about the army. I didn't stay long, but I didn't feel as though I needed an escort to reach my car afterwards, either. I felt better, despite the storm growing stronger and the sudden fear I would lift into the air.

I shuddered, thinking about flying and about the *bears*, and considered how reality had begun to conform to my nightmares.

Or maybe not.

Maybe every time I heard something odd, my subconscious dragged those things into the memory of the nightmare. I still felt feverish. My brain might be making me believe I had already seen some of these things in my sleep, which meant the *bears* hadn't been part of the nightmare. My mind added them into my memories of the nightmare as soon as I heard the story.

I wanted to believe this trick of the mind. I did feel ill, in fact and began shivering by the time I reached the car. I climbed in and kicked the heat on again, in the middle of summer.

I waved to Pablo as I drove past. I had the feeling he'd welcome me back if I had anything I needed to ask. Good. I drove out the same way I came in. The downpour grew worse, and the debris-filled water had risen over the curbs already. With the ground drenched, the water had nowhere to go. The rain cascaded off the trees, puddled on the sidewalks and made mud holes in yards. I saw kids standing on porches, forlorn as they waited for summer to return. I imagined a few parents feeling the same way.

And I thought of Pablo's family and the children huddled close by the television like little mice, trying not to draw attention. They deserved better than hiding in their house, frightened to make too much noise.

I had almost reached the Kennedy Freeway when I caught a glimpse of Kenwood's black Eclipse in the rearview mirror. At first, I thought I must be wrong, until the car raced at me, horn blaring, and swerved around in an area where he should not have been passing.

I stomped on the brakes and let him go past, cursing him in a couple different languages. He reached out into the rain and gave me the finger. Wow. How adult. He turned and disappeared at the next corner.

I gave a sigh of relief, but something told me --

Right. He came around the block and pulled the same trick, this time swerving closer toward my car as he went past. I had about six blocks to go to the freeway, for whatever good being there would do. I thought he might get a little crazier when he had a clearer path, but at least there wouldn't be people on foot. I suspected he never noticed the old guy starting to cross the street at the last corner.

He hadn't come around the next block, so I relaxed. Kenwood was an idiot. I hadn't realized how childish he could be, though maybe the Woo Woo News stuff should have alerted me.

I heard the squeal of tires as he charged at me from a side street. If I hit the brakes he'd slam into my car. If I hadn't been worried about an injury, I'd have been damned tempted. Instead, I eased down on the gas, trying not to slip on the wet road, and swerved a little to let him get past.

A *shame* he didn't see the cop car in the lot at the next the corner. The cop saw him, though, and hit the lights and siren. Kenwood stopped and the cop jumped out of the patrol car, not in a good mood.

I pulled over to the curb as well, letting calm settle over me as I took several breaths and repeated a mantra I'd learned from a Tibetan monk when I was ten. The cop waved me to go on. I hoped Kenwood had enough trouble to make him rethink some of his actions. He'd always been a pain in the ass, but I hadn't thought him dangerous.

I couldn't be certain how long the cop would keep Kenwood busy, so I headed for the Kennedy Freeway, followed it for a few miles in the pouring rain and wind before I cut across the city by a couple side roads.

The storm broke loose in a new fury and far worse than what I'd been driving through already. Lightning flashed brighter than a dozen paparazzi cameras. Hail hit the car and the wind snapped a branch off a few feet ahead of me. I wanted to reach the top of the next hill because I could already see a wide stream of water rushing along the road. If this weather continued --

Something huge moved across the intersection ahead of me and I hit the brakes in panic. The creature lumbered across the street in a slouched gorilla-like walk before the thing spun towards me, head coming up. I saw long, sharp teeth and red eyes.

I rolled down the window sticking my head out but the

creature rushed towards me, moving far faster than I would have believed possible. I yelped and pulled my head back in, rolling the window up --

I heard the shouts. Good someone else had seen this thing!

Horses charged at the creature, the riders swinging swords. The thing took off at a run down the side street and the half dozen riders followed, disappearing out of my sight.

I held my hands clenched to the steering wheel. Lightning flashed and thunder rolled through the air. Hail hit the car, chipped the windshield, and a tiny spider web design began to spread almost immediately. I watched the pattern, intent on not thinking about anything else.

I could not have seen . . . .

*Hell.* I hit the gas, and the car surged forward, the tires trying to find traction on the wet street. I turned at the side street where the creature and the riders had gone. Movement a couple blocks away caught my attention, though I couldn't see much through the rain. I almost stomped down on the gas, but remembering the crazy drive with Kenwood, I eased back and went a little slower.

A huge tree had come down in the middle of the street. If I hadn't already slowed, I would have plowed straight into the branches. The car skidded and half spun. Out of the side window I could see a single horse and rider making an impossible leap over the huge, old oak.

I sat with my hands clenching the steering wheel while the storm rushed over me. When the weather eased -- ten minutes? Half an hour? I had lost all track of time -- I backed around in a driveway and headed towards the office. I wanted inside. I wanted somewhere away from this crazy weather and everything else out here.

*Fever.* I felt ill with it, trembling with cold and heat. The illness had to be the explanation for everything I had seen, which also meant I had to get some place and park the car, and not drive until I was sure I had gotten past this illness. These kinds of hallucinations could be dangerous for me and for anyone else who happened to be on the road with me at the time.

Shivering (and not only from the fever), I drove at a sedate pace through the lessening storm, hoping Kenwood didn't somehow find me. I wanted somewhere safe.

A swarm of police cars swept past me, lights flashing. I pulled over and watched them disappear over a hill. I had no intention of following them to trouble. In fact, I took a side street and another, but after a couple more turns, I found myself right in the midst of the trouble after all.

*Karma.* I figured I had meant to be here, no matter how lousy I felt. I found a place to park a couple blocks away, pulled a jacket out of the back seat and shrugged it on, welcoming the little warmth over my already soaked shirt. I jogged over to the cop and held up my press pass.

"Damn, you people are fast," he said with a shake of his head.

"Chance. You passed me on the road. I tried to avoid the problem, but since I ended up in the same place, I figured I might as well find out what's going on."

"Summerfield!" I saw Officer Lenz heading my way, his face grim. "You're still on the cat story, I see."

"Am I? I showed up by accident."

He took a deep breath and waved towards a line of scraggly bushes at the end of the street. "We got a report of someone mauled to death and left in the underbrush."

"Damn." The news took me by surprise because, for some reason, I had been thinking the big cat was tame.

"We're warning everyone to stay inside while we try to flush the animal out. The death couldn't have occurred more than half an hour ago. The wise ones aren't out in this storm anyway." He shook his head as he looked me over. "We're getting trackers and trappers out, but with this weather, we fear we won't have much luck."

A car came to a stop nearby. Kenwood had arrived but at least he drove sedately, and except for a glare which would have killed a lesser man, he pretty much ignored me. It made my day better. Lenz gave him a nod, and I suspected he didn't know Kenwood had been pulled over for reckless driving a few minutes ago.

Lenz filled us both in on everything from the site. He would not let Kenwood take pictures of the body. I don't know why he would want to. No newspaper I knew would run shots of a mauled corpse.

"This is gang work," Kenwood said after Lenz finished. He shot me another glare. "There's more going on with the gangs than this fights they're having."

"War," I corrected, despite myself. "A fight is when you go at it *mano-a-mano* -- hand-to-hand. A war is when you take out the guns and knives and start killing off people in mass numbers."

"Should let them go at each other." Kenwood dared me to say something more, but neither Lenz nor I saw any reason to indulge him. "Obviously, the gang war has spilled over --"

"This wasn't done by any of the gangs," Lenz replied, maybe hoping to shut him up.

"And you know this because --"

"The teeth marks," he replied.

"Could be some animal they have."

"Could be some animal *you* have," Lenz replied and stared him down this time. "At the moment, you -- or Summerfield -- being in the neighborhood, would make more likely suspects. However, we think this is the work of a wild animal and we're going to try and track it down. I have work to do."

I recognized the sound of dismissal, though Kenwood

didn't. I headed to my car. Kenwood left a moment later when no one would talk to him. He'd parked closer than me and pulled away while I unlocked my door. He glared, of course. I grinned, because his actions had been so sophomoric, and filled with schoolyard theatrics, I couldn't help myself.

He hit the gas -- though not very much -- and drove off. I watched him disappear around the corner so I could mark a path and go in a different direction, though it would take longer to reach to the office.

The smile faded a moment later when I heard something rustling in the bushes beside the car. I had the door half open, and I turned my head.

"Drgg . . . drgggg."

I pulled myself into the car and slammed the door, fumbling for the key and glancing into the rain drenched bushes where something moved. I eased out of the spot and into the driveway across the street, turning towards the police. Lenz had started to walk away, but I reached out and waved him over, doing my best not to look like a crazed-Kenwood driver.

"What now?" he demanded as he walked to the car.

"I think there might be something in the bushes where I had been parked," I said softly. "Might be a big dog, but --"

I saw him stare, eyes narrowed. "Son of a bitch. I think you're right. Stay here. Keep an eye on it for me."

I felt an odd welling of relief. If he saw something, at least this wasn't my imagination. Good. I stuck my head out and watched the bushes. Something moved, and for a moment I thought I saw a huge shape. I shivered.

The police spread out, but Lenz returned a few minutes later and I knew they'd lost the trail. He came to my car, wiping mud from his hands and shaking his head.

"The thing disappeared. Damned cagey animal. Thanks

for the help.  And here is a little tidbit for you.  The prints didn't match the cat ones though I have to believe they're still the same animal because having two things loose in the city seems a bit too much of a coincidence.  The rain and the rest of us tracking through there destroyed them, though, so you're not going to get any pictures.  So, time for you to leave."

I headed out of the neighborhood, hoping they caught the creature soon.  This would start a worse panic than any gang war would.  People enjoyed reading about the unknown, but they didn't want it visiting their backyards.

The storm had eased by the time I pulled into the lot and parked by Jacobs' car.  I almost felt better until I glanced down the alley and saw glowing green eyes watching me for a brief moment before they disappeared.

I hurried into the office.

# CHAPTER 9

The rest of the day went quickly. I worked on reports and found material to research which led (willingly) to other material. I buried myself in the work of studying wild animal attacks within city limits. Any city's limits. I don't know what stuff in Tianjin, China had to do with Omaha, Nebraska but I studied the information anyway. Hell, I even found myself flirting with a few mythology and fantasy sites and learning about places which had never existed.

Later, I talked to Julia about the Doppler stuff and what I'd learned from Rich Anderson. Her enthusiasm for the story overrode the worries I had brought to the office with me. I went to work researching unusual weather patterns, which proved marginally less nightmare-provoking.

Jacobs remained quieter than usual, and though I didn't trust his whispered words on the phone, I did appreciate the lack of loudness in the office. I calmed finally. The fever lessened and I felt as though I had at least a tenuous hold on reality.

I worked through until after six when Julia insisted I go home. I didn't want to leave but didn't want her to know that I feared the idea of being alone. Those words sounded stupid even in my head.

I collected my jacket and headed out. The weather felt better when I stepped outside, though the clouds remained dark and ominous. I started to walk home but decided to take the Subaru the few short blocks and leave it in the garage, rather than abandon it here overnight. With the window open it felt pleasant and I even dared drive around the Old Market and Riverfront area.

I didn't want to go home.

I called Glynis to say I felt worse and intended to head to my place for the night. She told me to get some rest and asked if I needed anything. It was sweet. I almost asked her to come over, but I worried about the fever, and if I passed this cold on to her, I'd feel worse. Besides, I harbored just enough machismo to know I didn't want our first night together to be her taking care of me.

I parked the car in the garage and took the elevator up and gave a quick nod of a greeting to the guy who lived across the hall from me as he went out. I still didn't know his name and today was not the day to get friendly.

I felt better when I walked inside my place, moving along the hall and stopping in the kitchen to drop keys, billfold and change on the counter, to put the cell phone in the charger -- to do all the things I did trying to bring normality back to my life.

I felt as though I had found a refuge from the storm. Quite literally as the rain suddenly fell, pounding my balcony and lightning etched a line across the darker sky. With night coming, the storms might grow worse. I checked the Weather Channel: Omaha appeared to be the center of the universe today if you counted the amount of time they spent pointing to it and drawing lines on maps. I watched several video clips from the storms in the area, too.

I sat for an hour on the sofa before I admitted I was staring at the TV to avoid going to sleep. The waking nightmares had been bad enough, but I feared what would happen the moment I let go of consciousness.

I admitted something to myself, finally. I felt scared,

wondering if I should call a doctor and get an opinion. I didn't want to tell anyone about the hallucinations, though. I figured I could stand another night of this. Maybe the nightmare wouldn't return.

I felt exhausted, and closed my eyes --

The nightmare proved *worse* this time. I suffered through a replay of the first night's story, but with far more intensity. Emotions rolled through me, along with bone-numbing exhaustion and the pain of wounds. I watched in horror as the dragon died and felt such loss and emptiness that I thought to throw myself into the mass of darkness and die with Vane, and take the rest of the clan with me.

But I had my duty to protect the egg, to maintain the clan and to move on. We took to the sky. We flew through the nether to somewhere else. I thought, for a moment, we would get away, but the enemy found us too quickly. Everything changed to chaos: the storm, the moment of death, and falling --

And I awoke with rain falling on my face. Lightning brightened the area around me, and thunder shook more water from the trees.

I stood outside on a dark, wet night. I thought I must be somewhere along 10th Street, and a long way from home. Well past Durnham Museum and almost to the zoo, in fact. I felt drenched, cold and so shaky I had to sit down on the ground.

Hell, hell, hell.

I heard movement close by in the bushes and found glowing green eyes, watching with an unblinking stare while I sat, frozen and unable get a coherent thought.

I heard another sound, this time to my left.

"Drgg . . . drgggg."

I had heard the same noise back at the place where the person had been mauled. The creature with the glowing green eyes had not made the sound, however. This one was farther back from the sidewalk.

Oh damn. I had to fight not to be outright ill.

I tried to struggle to my feet and made it as far as my knees. Shadows moved all around me and I couldn't tell creatures from the growing storm. I couldn't tell where the enemy might be. Or *what* it might be, either. I heard the same odd 'drgg' sound followed by a hiss that made my skin crawl.

I worked my way along the sidewalk on my hands and knees for about a yard before I feared I would pass out. I did *not* want to be unconscious. I didn't want to sleep. I feared to blink at this point.

Another hiss. I stopped, my heart pounding so hard I couldn't hear much around me.

I saw a car coming down the street. I tried to get to my feet, hoping for some help, and praying for a Good Samaritan. I got lucky, because it was a police car that arrived and pulled over to the curb, the lights flashing. God help me if they decided I was a drunk. My sisters would have hissy fits if a report of me, found drunk on the streets, turned up in the news. I tried to stand as the cop got out of the car and came around to help me.

"You all right, sir?"

"I wish I was," I replied and made it to my feet. At least my words didn't slur, and I knew I hadn't been drinking. Had I? How did I know what I'd been doing when I had no idea how I got here?

When I started to sway, the cop stepped closer and took hold of my arm. He gave me a startled look. "Feels as though you have quite a fever, sir. Come on into the car. I'll get you somewhere. Do you have ID?"

"If so, it's only by chance. I don't know how the hell I got out here."

I didn't have my billfold. I remembered putting

everything on the counter when I got home. The cop didn't seem to mind. He helped me into the car, and I leaned back on the seat, closing my eyes --

I woke up at the emergency entrance to Bergan Mercy as the cop opened the door. People were coming out with a gurney.

"Oh hey. I don't need --"

"You passed out, sir."

"Summerfield," I said, feeling odd, woozy and disconnected. I started to get up and fell back on my ass. My legs felt as though they didn't belong to me and I kept experiencing the sensation of flying. Or falling. "Yeah, maybe you're right."

I let them take me inside the building and on into emergency. They worried over the fever. I answered a few questions -- but I passed out before we got very far.

# CHAPTER 10

I felt better by mid-morning of the next day. I pretty much had to, because they'd filled me with so many antibiotics and done so many tests, if I hadn't felt better, I feared what they'd do next.

Dr. Penn found me as soon as my name appeared on the reports. He came into the room about nine in the morning, shaking his gray-haired head. He'd been one of the family doctors forever and I felt better seeing him. The others had started ignoring my questions and a few had gotten downright surly. I'd been tempted to call on someone who would get answers from them, and they wouldn't be happy to see her, either.

"Hey kid," Dr. Penn said from the doorway. He smiled as he held up the chart in his hand. "You gave them quite a run for the money last night."

"Any idea what is going on?"

"We suspect nothing more than a bad fever. None of the tests showed a sign of flu or pneumonia and I have had all of them run twice. You aren't taking drugs are you? Drinking a lot?"

"Never have," I replied, frowning because I hadn't expected him to ask such a thing of me.

"Didn't think so, but the resident last night jotted it down as a probable cause of the problems. You had some strange hallucinations, I guess. But as far as we can tell, everything was fever driven. How do you feel?"

"Far better than last night, but not as good as I would hope."

Dr. Penn came over to do his own check, including, yet again, taking my blood pressure. They had done the check far too often the night before. Personally, I could have done with less prodding and poking and more sleep. Here in the hospital, I had escaped the nightmare -- or at least I didn't remember having it. The resident must have picked up on something, though.

"You're in better health than your sisters," Penn said with a shake of his head. "If Rose doesn't get her blood pressure under control, she's going to be spending some quality time contemplating the ceiling in a hospital room. And Rose isn't much better. You're good, though."

"Can I go, then?"

"What, you don't want to take a nice rest here and wait for your sisters to come and see you?" He laughed and lifted a hand before I could speak. "Yeah, I think you can go home. I'm going to get you a prescription for some antibiotics. You need to watch the fever, and if it gets worse, call me or come straight here. I'll have a standing order to call me in if you show up."

"Thank you. The sleepwalking stuff bothers me," I admitted, feeling chilled at the memory of finding myself out on the street.

"I find it troubling, too, but I suspect it won't happen again since we have the fever under control. I suggest you spend a few days with family to be safe, though."

"With *my* family?" I demanded. "Are you crazy? I thought you wanted me to get better."

He laughed but didn't disagree. "Okay, stay with friends."

"You won't mention this to the Unholy Five."

He frowned and shrugged. "You're an adult. If you want to try and keep this from your sisters, fine. And I stress the word *try* because they will find out. They know everything that happens in this city."

"Man, it's not just me who feels that way?" I asked.

"No, you're not paranoid. Or we all are." He stepped to the door and stopped. "Look, kid, this could be serious. If anything else happens, I'm going to want to do serious testing and find out what's going on. Where are your parents?"

"I think they're on some tiny South Seas Island learning about a local Goddess, but I could be wrong."

"You have strange parents."

"Really? Wow."

He chuckled as he left. I checked out of the hospital within the hour and took a taxi home. I had to go up and get money for him, but afterwards I went back to my place and settled on the sofa. I called Julia to apologize for being late. She didn't ask why, bless her.

The TV still showed The Weather Channel, as it had when I went to sleep the night before. The whole feel spooked me. I took a shower, ate some toast . . . but I wanted out.

I decided to risk driving. A trip to the pharmacy got me the pills I needed. I went to work because I would do better there rather than sitting on the sofa, fearing to sleep and wondering where I'd wake up. I'd have to find someone to stay with tonight.

Julia had her apartment upstairs from the offices, and I knew she had an extra bed. I also knew she would take me in without any lecture, question or complaint. Odd, but I felt I would be safe staying there.

As I got out of the car, I took note of the weather and feared we might have rain soon. I hurried inside, giving a wave to Julia who talked to someone on the phone as I went past. Jacobs looked up from a porn site and dared me to say anything as I came into the room.

"Well, lookee here. The wonder boy shows up late. You must have really hanged one on last night. Bossy won't like this much, I bet. About time you took a step down."

I glanced at him for a moment wondering if his brain ever connected with his mouth. Or if he had a brain. He'd messed with things on my desk and when I found some porn in my drawer, I set up the paper shredder. I thought he would hyperventilate, especially since Julia came into the room and he couldn't do anything to stop me.

"You feel okay, Summerfield?" she asked, frowning.

"Much better than I did last night when I passed out at the hospital," I replied and waved a hand before Julia spoke. "The doctor says I had an odd reaction to a bad fever, but they got it knocked out of me."

"You should go home," she said.

"I wouldn't be any better there." I put the magazines on the side of the desk, started up the shredder and began removing staples. Julia grinned, glancing once at Jacobs to let him know she understood the situation. "Well, as long as you don't work too hard. If you feel worse, let me know."

"I will." I began to shred the first magazine.

Julia left and I happily went back to the shredding. By the time she cleared the door Jacobs had jumped from his seat.

"Sit down. I told you what I'd do if you kept putting this crap in my desk. Not even as classy as Playboy. You have no taste."

"You don't have the right --"

"I said to sit down."

I don't know what he saw in my face, but Jacobs backed away so fast he fell into the chair. I shredded the magazines, having more fun than I'd had in a couple days.

By midafternoon the medications had kicked in and I decided to have a late lunch, fearing I wouldn't feel this well for much longer. Humidity had gone up several notches and a few clouds moved slovenly across the sky. I stepped outside the door and sucked in the air, feeling better despite the weather.

I might have been whistling when I came around the building and crossed to my car.

A shadow moved.

I spun and ducked under the swing of a huge hairy arm with a hand almost the size of my head and ending in long claws. I didn't have time to make a sound of surprise. I threw myself to the right and focused on what attacked me.

The creature from my dreams: red eyes, pug face swiveling on a thick neck. The sound of a car horn a block away startled the creature. He opened his mouth to show a double row of incisors, ready to snap at me.

My mind said this wasn't real.

Lucky for me, my body wasn't listening. I leapt away as the thing swung claws across my upraised right arm. I felt the sting of the cuts. I ducked under the reaching arms and felt claws catch me in the shoulder, tearing cloth and skin.

And then a huge golden-brown cat charged at me. I threw myself aside, but the cat ignored me and leapt onto the back of the creature with claws and teeth digging into the larger animal's neck. The thing bellowed -- a sound like a big truck picking up speed. No one would notice. The two creatures hit the ground, rolling away as I inched towards the sidewalk, hoping to escape into the building.

The first animal reached around and caught my leg, pulling me down with a bone-wrenching thump against the hard cement. The cat hissed and attacked once more although he already bled across the chest. I could hear a growl, a sound deep in the throat of the cat as he sunk teeth into the neck of the other one once more. Blood ran this time as the cat viciously shook his head from side to side, tearing at the neck.

The creature rushed to its feet, shaking the huge cat off in panic. I scooted backwards on my ass, trying to tell my body to get me up off the cement and inside the building.

Red glowing eyes glared at me, and the mouth opened, showing those dagger teeth once more. "Drggg. Drggg."

It took one step toward me but the cat got between us, ears back and tail swishing. . . .

And the big thing spun and fled. The cat followed for about two yards until the animal disappeared into the alley. I thought I heard an odd woof of sound and saw a little flash of light.

The cat stalked towards to me, having won the prize. I scrambled to my feet, but I knew I wouldn't outrun him. I stared into the glowing green eyes --

And the cat changed in a slow, odd melding; a swirling of reality . . . or whatever this was. I blinked. A tall, thin man with shoulder-length golden-brown hair and green eyes stood before me. He wore neat jeans and a tee-shirt with a tear across the shoulder, showing a line of blood. He blinked and grimaced, a hand going to the wound.

"You better get inside before another shows up. We'll talk later," he said.

I nodded. He held out his hand and I took it, letting him pull me to my feet. I stared into his face, trying to find answers, but we both jumped at the sound of something in the alley. He frowned and gave me a little shove.

"Go. Get inside."

"We should warn people," I said, my arm waving towards the alley.

"No. You're the one they're after. Go. We'll talk soon."

I had to call the doctor because the hallucinations had taken a really bad turn, and I wasn't safe out on the streets by myself. I gave one more nod to the cat man and walked away, limping a little, and headed back into the building.

Julia saw me and leapt from her desk so fast, she startled

me. "What happened! How did you cut yourself?"

I glanced at the cuts.

I could not bleed from a hallucination.

*Hell.*

I don't know why this made me feel better, because it made things so much worse in ways I couldn't even begin to understand or explain. I grinned which worried her.

"Come in and sit down, Summerfield." She pulled a chair away from the wall, breaking up the perfect Feng Shui of her office. I dropped onto the seat and took the paper towel she handed me, dabbing at a wound.

"I slipped," I said, knowing the explanation sounded odd and improbable. "A branch had caught under my car. I thought I heard something when I drove in today."

"Those look like claw marks," she said, frowning.

"Do they? Just twigs. "

The fact I sounded so upbeat helped. My mood came from an adrenalin high, mixed with an odd belief I wasn't insane, or at least not in the way I had first imagined. I tried not to think how sitting here with Julia might be more of the same hallucination.

"The things some people will do to get in good with the Bossy."

Jacobs stood in the doorway; well, slouched there, anyway, which made me think this was reality. I wouldn't have invited him into my dream world where even red-eyed monsters with dagger teeth didn't annoy me as much as he did.

I had traveled with my parents for a good portion of my life. They'd sought out the little known and exotic spiritual connections to the world and I'd seen some strange things, which made me a good reporter for Woo Woo News. My background also made this bout of craziness a little easier to accept, though it made no sense. A lot of things in the world don't make sense, but we all still live with it. I just never expected to have to deal with it on so intimate a level.

Julia got a first aid kit from the bathroom and cleaned up my cuts and scratches. I talked to her, joking. I don't know what I said. My brain kept my mouth moving while my thoughts tumbled through the events of the last few days. If the creature out there had been real, then my dreams were, somehow, real as well. Dragons. Flying on horses. Falling.

The door to the building opened. I hoped this would be someone to take Julia's attention, at least for a while. I needed some time alone with my head.

"Tessa!" she said with delight. "You've never come here before!"

Great. The astrologer. Well, maybe she would keep her busy.

I turned and started to nod a greeting.

Tall, golden-brown hair, green eyes. He still wore blue jeans, but he'd traded the tee shirt for a looser shirt without bloodstains and rips.

I had always assumed Tessa was a woman, but I'd failed to take into account one of Julia's odd eccentricities: she calls everyone by their last name. I hadn't expected the astrologer to be a man, and I certainly hadn't expected him to be some kind of shapeshifter with a double life as a huge cat with glowing green eyes.

"I don't think you two have met," Julia said, oblivious to my moment of shock. "Tessa, Summerfield."

"Pleased to meet you at last," Tessa said and held out a hand. I shook it. Felt real. He appeared amused at my obvious shock and dismay. I supposed it looked comical at this point, at least from an outsider's view.

Julia went to put the first aid box away, giving us a few brief moments alone.

"We need to talk somewhere," Tessa said.

"We? You? You are?" I asked, trying to frame some sort

of question.

He pulled aside the collar of his shirt and showed bandages and blood. "I am. We can't talk here."

I agreed and started to stand. He shook his head.

"We need to be a little more subtle. I have a plan."

He didn't say more since Julia returned. Tessa began to talk to her, and I sat back and tried very hard not to think about rooms with padded walls.

"I came over because I need a favor," Tessa said drawing my attention. "I need to get across town and wondered if you could take me."

I recognized my cue. "I'm heading out. I can take you."

Julia glanced my way worried about my state of mind, or health or something. I gave her a bright smile and stood without falling over. Tessa agreed before Julia could say anything, and in a couple more minutes we headed out of the building and into the humid, dangerous world outside.

# CHAPTER 11

I stopped by the side of the building, intending not to go any farther until he talked to me. "I want answers."

"Not here." Tessa glanced towards the alley and I remembered seeing something there the other day. "I do not ride in cars, but this time we need to get clear of the area, where the enemy is searching for you. So the car it is."

"Enemy?" I asked as we crossed to the poor, battered Subaru. "What enemy? What is going on?"

"We'll go have food and talk," he replied, as though I hadn't any say in what happened. I gave him a sharp glance and Tessa lifted his hand and appeared contrite. "My apologies. My manners are lacking at the moment. I need food. Shifting uses considerable energy and I want to replenish before we run into more trouble."

"And we will."

"Oh yes."

I unlocked the car and climbed in, sitting alone for a moment before I reached over and pushed the passenger side door open since he stood staring at it with some trepidation. He climbed in with the same sort of worry a first time rider might give a horse.

"I don't travel in cars," he repeated as he settled into the seat. He eyed the interior with a little surprise, I thought. Maybe a bit more plush and comfortable than he expected.

"Seatbelt." I pulled mine into place. He did the same and

appeared to take some comfort in feeling more secure. "Where are we going?"

"Wherever you think best. Away from this area." He glanced out the window and I couldn't tell if he felt more worry about what might be lurking out there or at riding in the car.

"You want to tell me what's going on?" I asked as I started the car. I glanced at the alley.

"Not while you are driving this thing. I prefer you have your attention on the matter at hand."

I wanted to argue, but I decided the time driving might give me a better chance to frame my own questions. I thought about where we could have a meal talking about things maybe I didn't want anyone else to hear. Nowhere too fancy with the wait staff hanging close by. We needed somewhere quiet, though.

Or else somewhere very noisy.

I drove to a Red Robins most of the way across town while Tessa gradually became more comfortable with the car and stopped gripping the seat, and I did my best to avoid any of the busier streets. I didn't want to know what would happen if someone startled him. Most of the streets were cleared now, too, which helped.

The restaurant was just starting to fill and the loud sounds startled Tessa when we first stepped inside. Then he gave a nod of understanding. We took a booth by the windows though we had to wait a couple minutes for one. In the booth, at least we wouldn't have anyone sitting too close. And the noise would drown out our discussion.

"Chicken. Good." Tessa looked up from the menu. "I like chicken."

"Right. So, first question: Are you a human or a cat?"

"Neither. I'm fae."

I took a breath to demand what the hell he meant, but the

server brought our iced teas and took our orders. Everything felt too damned mundane, and I kept wondering about my sanity level. Was any of this real?

I had no choice but to play along. I leaned forward and prepared to ask questions.

"There is another reality which brushes up close to your world," Tessa began before I could ask. "The area can be breached through magic, but it's rarely noticeable. Some problem seems to have leapt into this world big time, though. There hasn't been an incursion this serious since before the Industrial Age."

"Why am I involved?"

"Because you have something magical." Tessa lifted a hand and frowned. "Something which belongs to one of the clans, though I'm having trouble reading what it might be."

"I haven't --" I reconsidered the situation. "Could this be the same thing you searched for after the storm? That was you, right? There isn't another huge cat with glowing green eyes around town?"

"I am unique." He said the words with an odd little tilt of his head but went on before I could say more. "Yes, I was the one searching. I felt something fall in the storm, but I couldn't locate it in the mud and muck. I could sense the magic and knew it didn't come from my clan. I had hoped to grab it before someone else did, though."

"The medallion. Round with a dragon design?"

He froze in mid-move and appeared truly worried for the first time. "Dragon Clan? We're dealing with Dragon Clan problems?" he asked softly.

"You're doing your best to make me feel better about this, aren't you?"

He blinked and grinned a little, though he still appeared shocked and worried. "The Dragon Clan is the most powerful of the five clans. Mine, the Cat Clan, is the least powerful. I don't want to find myself in the middle of some Dragon Clan trouble, though I fear I have no choice. And neither, I suspect, do you since you have the medallion."

"I don't have it anymore. I lost it before I got back to the car."

"No, you didn't lose it. Magic. It hid from you to remain safe." Tessa reached towards me, and did a little flicker of his fingers. I felt a whisper of cold at my neck and chest. When I reached, I could feel the silver chain beneath my fingers.

Tessa sat back with a start; his green eyes went wide this time. "This isn't a medallion. Key. Gods."

"Key?"

"A piece of magic they'll need to get back home. The leader of the clan wears the key. If he has lost this --"

"Is this why I'm having the nightmares?"

"Nightmares?" he asked, though he had the look of someone who didn't want to know.

"The ones about the battle, the guy turning into a dragon and then dying."

"Son of a bitch." He did grow pale this time and sat still for a few seconds while he took deep breaths. "Tell me everything about the nightmare."

I recited as much of what I'd seen as I could. Tessa's reaction didn't make me feel any better. I had just finished when the food arrived. Tessa picked up his sandwich, sat it back down, and stared at me.

"I knew some magic had fallen from the storm -- something strong since I had picked up on it even in the mass of spells and powers circulating in the weather. I didn't realize I was searching for a key." He shook his head, upset. "I didn't expect this to be related to the Dragon Clan, and having heard about the battle -- damn, this isn't good."

"I don't want the key." I would have taken it off if I could have found it. Damn sneaky *thing.*

"I can't take the key," he said with regret. "The wrong clan; the wrong magic. I could have handled something not as powerful from the Dragon Clan, but not this. If I tried to take it, the results would be . . . well, more spectacular than you and I could explain, providing either of us survived. The key allowed you to find it because you aren't allied to any clan. Unfortunately, you aren't fae, either. You're feeling ill because the key is pulling power from you, and not being fae, you can't replenish what it has taken."

"So what am I supposed to do?"

"I can help while we figure this out." Tessa reached over and touched my tea glass. I saw the drink fizz a little. "Drink this. It'll give you energy for a while."

"You don't sound too assured about this trouble." I sipped and felt better almost immediately.

"This is something I never thought to see," he admitted. "Dragon Clan has held the power in the fae lands for centuries. They held power before your Rome fell. To have them fall . . . this is not a good sign. I'm going to try to contact others and see if we can decide what to do."

"How many of you people are there over here?" I asked, nibbling on fries.

"Not many. My clan . . . well, we're not friends with Dragon Clan. We fought a major war about two hundred years ago and they left us trapped on this side. So there's no love lost between Dragons and Cats."

I had a question on my lips, but I didn't know if I wanted to ask. He had explained the situation as though he suffered a personal affront as though he had been one of the ones trapped here. I decided I had enough to deal with already and didn't ask.

"So, you don't care what happens to these Dragon Clan people?" I asked instead.

"I shouldn't, but . . ." He ate some of the sandwich and I

left him to think through his own problems. I drank more magic tea and ate my hamburger. I had enough trouble to consider all of my own.

"I shouldn't care about what's happened to the Dragon Clan, but my instincts tell me this is bad for all of us," he admitted at last. He'd eaten some of his sandwich and seemed better for it. "We don't want the Dragon Clan on this side, not even in this weakened state. And there are the trolls. That's what we fought earlier."

"The trolls work for the Dragon Clan?" I asked.

"Not according to your tale of the battle since they killed many of the clan. Something else knows you have the key and they're trying to get it."

"Another clan?"

"I would think so. We don't need a third faction in this mess. I don't know who the Dragon Clan fought. I can't imagine any of the other clans being strong enough to kill their totem."

"Totem?"

"*Vane.* The dragon." He shook his head and I thought I saw sorrow in his face this time, even for what had to be an enemy. "Dragon Clan is no friend of mine, but I think whatever chased them here is worse."

"You were there on the street when I woke up, weren't you? You and a troll?"

"Yes. I felt something magical on the move and hurried out and saw you. I used a little magic to nudge you awake when the troll arrived but stayed in cat form in case I needed to fight."

"Thank you. So, what do we do?" I asked.

"I'll stick close to you while I figure this out. Will this be a problem? I have a small apartment over my shop and a futon where you can sleep."

"Not a problem for me," I said, though I didn't ask the

timeframe on this trouble. I knew he wouldn't have an answer yet. "I wasn't too keen on spending the night alone and wondering where I would wake up tomorrow."

The rest of the meal went normally, as long as you didn't count the bits of conversation about shape shifting and magic keys. I'm not sure when I began accepting everything as real and no longer believed I had gone crazy. I'm not sure I had made the wise choice in this belief, but at least this odd reality gave me some choices.

When we left the restaurant, we both glanced at the sky. I could see patches of blue through the roiling clouds. Unfortunately, the temperature and humidity had taken another leap upwards.

I unlocked the car and threw the door open. Tessa did the same, stepping away in shock.

"Goddess Great," he said stunned. "This is an oven!"

"Give it a minute." I climbed in and started the AC running. He came into the car more slowly and leaned forward so the vents blew back his hair. He closed his eyes, looking very much like a contented cat.

"Ah. This is better," he admitted. He pulled the seatbelt into place without being told.

"So, fae have a problem with cars? Technology? Bad mix with magic or something?"

He frowned, perhaps thinking I shouldn't be driving and talking at the same time, but since I hadn't pulled out of the parking spot yet, he must have decided we were okay.

"There's no problem between magic and technology. This is more of a cultural reaction, and hard to break. I sometimes carry a cell phone, though I seldom use it. We tend to consider technology crass and lacking in the beauty of magic. I begin to think this might be an outmoded way of thinking." He leaned towards the vent once more.

I drove back to the office, keeping the talk to a minimum

so I didn't upset my guest. Tessa relaxed finally, though he did keep watching the sky. I felt as though I should be watching for UFOs. Or flying horses.

As though my life hadn't been weird enough already.

I parked at the office and went in to tell Julia I was heading home, though my car would stay. I wanted it nearby, but not parked in front of Tessa's place. Jacobs protested the idea of me taking off, as though I hadn't already been leaving a few hours before. I hurried out before I heard too much of the disagreement and found myself taking out my frustration on him. I let Julia have the fun instead. After all, she'd had to suffer with him in the office all day.

Tessa had walked ahead to his place and waited by the door keeping watch and reminding me how some*thing* had tried to kill me not so long ago. Walking the couple blocks felt close to suicidal. I glanced over my shoulder at the sound of voices and spotted people a block away, but they looked normal enough. A couple cars passed by: crass by fae standards, which made me safe from them. Good to know.

I'd never been inside Tessa's little fortune-telling shop. I passed the doorway and shivered as the hair on my arms rose --

"You came through a ward," Tessa explained. He stood by a table, glancing down at Tarot cards laid out on a gold cloth. "You felt the power because of your link to the key. Most people never notice."

"Why this work?" I asked, waving a hand towards table. Arcane symbols, neatly framed, hung in pleasant patterns. Nothing here screamed charlatan.

"I have to make a living somehow. Using magic for everything is too noticeable these days. Since technology doesn't suit me, I have a hard time finding work I can do. And I am good at this. I've always had a feel for the currents of time and the blending of now with the possible future."

He stared at the cards for a moment more, and then crossed back and locked the door. We took a flight of stairs to a small, well-kept and rather sedate apartment. I found myself relaxing the moment I entered the living room.

"I get the feeling . . . ." Tessa gave a little shrug though this time he winced and touched his chest, reminding me of his wounds. "I get the feeling we're going to face trouble soon. Maybe not tonight, but within the next couple days. I suggest you get some sleep. You've not had much the last couple day, and you're going to need rest."

I didn't argue. He brought me a blanket and a pillow, and I settled on the futon. I felt exhausted.

"I'm going to contact some people." He already looked harassed, as though he knew this wasn't going to be easy. "I'll try to stay quiet."

"Don't worry about me. I appreciate the help."

I kicked off my shoes and stretched out, feeling more comfortable than I expected. Maybe that came from magic. Despite the early hour, sleep came almost immediately.

I heard Tessa talking during the next few hours and began to realize he didn't do so by phone. He grew angry at times, which couldn't be good.

But I slept and wondered what the new day would bring.

# CHAPTER 12

When I awoke sometime after dawn, I found Tessa pacing by the window overlooking the street. I didn't think he'd slept. I grunted a few words and he directed me to his bathroom and shower. He had my clothing clean and *magically* sitting by the shower by the time I came out.

"That must be handy," I said, brushing my hand over my shirt.

"It helps," he agreed and settled on a chair by the futon. I settled on the futon, ready for whatever knowledge he would impart. I'm a reporter. I'm good at listening.

"My clan are fools," he said at last with a little wave of his hand. "They will not come to help the Dragon Clan, even if in helping them, they might save this world from considerable trouble. I shouldn't take this so badly, but I thought they would come for *me*." He shook his head and handed me a glass from the table beside him. "Drink this. It'll help you through part of the day."

"I'm sorry about your clan," I said. I worried, wondering what the two of us could do. I sipped the orange juice, feeling better almost immediately again and wondering if a person could get addicted to magic.

"My problem with the Cat Clan doesn't matter in the long run," he admitted and leaned back. "There are no more than two dozen of us left in your world. I understand the anger they feel towards the Dragon Clan, but sometimes a person has to move past anger and do what's right."

"And what's right in this mess?"

"I don't know yet. I am going to go prowl around. Yes, literally prowl in my cat form. You can stay here, but it won't make you any safer if I'm not around."

"I'll go to class this morning. I'd like a little normality in my life."

I wanted to see Glynis, though I didn't say so to Tessa. He didn't argue though. I walked to the Woo Woo parking lot, him tagging along. Nothing attacked us, and in a couple minutes I drove away. I glanced in the mirror to see the swishing tail of a very large cat as he darted into the alley. The tail gave away more of his agitation than anything had in his human form.

I don't know why I felt better. Considering the magnitude of the trouble, and how little prepared I was to deal with any of it, I should have panicked. However, I had a clue and an ally who at least had some measure of power to keep me safe while we figured things out.

And I had a key hanging around my neck, though I couldn't see or feel it. I tried to banish the idea of a noose. The Dragon Clan would want the key and I think even Tessa wanted them to take it and leave.

I pulled into the garage at the apartment and ran upstairs -- took the stairs in fact since I hadn't been getting a lot of exercise lately -- and grabbed my pack with my school supplies. My mind wasn't on Terrestrial Ecology, though. I wondered about the old war between the Cats and the Dragons. I'd have to ask Tessa. Since I knew something existed, I wanted to understand it all.

Maybe they had college courses for people like me.

Glynis stood by the tree, waiting for me. She didn't appear happy, which made me slow for a moment, wondering what I had done. And then I knew.

"I'm sorry," I apologized before she could speak. Her pretty eyes narrowed. "I missed our study date at the library last night. It slipped my mind. I was in the hospital --"

"Hospital? You were in the hospital?" Her hand went to my arm and I saw worry in her face.

"The night before. I passed out," I said and patted her hand. "Nothing serious. They gave me medications and things just got odd or I would have remembered at least to call you."

"Oh. Well." Her face softened. I hated the little bit of a lie I had slipped in there. "You're all right?"

"Doing better. Well enough to remember to come to class, at least. Let's get in. We can talk afterwards."

"I'm glad you're feeling better." She put her arm in mine.

The day would have gone well if I hadn't been sitting by the window during class. I kept seeing things in the sky. I don't think anyone else saw the odd shapes moving through the clouds. I wondered if Rich Anderson sat at Doppler pulling his hair out this time. Glynis noticed how scattered I seemed and suggested I go home and sleep. I promised to call her later.

Later, after all this insanity had passed. I realized the danger following me could pull Glynis in as well. I hurried home, got in my car and drove away, glancing upward at the first stoplight. I'd been stupid to walk to class and not think about the enemy. Plainly, I had not quite come to believe yet.

Tessa's shop showed the closed sign. I tried the door anyway. I think if he had been around, he would have noticed me. I headed for the Woo Woo News office as my second choice since I knew Tessa could find me there. I parked so I could see the alley. Nothing moved. I judged the distance to the front door as I got out of the car and hit the lock. I backed away for the first few steps, keeping an eye on the shadows. I didn't want to appear too crazy though, so when I heard someone on the sidewalk, I hurried to the front door.

Julia was filing something when I came in. She came to the doorway, frowning a little. "You sure you want to work today?"

"I have some writing to do," I said. "Anything new out there?"

"No. Tessa says we should stay quiet for a few days and the story will come to us if we're patient." She gave a sigh. *Patient* was not one of her favorite words. "He also said he thought the two of you would get along real well."

"I think so," I agreed and headed to my desk.

Jacobs had been speaking on the phone, but he hung up when I arrived which meant it hadn't been work-related. Should I be surprised?

"I figured out why Bossy lets you get away with all this shit all the time. You two have something kinky going on."

"You should mention that to her. I'm sure she'll find it interesting."

He smirked, as though I had blurted out the details of a clandestine affair. Some people hear what they want. At another time I might have taken him to task. Today, he wasn't more than a passing gnat of annoyance.

I worked for about an hour, got one report done and the outline for another written before Tessa arrived. I could hear him talking to Julia and began closing my work before he came into the office.

"Hey, Summerfield." He nodded a greeting, glanced at Jacobs and back to me. "I hate to impose, but Julia said if you're done with work you might give me a ride. If not --"

"I'm done," I said. Jacobs' head came up and he swiveled in his chair to look from Tessa to me. I could see whole new insinuations about my sex life lighting up his eyes, and I still didn't give a damn.

Later, though . . . later we'd have a discussion about his

bad manners.

I put the laptop in the drawer. Since the computer is password coded, Jacobs couldn't get into it to take my work, which he had done once early on. He hadn't fooled Julia and he'd had to work hard to write something of his own in the next six hours.

I didn't say goodbye to him. Tessa and I both made quick farewells to Julia and headed out into the lot. The day had grown hot and sticky. What a shock.

"What is the little creep's problem?" Tessa asked, glancing back at the building.

"Other than he's a little creep?" I asked, hurrying to the car.

"Good point." He stared at the building. I would rather he watched the alley. "He had some bad currents going on around him. I get the distinct feeling he's going to be a very unhappy man soon. I can sense such things sometimes."

"Karma catching up with him," I said, and Tessa nodded. We both understood how it worked. "So, what are we doing?"

He finally glanced at the alley and crossed quickly to the car. I don't know if he saw anything or not, but I decided not to waste any time and followed right behind him. We drove away and I turned to him at the first stop, waiting while the heavy foot traffic in Old Market crossed in front of us.

"I have been trying to move around town to get a feeling for the magic," he explained and sounded a bit annoyed. "There's too much magical energy centered in Omaha, and the powers are overlaying each other. I'd need to get about fifty miles out of town and do a reading, which should help me sort out the areas. I could have gone as a cat, but I think it better we stick together this afternoon."

"Not a problem. What direction?"

"It doesn't matter."

"Since we're on the north side of town, we'll head up I29."

I started that way and dared to speak, even with the car moving. "Anything else you've picked up?"

"I sensed a considerable amount of magic moving this afternoon. Something is about to happen."

"When I was at class, I thought I could see things in the clouds."

"I'm not surprised." Tessa brushed his hand through the air, as though he could feel something near me. "Yes, the key is making you more attuned to magic, which might be good. You'll have more warning when something is coming for you."

"And what should I do then?"

"Run like hell. You don't have any real defense, and I don't think I can make you one which would work against even the lowest member of the Dragon Clan."

Not the answer I wanted to hear, but at least I knew where I stood . . . which wasn't good, of course. Tessa and I stood against a lot of forces I didn't understand, and I couldn't fight anyway.

"Any luck with your clan?" I asked.

He snarled. The very cat-like sound startled me, and I glanced his way.

"Sorry. No, I haven't had any luck with them. They're too happy to see the Dragon Clan trounced to care what the larger picture means."

"You and I aren't going to be much of a force to fight anything."

"I plan to do my best to avoid any battle. I'd avoid contact, too, but since you have the key, I think we must deal with someone from the Dragon Clan eventually."

"Or whoever is chasing them? Since you're no friends with the Dragon Clan, should we ally with their enemies? The enemy of my enemy is my friend?"

"Yes, well, things don't work that way with the fae," he admitted and sat back. He seemed more comfortable with the moving car and talking at the same time. Or perhaps he knew he dared not waste time while he helped me understand the situation. "From what you told me about the nightmare, I suspect whatever clan attacked them has allies from the Other Side, which is a mass of realities far less akin to the fae and human worlds. Those are dangerous groups to deal with because we can't understand their needs and wants. Someone has gone to them and brought them into the fae lands."

I didn't ask more questions. I figured he had enough to think about already.

We had light traffic once we got past Missouri Valley. I pulled off at Modale, and Tessa checked with a hand out the window and shook his head. We went on to Mondamin, but he said it wasn't much better. Clouds had rolled in over us and a steady drizzle began to fall. The windshield wipers amused Tessa who had a momentary fascination with their movement. Wind gusts jabbed at us and I could tell we'd soon face another bad storm.

"Better traveling through this in a car than on foot," Tessa admitted as rain began to fall harder. A glance in my mirror showed a massive black cloud hanging over Omaha. "That's a major admission for me, you know. I rode in a car once, a long time ago. They've improved since then."

I considered asking about time and the fae, but I still couldn't quite frame the question properly. We reached the turn off to Little Sioux and Tessa glanced up at the huge sign at the side of the road.

"Prepare to Meet Thy God," he read aloud. "Wow. I didn't know he lived so close to Omaha. You'd think the place would be more popular."

Lucky for me I had already slowed for the off ramp. I snickered and saw him grin. The humor lightened the mood.

On one side of the freeway sat a small cluster of buildings and on the other side was a huge campground. I had never seen anyone moving at the campground, though. Today, given the way my life had been going, I wondered what lived there. I was tending toward an alien enclave. Anything was possible.

"This is good," Tessa said. I pulled over and parked. He got out of the car and moved off the side of the road where he sat down with a clear view of Omaha back along the Interstate. I hoped he didn't take long and we didn't draw too much attention. I didn't think they got many people communing with nature in the middle of rainstorms around here.

I got out as well and stood by the Subaru, letting the light rain brush over me. I felt better once we left Omaha, probably because I no longer felt the weight of magic hanging over the city.

Tessa sat with his eyes closed and his hands in his lap. I had seen monks sit in the same position for hours. I had learned patience in a small, overlooked temple my parents had sought out in their quest for enlightenment. Closing my own eyes, I felt the peace of the distant place wash over me. It helped as well.

A few minutes later, Tessa stood, brushed rain, grass and bugs from his clothing, and headed to the car. I regretted leaving so soon. I'd enjoyed the calm and quiet of the place where the sound of the passing of cars on the Interstate became almost as soothing as the sound of the breeze.

"I can read two hot spots," he said as he reached by the car. "One is out in Fontenelle Forest. I should have thought to search there long before now. The wildness area makes it an excellent place for fae to hide. The second is more worrisome. I can feel something forming, coming in on the storm. I think we're in for one hell of a lot of trouble tonight."

"So, we head back?" I asked, half hoping he'd say no.

And I saw the moment of indecision on his face. He turned towards Omaha, the wind blowing back his long hair.

He lifted his hand to test out the magic. "Yes. We go back. I have to. I can't let this go without trying to help set things right and get the trouble out of here before these fools do the kind of harm humans can't ignore. The trolls are inexcusable. No one should have let them loose in the human world. And you are still safer with me in Omaha rather than out somewhere else alone. I'm sorry."

"I appreciate the help," I said as we got into the car. "Without you, I wouldn't have survived this long."

"You need more energy. Is there somewhere we can get something to drink?"

I found a little gas and shop, filled up and bought us a couple sodas. I drank mine after Tessa imbued it with magic. Like him, I had the feeling I would need the strength. Then we headed back towards Omaha.

The storm grew worse as we headed south and by the time we reached Missouri Valley, I had trouble seeing through the deluge. We'd passed one car off the side of the road, but Tessa checked and found no one injured. I don't think the sight improved his feelings toward cars, though.

Just short of the North Omaha bypass, I felt something else hit.

"Magic!" Tessa warned, startled. I slowed and pulled off under the ramp, which was not an uncommon thing to do in a storm this serious. Tessa leaned forward, hands against the windshield while the storm went crazy. Wind howled past us, and rain turned to hail in a heartbeat. Other cars pulled over, worried people all around us.

The storm eased a moment later.

"Go," Tessa ordered. "We need to get moving. Head towards Fontenelle as quickly as you can -- as quickly and *safely* as you can."

I pulled out. Someone else took our place as I drove away on the slick and wind-swept road. A few of the big trucks had pulled over and one had jackknifed into the center, but we got past him without trouble.

I headed for the south of Omaha, taking 80 West, which was an iffy choice if we hit traffic. From there I went south on the Kennedy Highway. The weather hadn't improved, and I worried about what I would find on the regular streets, but we soon had no choice. I headed into Bellevue.

We didn't get very far.

None of the stoplights worked. Cars had stalled out in the half-flooded streets, and the rain and hail grew worse. I saw people huddled in doorways and a cop car abandoned in the middle of an intersection with water up to the doors. I started to slow.

"Go through. I'll get us there," Tessa said. He placed both hands on the dashboard and I could see a little sparkle of light around his fingertips. I went through the intersection with my breath held.

At the next intersection we ran into a different problem. Something huge galloped through the street ahead of us, and made a skidding stop and spun our way.

"Hell," Tessa whispered

I knew enough to back up, but the horse and rider moved too quickly. Then I realized --

"Centaur," Tessa hissed as the creature charged the car, rose up on back legs and smashed down. The hood dented and the engine squealed in protest. I hit the gas, still in reverse, and we retreated a block, the centaur coming after us, stalking forward with his head down while trying to see inside the windshield.

"This is the best chance to get past him," Tessa said. "Roan's not used to cars. Go forward and go fast. I'll throw him off balance."

"I'm not sure how far the car will get," I admitted as I started to shift gears, the engine protesting.

"As far as we can," Tessa replied and shook his head. "Centaur Clan. They should *never* have had the power to take on the Dragon Clan."

He sounded considerably more worried, which didn't help. I hit the gas as the centaur rose as though to trample us. Tessa waved his hand; magic cracked the window, and the centaur lost his footing and tumbled backwards as we swept past.

The engine howled in protest and I heard something snap before it died.

"Out," I said. "We can't stay in here!"

Tessa didn't argue. He leapt out his side and reached me before I stepped into the cold, over-the-ankle, water.

"Get to cover!" Tessa ordered. "I'm going to change and get clear. I'll find you later. Summerfield, don't admit to anything if they ask you. Whatever you do, don't mention I'm a shape shifter or that you have the Dragon Clan key. Those are secrets we can use!"

He expected them to catch me. His ability to get away might be the best hope I had, so I sloshed towards the sidewalk and higher ground. I saw Roan, the centaur, getting back to his feet, and I thought I could hear shouts of others heading towards me.

I saw Tessa bounding through the water and into the shadows, which would have been handy. I felt ungainly, slipping in the mud and going down on my hands and knees. I scrambled back up and ran as best I could.

I knew I wouldn't get far.

# CHAPTER 13

For a little while, I harbored an insane belief I might get away. I ducked between buildings too tight for the centaur and kept out of direct sight. I found few people on the street, which didn't help. I had the feeling if I could get to a crowd, Roan would be slow to show himself. I spotted someone, which I thought a good sign until the person lifted a hand and I felt magic in the air. I threw myself down as warmth brushed over the top of me while the water felt uncomfortably tingly. Scrambling up, I looked around and darted in another direction, but the person followed. The centaur had help.

I began to run out of energy and this time I couldn't blame it on the key. Slogging through half-flooded streets while being chased took regular, human energy. I knew I had to find some kind of cover. The water flowed to the right; I turned to the left and worked against the flow, hoping to get to higher ground where I could move easier.

Someone ran ahead of me, though he limped, a cloth tied around his wounded leg. I almost caught up with him when he spun, his hands lifting -- more magic. I yelped and dropped, turning the fall into a roll and caught him in the legs. He gave a grunt of pain as he landed. He tried to scramble away, which was fine by me. I didn't want to stop and fight.

The centaur appeared half a block ahead of us.

"There they are!" he yelled, arms waving in our direction.

I struggled back to my feet and started to run.

*They?*

The guy I had taken down still struggled to reach his feet. I could hear people coming in the rain and they didn't sound as though the storm slowed them.

This guy was not my enemy.

*The enemy of my enemy is my friend.* Maybe things didn't work that way in fae, but we were in my realm right now, and I could at least pretend we played by my rules. I caught him by the arm and pulled him to his feet. With an arm around his waist, I dragged him off in a direction I hoped would get us clear of this mess.

"Who are you?" he whispered, his face ashen white.

I thought about saying something witty about being the keymaster, but I had the feeling human cultural references would be lost on him. He wasn't from around here -- not from around here by a long shot by the look of his hand sewn clothing and intricate embroidery.

"Summerfield," I said. "And you?"

Shock showed in his pale face. "You're not Dragon Clan."

"No. You?" I half recognized him from the link, but I couldn't reach the information. He had not been present in the dream like some of the others.

"I'm the . . . . He stopped speaking, as though he thought he might say something he shouldn't. Then he gave a little shrug. "I am York, the Dragon Clan bard."

By the way he said those words I knew he shouldn't be out here and about to fall to the Centaur Clan. "Why aren't you with the others?" I asked, sounding, I suppose, as though I had a clue about what was going on.

"I am trying to reach them, but the city is bathed in magic," he said, his hand held out. "I couldn't find them. You aren't Dragon Clan. Why are you helping me? Who -- what --"

He reached out and brushed a little magic over me and yelped, trying to pull away.

"*Cat Clan.* Cat magic. Where are you taking me?"

Cat Clan and Dragon Clan had their own battle, and he must have felt the magic Tessa had given me to drink. I wondered why he didn't feel the key, except I thought the key wanted to stay with the stronger person. Odd, to think of the medallion being intelligent enough to make those decisions.

And worrisome to think I was the stronger of us: clueless, magicless me.

I grabbed the bard when I heard shouts closer.

"I'm taking you away from *here.* Don't worry. We're both running from the same enemy."

He glanced over his shoulder and didn't argue when we began to move. I could feel him shudder with each breath and knew he held to consciousness by magic. I did my best to get him away, but at the next block I found another problem. They'd brought out the trolls, and those huge, hulking creatures weren't slowed at all by the water. I tried to change direction and found two more trolls bounding towards us like puppies in a spring rain.

The bard lifted his head . . . and sang.

The sound might have held words, but I didn't hear them. I felt the magic instead. The sound brushed over the world as peaceful magic spread out around us. The trolls paused and listened, heads canted to the side, eyes blinking. I thought I might have done the same, except I held enough fear to know we had to get moving. York stopped singing and slumped against me, but we got away from the trolls. I wished Tessa would show up. I wished I had real magic to help.

The Centaur Clan captured us at the next street. I slid around the corner and found myself facing five people formed up in a square with one in the middle. The moment we appeared their magic spread out in a wave of sparkling light, catching us in an enchanted fish net.

The bard fell to his knees as the magic swarmed around us, a force so strong I found it hard to breathe. My sight fuzzed, and the world slipped away a little. The others dragged the bard and me off through the rain. It hurt when I banged my legs against the curb, but there wasn't a damned thing I could do. They controlled me.

I closed my eyes for a while and fought them open because I realized I needed to know where they took us. If we could get away, I might be able to get us to safety if I knew which way to run.

I could see the enemy through the haze of magic, and they appeared to be very nervous fae. Every time lightning flashed, they jumped. They formed a square around York and me --

We went up into the sky. I thought, for a moment, I would be ill. Riding a horse through the clouds had felt different, with a sense of comfort and protection beneath me. I feared they intended to drop us.

Even with the shield of magic around the bard and me, I could still feel the wind blowing past my face. We went into the clouds and I had expected they'd go higher, but I think they meant to hide in the mass of gray. We skimmed through the storm with four people at points around the two of us, and a fifth moving overhead. I could see the lines of magic woven around them and us.

A shame I had no way to attract attention. I could turn my head enough to see several more of the Centaur Clan, though not Roan himself. I could see York, too, and the blood flowing down his leg.

We didn't fly for long. I recognized the outline of north Omaha as we came out of the clouds. I thought we headed for the Lake Cunningham area. We skimmed too close over the tops of trees and dropped into an open glade, the bard and

I hitting the ground with more force than the others. The magic eased for a moment, but hands grabbed us and dragged us both off. I tried to fight.

That didn't last for long.

When I regained consciousness, I found myself in some kind of odd stockade. Small trees had grown in a perfect square around a flat, muddy patch of ground. Lines of glowing magic twined around them.

Given the darkness of the night and the stiffness of my muscles, I knew many hours had passed. I rolled over and sat up, grimacing at a new pain through my back and shoulders. I wasn't alone: The Dragon Clan Bard sat a few feet away, his legs pulled up to his chest and looking forlorn and lost. I couldn't sense the magic I'd been feeling for the last couple days, except for a bit from the area around the trees. I suspected the enclosure made us invisible to anyone who might be searching for a lost bard. Or for me.

"Hey," I said softly, not certain if I wanted to draw too much attention.

York lifted his head. I thought he must be young and someone who hadn't dealt with trouble very often. Or perhaps, being a bard, he just hadn't had to face it on his own. I didn't know, and I wasn't comfortable asking anything which might alert him to the fact I wasn't fae. So far I didn't think anyone had noticed. Tessa's magic and the key must have imbued me with enough magic they never considered I could be human, which probably saved my life.

"We . . . we won't get free of this, I fear," York whispered when I moved closer. He glanced around and shook his head. "You should have left me. You would have had a chance."

"It wouldn't have been the right thing to do." I took a deep breath, calling on my inner calm. I didn't want to think we hadn't a chance at all. Besides, he didn't know about Tessa. "What do you think we should do?"

"Pray to the gods --" He stopped as the trees in front of us parted.

And they brought in Tessa. I know I made a sound of worry as Tessa landed on his knees in the mud. He stayed there for a moment as the prison walls went back into place, before he crawled over to us.

"Well, this is bad, isn't it?" I asked.

"Oh, not as bad as it seems," he said softly, and gave a quick, feral little smile. "We have to move quickly, though. The Centaur Clan leader is on the way, and he's bound to note I'm not as magic-less as they think. And you are?"

York frowned and shook his head. "You're Cat Clan."

"Yes. And you're Dragon Clan, and from what I can guess, your people are in a hell of a lot of trouble."

"We were attacked." He swallowed, as though he thought he shouldn't say anything. He glanced around at the trees and must have decided he didn't have anything to lose. "We were attacked, and the dragon died. We tried to get away, but they came after us. They have help."

"I guessed as much. Centaur Clan never had the ability or the power to pull this off."

"We weren't ready for this trouble, neither there nor here. We scattered in this damned city, and I've been trying to get back to the rest of the clan. I couldn't trace them in this morass of magic from the storms. I ran into trouble on the streets with some locals and then more trouble with the Centaur Clan." He held his head a little higher. "I'm York, the Dragon Clan Bard."

"Oh hell. We need to get you out of here."

York seemed startled by the reaction. "Why would you care?"

"Because I don't think whatever battle we had in the past matters in the present circumstances. Can you stand?"

"I'll manage." He had already ripped more cloth from his

shirt to wrap around his leg, but the wound still bled a little. "How are you going to get us out?"

Tessa glanced over his shoulder, making certain no one watched too carefully. I could see the movement of shadows beyond our little square and guessed we had less than an hour before dawn. Just as well I'd had such a long rest.

"The leader of the Centaur Clan arrived," York said when light flashed and died. "We're out of time."

Tessa reached into his shirt and pulled out a little orb of light. York smiled with pleasure.

"Oh yes, you will take them by surprise," York said.

I couldn't ask anything, of course. York's assumption that I knew what would happen hung there in the air. Tessa patted me on the arm. "Help York. I'll do the magic. York, I sensed some of your people not far off the south. Probably in Florence."

"Florence?" he asked, confused.

"I know where," I said. We hadn't any more time to discuss what to do. I could see something happening outside the walls of our tree prison, and I knew we dared not stick around any longer.

Tessa stood and spun, the hand holding the globe of light moving, and the magic spread outward in waves, like a rock dropping down in the middle of a pond. The power brushed over us. I pulled York to his feet as the light hit the trees and pushed them aside as though they were rushes at a pond's edge. The waves of light hit the nearest fae and mowed them down as well.

Tessa grabbed me by the arm and we went *up* without any warning. It had been a good move since magic hit where we had been a heartbeat before.

We rose so fast into the clouds that my ears popped. I could feel the damp, clammy grasp of Tessa's hand on my arm. We wouldn't go far unless we intended to make a very quick and messy drop. Florence wasn't too far away, but dropping three white guys into the midst of Omaha's black community might not be wise, either.

No choice. We went down, and a little too fast for my tastes, though Tessa slowed for the last few feet. We landed beside an abandoned building, the lot filled with glass and broken bricks. Tessa went to his knees and I sat down for fear I'd be sick.

Oddly, York stayed to his feet this time. He lifted a hand.

"I know. We're in trouble," Tessa said, still sounding breathless. He tried to stand and failed. "Damn --"

People rushed towards us. I got to my feet, for all the good I would do. I tried to find a nice, mundane weapon like a broken board, because I wouldn't let them drag me away without a fight --

"York!"

The people had to be Dragon Clan, though that didn't make some of us safer. I moved to stand by Tessa.

"Cat Clan!" Someone yelled and I saw weapons move towards Tessa and me. "In league with Centaur --"

"No!" York leapt in front of us and I think he must have saved us from something seriously bad. I heard a lot of yelling for a moment before Brandis stepped forward. It felt odd to recognize him. He looked worn, frayed and worried. I thought the key would want to go to him and I was ready to step away from this insanity.

But we could hear trouble arriving.

"They saved me," York said. He grabbed Brandis by the arm. "They got me away from the Centaur Clan. Leave them safe."

Brandis appeared confused and perhaps relieved to know he didn't have another enemy clan to face down. We could hear the shouts of Centaur Clan coming closer. Tessa got to his feet and started to take a few steps backwards.

Brandis waved a hand towards some of his people. "Hold them off. We'll get York out of here. Don't commit to a battle and try to stay clear of the locals. You two --"

"We're going," Tessa said.

Brandis gave a curt, almost dismissive nod of agreement as he took hold of York and disappeared into the rainy pre-dawn with the rest of his people, some heading towards the trouble and some away. All too soon, we stood alone in the lot.

"Damn, damn." Tessa bent over, hands on his knees, gasping for breath. I could hear dangerous, loud sounds and far too close. "We have to go. On foot and quietly. I don't have the magic for anything else."

"Thank you for getting us out."

"This is crazy. But they needed their bard if they're ever going to get out of here. They need the key, too. The reason they didn't notice is all the other magic on the loose."

"York believed I'm a member of the Cat Clan. I think from your magic."

"Ah. Makes sense. Come on."

We headed down the street, then backtracked and headed another direction to avoid a group of locals standing under an awning by a door.

"Damn mess," Tessa said when we reached the doorway of another, dark building. We could hear trouble elsewhere and I silently wished the Dragon Clan well. I thought I heard shots, farther off. The pale light of dawn cast the world in shades of gray, and I glanced at my watch. It had stopped working at some point.

"We can get back to the Old Market area." I sounded far more assured than I felt. "Hell, considering everything else we've gotten out of, I think this walk shouldn't be so bad."

He gave a little laugh. "I'll have more magic soon."

I didn't mention how ill I'd started to feel as the magic he had given me earlier wore off. I concentrated on moving and ignoring the fever and cold trembling which took me by turns, not helped by the downpour of rain. Maybe the weather would quell some of the tempers in the area, though, and get people back off the street. From the growing clamor behind us, I could tell the trouble had passed beyond the encounter between two fae clans.

We didn't dare head down North 30th, the main road through town and the fastest way out, which would also be the fastest way to run into trouble from the sounds of traffic there. I heard sirens and thought about trying to get to the police, though I couldn't be certain heading for them wouldn't take us right into the heart of the trouble.

We dodged in and out of yards, startling dogs, stray cats, raccoons and possums. We avoided people, but as the day grew lighter, staying invisible would be impossible without Tessa's magic, and he still seemed shaky. I thought we could get to Fort Omaha and the college, which would be the best place to get out of sight. I just kept moving.

"I'm going to say something I never thought to hear myself say," Tessa said as we stumbled along. "I wish we had your car."

He made me laugh. The daylight helped us choose our way and we made better time. I even thought we had reached some sort of safety, right until a car came roared up behind us and hit the brakes. I spun to find a young black man with his head out of the window.

"What the fuck you doing here?"

"Got stranded back there," I said, waving a hand towards the sound of trouble. "We're doing our best to get clear."

"Shit. Get in. I'll drive you out. Keep low and don't make no trouble."

I grabbed Tessa, jerked the car door open, and propelled him into the back seat before he could argue. I knew he wouldn't be too happy about getting into the gaudy low-rider, but I didn't care. I had to trust this guy and hope my karma points were still in good standing. I slid into the front seat and down as far as I could.

"Stupid ass people making trouble," he mumbled as he put the car in gear and headed down the street. "This isn't going to help anyone. Someone is playing us and I don't like it."

I nodded. I hoped Tessa kept low because I could hear angry shouts out on the street.

"I'm heading over to the main drag and going south. The trouble's up north. Some stupid ass wannabe gang bangers making trouble. They aren't going to be happy when I'm done with them."

He grunted a curse as a police car swept past us followed by an ambulance. We kept moving away from the danger. I found I could breathe easier.

"Time for you to get out."

I could see a roadblock ahead stopping people from going in, though not coming out. As soon as we went past, our benefactor pulled over to the side. I got out, amused to see Kenwood standing by the police. He stared at me with shock and then anger for some reason.

I reached back in while Tessa got out and gripped the young man's hand. "Thanks."

"Keep your ugly white ass out of my neighborhood or I'll shoot you myself next time."

I nodded and he drove off. Tessa and I started to walk away as the rain lessened. I thought the police might come to talk to us, but they seemed to be too busy with other problems.

"Back to my place," Tessa said. He started walking faster. "We're too vulnerable still."

I glanced at the sky, grateful that all I saw was more rain.

# CHAPTER 14

We bypassed my apartment and headed straight for Tessa's place. I had thought to go home instead but street flooding cut us off and Tessa pointed out his place was safer. The city had begun sandbagging around the Old Market, where water ran ankle deep across the cobblestone streets. Few cars moved in the area just after dawn and none of the local eateries had opened or I would have suggested breakfast so I could get a chance to sit and rest.

We trudged up the slight hill to his shop. His hand fumbled with the key and I realized Tessa hadn't any more strength left than I did. I caught his arm on the way in, locked the door behind us -- as though something so flimsy would stop trolls and centaurs -- and helped him up the stairs.

"Go shower." He waved a hand towards the bathroom. "Go ahead. I need to sit first."

"You need to sleep."

"Not yet. Not quite. It would be too dangerous."

I didn't ask why. I took my shower and borrowed some of his clothing this time. Good clothes, a little large on me, and all bought at a local shop. I had almost expected something made of magic instead.

"I'm going to try to reach my people again," Tessa said after he'd showered and changed. I could see the signs of weariness in how he slowly lowered himself into a chair. "I don't think you want to be here, because this could get loud and maybe dangerous."

"I'll head to work."

"Good." He ran a hand through his wet hair and shook his head. "Centaur Clan should never have been able to take on Dragon Clan. And they shouldn't be pushing the trouble into this reality. I need someone to listen to me."

I headed out, Tessa watching from his doorway until I reached the Wolton World News building. I suspected even the trolls had tired of the rain, though. Nothing moved.

Julia had to unlock the door and let me in.

"Fresh tea and rolls in my office," she said.

"You are an angel!"

"You still don't look well," she replied with a frown. "Why did you walk today?"

"Car problems last night." I had, in the midst of all the other insanity, forgotten my poor abandoned Subaru with the oddly dented hood. I wondered if anyone had towed it off yet.

"Bad weather. I wonder when this is going to clear up." Julia settled at her desk and glanced out the window while I got us both cups of tea. "Thanks. Do you have anything to work on today?"

"Enough to keep me busy for a while. Besides, how could I miss your rolls?"

She laughed. We both saw Jacobs driving past and into the lot. I hadn't expected to see him today since the guy took every chance he could to avoid work. I wondered what could have drawn him in on a day when even I would have thought twice about coming in, at least under normal circumstances.

Jacobs stomped through the door and stopped at Julias' office. The scowl on his face changed to a snide smirk. He grabbed a roll from the plate.

"I didn't see your car, Summerfield."

"I walked," I said.

"Yeah, right. In this weather."

"There's flooding down by my place."

"Yeah. Right."

Julia glanced at him, frowning as she sipped her tea.

"He thinks you and I are having an affair," I told her.

She spurted tea while Jacobs turned a color red I had never seen before as anger came to his face. His mood didn't improve when Julia began laughing and couldn't stop. Jacobs stomped back to the office. I'd like to say I felt contrite about what I'd done, but I won't lie.

I went to my desk a few minutes later and began working. Jacobs muttered and cursed. He appeared less tidy than usual and I wondered if Pam had gone off somewhere on vacation. I wouldn't think Jacobs would let her off the hook from taking care of him.

I went to work on a story, trying to force myself to think about a haunting in a lost temple in the wilds of India. I buried myself in the research and noticed nothing in the real world until three men came into the room and walked over to my desk.

"Mr. Summerfield? Would you please accompany us downtown to answer a few questions?" One of the men held out a badge: Detective Myers.

"Pardon?" I asked, startled. This had to be a joke.

"If you don't mind," the man said, but clearly didn't mean those words.

"Questions about what?" I asked as I hit save on my work -- an automatic reaction. I saw one of the men reading the material and he didn't complain when I shut the computer down. Obviously, this wasn't about ghosts in India.

When I looked back at Detective Meyers, he gave a quick nod. "We would want to discuss your association with gang members whom you have had recent associations with, and specifically your contact today. This *shouldn't* take long."

The *shouldn't* implied it would take a damn longed time if I didn't have the right answers. I knew better than to make any protests, though. I'd done nothing wrong, unless there was some law about consorting with fae. Considering the depth of my research into the unusual, I kind of doubted such a law would have slipped past me.

I glanced over to see Jacobs leaning back in his chair, smiling brightly. Karma's a bitch. I should have remembered that when I felt so smug about his own discomfort this morning.

Julia stood in the doorway to her office. I had never seen her so livid. I patted her arm.

"Call my sisters," I said, stopping her tirade before she started. She nodded and headed back to her desk.

We went outside. The rain had ended and the humidity had returned with a vengeance. I hoped to hell this weather cleared soon, along with everything else plaguing my life. A plain black car sat parked in front of the building. They maneuvered me into the backseat without any visible effort. I'd have expected my fae friend to come and get me but not the cops.

Unless . . . no, I couldn't sense a bit of magic in them, and the key would have given me warning. We went past Tessa's place and I looked towards the building, hoping for a sign. I saw nothing to indicate he had noticed.

We didn't have far to go to the 15th Street offices of the Omaha Police Force. However, with the rain and blocked streets, the trip took us almost twenty minutes. I sat with a cop to the side of me. No one spoke. I tried to figure out the problems. Me and gangs? The Rojos, yes -- but today? Someone saw me coming out of Florence, and they'd made some odd connection, I suspected.

The building always reminded me of a converted parking garage, with far too much concrete and a feel of austerity that gave me a chill today. We went upstairs to an office with a view of nothing particularly good. A dark man with short gray hair glanced up from his desk and waved to a chair. I sat without any complaint, glad to be off my feet. All but Detective Meyers left, which made me feel a bit better.

"You're --?" He glanced at some paperwork and frowned.

"I'm Summerfield, yes."

"I'm Detective Nickols. I want you to answer some questions about the gang problem we're facing. We have a reliable source saying you know a lot more about what's going on than maybe you should."

This was true, but I didn't think what I knew was what he wanted to hear. If I started telling him about fae wars, trolls, and magic I had the feeling he'd lock me up in one place or another before long.

"What makes you think I know anything about the gangs?" I asked. "I did have a discussion with the Rojos, but I went there as part of the job. I am, after all, a reporter."

"Yes, but for the Woo -- Wolton World News." He shook his head, either at his near mistake or my place of employment. Maybe both. "Your newspaper isn't the type to cover breaking news."

"Are you going to tell me there's nothing unusual going on?" I asked. His eyes narrowed but he couldn't deny anything since the police had already passed around information. Perhaps I could turn this into a new angle for the report. "Really, you don't think there are aspects of this gang war which would attract Wolton World News?"

"Maybe," he admitted, leaning back in his chair. He seemed tired. I suspected he wasn't getting much more rest than me, though for other reasons.

"What is the problem?" I asked.

"This." He pulled two sheets of paper from the top of his desk and handed them to me. They were computer printouts of pictures. One showed me outside Pablo's house, several of the Rojos close by, though in the other yard. I stood by Pablo and his wife. The second picture showed me getting out of a car, a young black man in the front seat. Tessa had started to climb out and I couldn't see his face.

I only had to think for a moment.

"You got these from Kenwood."

"That's not the point."

"Oh, it might be. We're both reporters. He's been unhappy I've gotten into places where he hasn't."

"And how did you manage to do so? These two men are well-known gang members. Your association with them --"

"I met both of them once. I knew about Pablo being associated with the Rojos. My boss set up a meeting through his wife who subscribes to Wolton World News." I touched the other one. "I have no idea who this other guy is. He gave me a ride."

"And you'd never met him before."

"No."

"Where did he pick you up?"

"In Florence, where I shouldn't have been, even as a reporter. Things got out of hand and I had to hike out."

"There's someone else in the car."

"Yes. He was with me. It was stupid for both of us."

"Why would someone who is a known leader in the Black Knights help you?"

"You'd have to ask him that question."

"You had no contact with him about the war and riots."

"You know, I think we'll sit here for a while and wait for my lawyer to arrive, which shouldn't be too long," I decided. "I suspect things might go better for both of us."

"He called a lawyer before you brought him in?" Nickols asked, frowning.

"No sir. He did tell his boss to call his sisters."

"His --" The detective's mouth clamped shut and he

picked up a paper on his desk. "Oh hell. *Summerfield.*"

This kind of reaction makes it worthwhile being the younger brother of five very aggressive sisters. I gave the man a little smile. He had already pushed away from his desk, rethinking this strategy. He was too late. I could hear the steady step of feet out in the hall followed by a quick rap of fingers, and a moment later the door opened.

Not one, not two, but *three* of my sisters came into the room.

"Detective Nickols? We represent Summerfield, Summerfield, and Brown." Violet crossed to the desk with Rose and Aster side-by-side at her back. Aster put a hand on my shoulder. Detective Nickols acted as though three wolves had just stepped into his room.

Oddly, a lot of people have the same reaction.

"There's no need for any trouble," he said with a wave of his hand. "I wanted to ask Mr. Summerfield a few questions."

"Perhaps you should have considered asking them at his place of employment," Violet replied, her voice edged with acid. "Rather than dragging him here like a criminal."

I knew Violet's tone too well and realized she would soon be in a full-blown rant. I didn't want to annoy the police. I reached out and touched her on the arm, drawing her attention.

"The Detective had reason to think I might know something important," I said. "And don't you dare make that little snarfing noise at the idea."

Rose laughed, which drew Violet's look of reproach from me to her. I had broken the spell, though. She took the two pictures from my hand, frowning.

"These are the problem? Do you have any idea who took them or why?"

"I'm not at liberty to --" Nickols began.

"His name is Brian Kenwood and he's a freelance reporter

who doesn't much like me," I said. "He was present at the meeting with the Rojos, and I noticed him when I got out of the other car this morning. He had his camera both times, and the angles are right."

Nickols said nothing, but I could see calculation in his face.

"This is the same guy who tried to have your press pass revoked, right?" Rose asked.

"Yes."

"I'd say we're dealing with possible harassment here," Violet said, a finger tapping her lips. She focused on the detective. "It's unfortunate he pulled the police into this personal problem."

Nickols frowned and glanced at me. "You don't know anything about the gang wars."

"Nothing more than you already know. I know there's something odd going on and there may be a new gang moving in."

"That's not common knowledge."

"No, but the Rojos are aware of it, having lost a few members in the first fight."

He nodded, glanced at my sisters, and dared another question. "Do you know anything about a new gang, Mr. Summerfield?"

Lucky for me, I could answer truthfully. I hate lying about anything which might come back and bite me.

"I know nothing about a new gang," I replied. They weren't a gang. Really. Fae Clan. Two of them.

I hoped I wasn't going too far over my Karma limit today.

"Sorry for the inconvenience."

Violet took the capitulation well and looked at me for the first time. "Are you okay, kid? You were in the hospital and didn't let us know."

"Only overnight." I had known they would find out.

"And you're back to work already?" Aster demanded.

"I'm fine." I waved my hands as though to shoo them away. "Go harass someone else for a while. I've got to get back to work."

"When are you going to get a real job?" Rose asked. "With your degrees --"

"I enjoy my job," I interrupted. I could see Nickols getting far too interested in my family discussion. "Go, go. But thank you for coming by."

Rose glanced at Nickols. "Are we done here?"

"Yes. I'm sorry for the inconvenience, but we do have a volatile situation, and we thought your brother might have had information. We're desperate for anything to help settle this problem."

"I understand," I said before any of my three sisters could speak. "This is a rough job with all the other trouble going on. If I had anything I thought would help you, I'd let you know. If I didn't do so, my sisters would disown me."

He glanced at the three and back at me. "Is that supposed to be some kind of reassurance?"

I grinned and Rose laughed once more. Violet gave the detective a friendly nod before she and Rose started for the door. Aster paused, a hand on my shoulder. "You should consider resting for a while. And you'll be at Lily's birthday dinner, right?"

"Have I ever missed one?"

She smiled, patting my arm which was better than the usual pat on the head. "You're back in school, right? What are you taking this time?"

"Terrestrial Ecology at Creighton," I replied.

"Why?"

"Because it interests me."

She accepted the answer with a smile and crossed to join the other two, who waited halfway to the open door. I don't often call on my sisters to appear in person. It's like half opening the gates of hell to see if there's anything interesting inside: sometimes it's damned hard to get the gate closed again. I am, if not the black sheep of the family, at least the wayward lamb in their eyes. Once they get me in their sights, I have a hard time disappearing.

They (and just about everyone else I meet) give me trouble about my job, but overall, we get along well these days. I think they accept I am always going to be more akin to our parents than to them.

I hadn't expected Tessa to step inside the open door. He took one look at my three sisters heading his way and swiftly moved aside as though he thought he faced some fierce set of beasts. The sisters gave him nods in passing and went on out, their three sets of steps perfectly in sync.

Tessa peered out the door and then turned to me.

"Who the hell were they?" he asked, shaking his head.

"Three of my five sisters," I replied with a sigh.

"Five? You have *five* sisters? Five is a powerful number. That can't be good."

"Don't mess with them," I warned.

Tessa looked back out the door. "Absolutely not."

"And you are?" Detective Nickols asked a little perturbed by the new interruption.

Tessa crossed the room and held out his hand to the man. "Dion Tessa."

"Tessa," he repeated, trying to place the name.

"I'm the astrologer, up on 10th street," he replied as they shook hands.

Nickol's eyes flickered a little. "And you're here because?"

"I was at the newspaper and they told me you had picked up Summerfield, so I figured you'd want to talk to me, too."

Nickols glanced at me, one eyebrow raised.

"He was the other guy in the car."

"Ah. Well, we've settled the problem," he said with a shrug. "Unless you know something about the gang war brewing out there?"

"I could do a tarot reading, if you like."

"As good as anything else we're doing right now," Nickols admitted. I felt sorry for him. I did know more of what was going on, even though it was nothing he would believe or could use.

"I'll tell you something else," Tessa said. His face changed a little; his eyes dilated as he stared towards the wall. I felt startled at the change. "You're dealing with outside forces which will pass with the storm, Detective. The trouble isn't going to last, at least not this time."

"Right. I'll take that to my boss."

Tessa blinked and grinned, looking more himself. "I know, I know. But I might as well pass such things along in case they help in some way. You never know."

He turned away from Tessa to me. "You come from an important family. Are you going to tell me you believe in this stuff?"

I saw the way Tessa blinked at the 'important family' part, but otherwise he showed no sign of surprise.

"I work for Woo Woo News," I reminded the man. He snorted at the name and grinned brightly. "I do believe there are things happening out there which can't always be explained away with a few convenient facts. On the other hand, sometimes people hunt for the inexplicable when they should be studying those facts instead. But yes, I do think there are things Tessa can touch on which most of us can't."

"As much as I would love to talk with you two about metaphysical crap and the reality of the universe, I have work to do. Go."

I stood and we both headed to the door, but Tessa stopped there. "Your phone is about to ring. You're late for a meeting."

He headed out the door as the phone started ringing. I saw the startled look on Nickol's face.

We walked down the hall in silence.

"You shouldn't have done that," I finally said.

He grinned. I hadn't notice what a Cheshire Cat smile he had until now.

# CHAPTER 15

W̲e stepped out of the building into the hot, humid air of another miserable afternoon. I could tell the humidity had pushed the heat index far above tolerable for this area. Magic or not, this weather had to break soon. People glared at the sky, glared at each other and glared at us. We wouldn't need gang wars pretty soon; people would swing at each other out of pure frustration.

"How did you get here?" I asked as we reached the sidewalk.

"I ran. When Julia told me what happened, I had the feeling I should get to you. Perhaps I overreacted, though you can't blame me with everything else going on."

I understood the feeling. We walked a short distance. He stared at me when we waited at the first corner for the light to change.

"You might as well say it," I told him.

"You come from an important family." I could see shock hardly hidden in his face. "I should have known this. I should have sensed your background. Why don't you seem attached to them? Why aren't you linked to your five sisters?"

"Long story."

"We have a long walk."

I thought about saying nothing, but he would find out anyway. Besides, I had nothing to hide. Well, not much from him. The tale would take my mind off of what I had said, and not said, to the detective.

"My family owns considerable land and many business enterprises here in Omaha. Summerfield Estates, Summer, Inc., Field Corporation and quite a few more. I come from a big family." We crossed the street, Tessa silent, his eyes narrowed as he took in the information. "My father is the middle kid in his line, and he'd always been a bit of a rebel and dreamer. When he met my mother, he found someone with whom he shared a soul. They are both hippies and New Age followers, and they held to their beliefs, even in the face of family disapproval. They married and had five daughters and named them all after flowers: Violet Mist, Rose Wine, Aster Snow, Carnation Blush, and Lily Fire. They lived on a farm south of Omaha, growing all their own food, and making their own clothing. Solar and wind generated power and wood cook stoves -- the whole thing."

"And that's how you grew up?"

"Yes, for a few years. See, I was born late. My next oldest sibling, Lily, was already ten. My upcoming arrival came as quite a shock, and they had some trouble finding a proper flower name for a son."

"A son flow -- Oh gods." His eyes went wide. He'd stopped walking. "What is your name?"

I held out my hand. "I'm Sunflower Breeze Summerfield."

He shook my hand, blankness coming to his eyes. I hadn't seen the reaction in a few years since I try to avoid discussions about my family or my name if I can. People moved around us, giving us odd looks. Tessa drew his hand back and we walked on.

"Why haven't you changed your name?"

"And miss those reactions?" I asked and laughed. Then I relented. "I haven't changed my name because it's who I am."

"You're not like your sisters. They grew up the same way

--"

"Not exactly. See, when I turned five my parents decided they wanted to make a pilgrimage to Tibet."

"Tibet."

"Mountain country, Buddhist --"

"I know what it is. I know where it is. They took their family?"

"No. The oldest two sisters had already started college and the other three got the choice of going along or staying behind with Uncle David and Aunt Mary. They'd suffered through enough family pilgrimages in the US, and they opted out. My parents hired a tutor for me, and off we went. The month in Tibet became a year, and afterwards we traveled to a Coptic religious site in Egypt, and on to China and Japan. We kept going. I didn't come back to the US until I was twenty, though I had spent a few of those years at colleges. By then two things had happened: all five of the girls had adopted the more common family attitude towards income and power, and I had become far too much like my parents."

"Why do you work for Julia?"

I wondered if he had sensed the link, or if this was a natural question. "Because my parents asked me to help her out. They're old friends and my parents loaned her the money to start the paper. That's not known in the family. A few of them would come unglued if they found out any Summerfield funds helped Woo Woo News."

He laughed. "I don't know why I never thought about your background. I work with Julia quite often and your name always comes up. Besides, Summerfield is a known name in this area. You manage to stay out of the flow very well."

"All those years at spiritual shrines paid off."

"And you're lucky you didn't grow up in the shadow of your five sisters. Five is a very powerful number: a square with a center point, so power flows in all directions."

"I saw the Centaur Clan people form into a square with a person in the middle."

"When you see fae form a square, get out of the way as fast as you can. And if they form a square within a square, dig a hole and hide."

"My sisters don't have magic, though."

"Which is a damned good thing for your world. No, they don't have magic, but they do have power." He fell silent as we overtook a group of foreign tourists who muttered about the weather. The tourists hurried across the street hoping to get inside somewhere and cool off, and I couldn't blame them. I started to walk faster as well. "Your sisters have power. I could feel it in the three of them. If all five are united in action --"

"Oh yeah. You don't want to see what happens then."

He stood still and his pupils dilated while his face went slack for about three heartbeats. He slowed, shook his head and began to move quickly.

"We need to hurry. Something is going to happen, though I'm not quite certain what. I sometimes touch on the fields moving around me, actions started which will push other things into place. I don't always know what or where, though."

Worry drew his brows down as he stared ahead of us, though I couldn't be certain he saw what I did out there. I felt something odd: a tingling through my body and realized someone nearby was intent on what we did. I knew it, somehow.

"Someone is following us," I said.

Tessa made a little movement of his hand and I felt his magic move on a whisper of a breeze. He kept moving and then gave a slight nod.

"I think you have a link with Dragon Clan through the key," he decided. "One of them is following us, probably trying to figure out where Cat Clan plays into this mess."

"Is it good I can feel them?"

"The warning might give us a little lead time if there's trouble. However, they might also figure out you have the key."

If they wanted the key, I'd be just as glad to have them take the thing. I found my hand going to my neck where I knew the chain hung, though I couldn't see or feel the links. I couldn't get rid of the key on my own, and Tessa couldn't take it. At some point I'd have to deal with the Dragon Clan or live with this dragon-linked albatross for the rest of my life.

"You don't want them here," I said as we started the last block to his shop. "Shouldn't I give the key over to them?"

He remained silent for several steps. "Wait a little longer. The key is a power we hold, and we're in damned need of whatever power we can get our hands on. I don't trust anyone from the Dragon Clan or the Centaur Clan."

"I don't appreciate being pulled into this trouble," I admitted. I thought about trolls, centaurs, flying horses and sleepwalking nightmares. "At this point, I think I'd trade it all to go live with the Yak herders of Ladakh again."

"That doesn't sound pleasant."

"And this is?"

"Well, maybe not." He wiped perspiration from his forehead as we reached the door to his place. "Come in. I'll give you something to drink to get you through the rest of this day."

"It won't be a problem for you?" I asked.

"No. I'm better." Tessa unlocked the door and waved me inside. I took a step forward, feeling the tickle of the ward and glad to be inside with some protection --

*Not safe.*

I stepped backwards and Tessa put a hand on my shoulder to pull me out of the way. I didn't see the others until they moved out of shadows which shouldn't have hidden them so well. More than a dozen people stood in the room, all hard-looking men and women. I could feel the magic in them. They wore clothing of similar colors; grey pants and brown shirts, giving them the feel of clan outfits though all of the clothing was modern. They also wore knives in sheaths at their sides and the little magic I felt around them seemed dull.

Too long in this world. I realized I faced the people of the Cat Clan and from the way they watched me, I had a mouse-before-the-cat feeling stronger than I ever hoped to experience again in life.

A man with close-cropped grey hair, and a face lined by anger -- not age -- stepped forward and started to grab me by the arm. I pulled away in time and saw people going for their weapons, as though I had made some move against them. Anger showed in every face --

Tessa stepped forward. He waved his hand and everyone staggered backwards, shocked by the sudden magic. The man who tried to grab me glared, though he backed away very fast when Tessa looked his way.

"I will have manners in my home," he said, his voice harsh. "You will not treat my guest in this fashion. Have I made myself clear?"

Heads bowed in quick succession as Tessa glanced from one to the other, though the man who had tried to grab me did so with obvious reluctance. His defiant stare towards me didn't lessen.

"It doesn't belong here," he said.

"He belongs here more than any of you do," Tessa replied. His hand lifted and the man stepped away in haste. "Don't try my patience, Gryn. Don't push me already. We have a truce. Live by our agreement in my home or leave."

A truce with his own clan? Well, that didn't sound good though I wasn't surprised, either. I could see the difference between Tessa and these people who despised the humans they lived among.

For hundreds of years?

"Will there be peace?" Tessa demanded.

The others agreed with mumbled words, though little change in their attitudes.

"Better," Tessa replied. He waved me towards a chair. I would have rather gone outside, but I think he feared to send me alone when we knew a member of the Dragon Clan had to be close. I settled in the chair and he stood beside me.

Gryn started to speak, in a rush of words I didn't understand.

"English," Tessa said.

"Why? Have you forgotten what you are?"

"Oh, you don't truly want me to answer such a question, do you?" Tessa asked.

The others had gone from glaring to appalled at Gryn's words, and then worried at Tessa's. I sat with my hands still and hoped this didn't turn into a blood bath. I wondered if I shouldn't start carrying a knife and then considered the reaction from the locals.

I decided I was far too caught up in fae stuff.

The others lounged back against walls, the table, and one sat on the stairs. Everyone seemed worn and weary. Gryn held his ground. I realized he must be the leader of the group, though he vied with Tessa for control. I couldn't decide where the others stood, except they came with Gryn.

"We've come to your summons," Gryn said, the words in English. "The others voted to do so. If the Dragon Clan is in such dire straits as your messages indicated, now is the time to strike our blow of vengeance --"

"No."

Heads snapped up, faces staring at Tessa in disbelief this time. Even Gryn took a step backwards, stunned by the single word. I didn't want to witness any more of this trouble.

"You can't seriously mean we aren't going to get our chance at them," a woman said. She pushed herself away from the wall and I saw not so much anger in her face as loss and disbelief. "After all the years we've been trapped here, cut off from our own people, we deserve revenge. We didn't deserve this."

Gryn nodded, quick and decisive.

I saw Tessa's emotions softening from the glare he'd held since we came in. "We didn't deserve this, you're right. And Dragon Clan will pay. But now . . . now is not the time to strike. I don't think you realize the implications of Dragon Clan arriving here, in such trouble. They were attacked by something from the Other Side. Something allied with Centaur."

"You're certain?" the woman asked and seemed troubled.

"Yes. And worse still, the enemy killed the dragon."

Shock spread through the entire group -- except for Gryn. He smiled with a brightness that turned my stomach, and not because I had suffered the loss of the dragon on a personal level. He didn't take joy in anything good.

"The dragon's dead! "This is the time to strike! We could wipe them out if their totem is gone and destroy the dragon for good! This is the perfect chance for our vengeance!"

"And if we did, what would such a loss mean for the fae lands, with the destruction of so powerful a clan?"

"What do we care?" Gryn growled.

"If we didn't care about what happens in fae, then being exiled here is not reason enough to fight the Dragon Clan for vengeance's sake." Tessa stood and took a step closer to the man who held his ground this time. I saw Gryn's fists clench in rage. "Think beyond yourself, Gryn."

Gryn glanced at his companions and took his cue from them this time, no doubt seeing he would lose their backing if he didn't stop the attack.

"Summerfield and I are stepping out for a few minutes. This will give you time to discuss the matter amongst yourselves." Tessa started for the door and I followed, hoping I didn't appear too anxious to get the hell out of this lair of cats.

He signaled me out first but glanced at the others before he shut the door. "Be wise," Tessa said.

Gryn clamped his mouth shut and glared. We took several steps down the sidewalk before Tessa shook his head, obviously more unsettled than he had let on.

"I didn't expect them to come," he admitted. He leaned against a building, and I had the feeling he wanted to stretch out the time before he went back in. "When I talked to Gryn, he said he wouldn't bring the last of the Cat Clan warriors to me. I sent out a general call instead but heard nothing. And yet, here they are, though they thought they came to fight an old enemy."

"Why did the Dragon Clan leave you on this side?" I asked.

"There had been an old war between us, which had spilled over to this reality. There used to be considerable traffic between the fae world and here before your people chose the path to modern technology. The fae found the Industrial Age annoying and distasteful. The gates we'd held open for eons began to close as the clans lost interest in this place. The Dragon Clan and the Cat Clan alone remained with people on this side. Dragon Clan got the upper hand in the battle and did something none of us expected: they pulled the gate closed and told Gryn we could go to hell, leaving us trapped here since they took our key."

"And you couldn't make another one."

"We've tried." He pushed away from the wall at last. "For several hundred years, in fact. But we're few, and we have no bard to sing the magic. I needed to get you away from them because if they had sensed you have the Dragon Clan key, I think Gryn would have killed you. I don't want the Dragon Clan people trapped here, which would not be good for this world with the two of us in the same place, and returning to our old wars."

"You've accepted being here, but the others haven't."

"I suppose so." He fell silent until we headed towards the door to the newspaper. "The others all left family behind in the fae lands. Most of the warriors died in the battle or remained trapped here so those of our clan still in the fae lands cannot have survived for long. Dragon Clan's actions were unforgiveable. But even so, I'm not going to seek my revenge now. I don't know if I can get my people to help, but I won't allow them to become more of a problem."

We reached the Woo Woo News building. A rush of cool air blew out around me as I opened the door and turned to see Tessa already heading for his shop. I felt grateful to be out of the Cat Clan battle, at least. I hoped he did well with them.

# CHAPTER 16

I worked through the rest of the afternoon, all the while feeling a growing sense of unease. I worried about Tessa and his Clan, though whatever decision they made wouldn't affect me since none of the Cat Clan would step forward to help a human. Though, rethinking the line, I realized a human who held the Dragon Clan key could become a nice little mouse to play with. I needed to avoid the group.

And all the other fae groups.

I tried to do my work, but my mind refused to connect to the words on the screen. I didn't pay much attention to Jacobs who snarled, growled, and cursed. He expected me to be arrested and turned surly when I returned and none the worse for the trip. Julia took notice of my worry, but I let her know the problem had nothing to do with the police.

Honestly, I had started to feel run down. I'd gotten used to Tessa's pick-me-up magic drinks and without one today, I grew increasingly weaker and feverish. I plugged away at the keyboard, forcing myself to stay focused on something and spent too much time backtracking, rewriting and wondering what the hell I was writing about. I deleted half a file with a curse.

"Problems?" Tessa asked from somewhere behind me. I looked back, relieved to find him here. "I thought we could discuss the project over dinner," Tessa suggested, sounding uncertain. "My guests have taken over my apartment and they're already driving me crazy. Want to walk to Old Market?"

"Sounds good." Quitting time anyway.

Tessa lounged by the door. I finished my work, but Jacobs managed to get out ahead of me. I stood -- and went right back down. Tessa gave a hiss of worry and crossed the room, dropping a hand on my shoulder. I could feel the surge of magic.

"Sorry. I wasn't thinking," Tessa apologized. "We should get you to dinner. I can do more with a drink than I can with direct contact. Feel better?"

"Much." My head pounded but I figured food would help. "How is it going with your people?"

"They're still arguing, which is a good sign since when they first arrived, I saw no dissent at all. They planned to joyfully go and kill all the Dragon Clan people they could find. I'm letting them have my place for the night and I'm staying clear."

"What are you going to do?"

"I'm going to prowl for a while. I'll sleep somewhere else -
-"

"My place. I have an extra room." I waved good-bye to Julia as we passed her office. She gave a nod, intent on her phone conversation.

I'd gotten used to the air conditioning. The step out into the heat and damned humidity came like a physical blow and I think I gasped this time. A group of people walking past the building gave me a nod of commiseration.

"Come on." Tessa tapped my shoulder, and I felt another jolt of magic. "Famous Dave's sound okay to you? I called ahead and got us a table, though they won't hold it for long."

"Sounds good," I agreed. They had air conditioning, good food, and it wasn't far from my apartment. The rain hadn't fallen much during the day. The streets had dried, the flooding retreated, and things almost seemed normal.

I *did not* look up at the sky.

Dinner went well. The drink helped, though I felt exhausted by the time we headed home.

Tessa eyed the condo building with some suspicion as we neared. "Expensive place," he said.

"Yes. I have family income, Tessa. I don't let Julia pay me."

"Ah. I can't get used to the part about you being rich," he admitted.

We took the stairs because Tessa disliked the idea of the elevator. By the time we reached the apartment, I felt exhaustion washing over me. Tessa glanced around and went to the balcony windows as I dropped things on the counter and shoved the cell phone into the charger. Mundane, normal things which had been part of my daily life and welcome at the moment. I wondered if I could reach the sofa.

"Great view."

"Best in the building." I rummaged through the drawer for another set of keys. "These will get you into the building and into my apartment. Don't spend the night somewhere else. I'll feel better if you're around here in case of trouble."

Tessa gave a reluctant nod. "Yes, you're right. I won't be gone for long."

"Thank you."

He went out the door. I called the building manager to say I had a guest who would be in and out so he wouldn't come unglued if he heard about a stranger in the building. He'd give the word to security.

I checked the guest room for Tessa. No one had ever stayed there before, but the cleaning people kept everything nice and neat. Sometimes I stand in my apartment and feel as though I have come to some alien place. I spent a lot of my teen years living in Third World hovels and sometimes following those yaks out into the fields as a form of entertainment. I remembered being the only Caucasian child in a hundred miles, as well as knowing the feel of sanctity at out of the way spiritual sites few outsiders have ever visited.

But I had never learned what it meant to be rich.

I went to the sofa and leaned back, intending a moment or two of rest, but I fell asleep.

And the nightmare returned at once. The depth of realism and emotion washed over me and I couldn't escape out of my sleep. I felt the horror, the disbelief and the loss. The wounds I took bled, but the pain was nothing compared to the inner turmoil.

I did my best to get them out, but I knew we would lose. I knew it both as myself and as Summerfield. I knew --

Something pulled me straight out of the nightmare. Tessa stood over me, a hand on my shoulder. I tried to say something, but for the moment I didn't seem to have control. My thoughts swirled from there to here, blended . . . and for a moment the apartment seemed more than just alien: This was not my place. I was leader of the Dragon Clan --

"Summerfield," Tessa said, leaning closer.

Me. Summerfield. Not -- not Karolan. Karolan had died. I had felt the death when he let go of the key. I knew he didn't mind dying, because it meant I -- *he* -- wouldn't see the defeat of his people. Maybe I gave up too soon.

"Summerfield!" Tessa knelt, looking into my face.

"I --" I lost the words.

"We have to get rid of the key," Tessa said. I felt my hand go to my chest, as though to protect what I couldn't feel in the real world. The worry on Tessa's face won through some of my haze and pushed more of the nightmare away.

"How do we get rid of the key?" I asked.

"We give it to the Dragon Clan." Tessa ran a hand through strands of his hair. "I think they might be out in

Fontenelle Forest -- but they are shielding, and I can't track them in there."

"And you're not certain you want them to have the key, anyway."

"I don't like the Dragon Clan any better than the rest of my Clan does." For a moment I saw anger in his eyes, but the emotion disappeared in a blink. "But I will not allow this world to suffer for *our* old war. The rest of my clan doesn't care about what happens here, as long as they can have their revenge. But I have. . . ."

"Assimilated," I said, with a little grin.

"Maybe so. I've adapted. And I have human friends, which few of them ever have had. I want this to go well, Summerfield. What's already happened has proven dangerous and destructive enough."

I glanced towards the sliding glass doors. A distant storm flashed to the south. I hoped the bad weather stayed away tonight.

"You need to sleep," Tessa said.

The idea of sleeping frightened me far more than facing trolls. "I don't think so. I don't want back in the nightmare. Every time I sleep, the dreams feels more real, and I fear I might not come back next time."

"I can block the link from the key to you for a few hours." Tessa reached out, though not to touch. He must have been testing the magic since I felt a little tingle along my chest. "This will take considerable power and I can't do the work often. However, you need to sleep and to rest. I suspect things are going to get worse tomorrow."

"Worse?" I tried not to moan.

"Yes. I have felt . . . something coming. I took four readings of the tarot cards this afternoon and none of them were good. Even the rest of the Cat Clan worried about what I saw in the cards. I can't say what trouble we'll face.

However, I want you as clear-headed as possible. You're an important part of this mess."

"Do it," I said.

Tessa's fingers moved through the air and I felt something lighten within me, as though I had lost a fifty-pound weight I'd been carrying around my neck. I took a deep breath and felt my headache recede before exhaustion washed over me in a wave. I leaned back, my eyes already half closed.

"You should go to bed," Tessa said, sounding amused.

"No." I yawned and waved away his helping hand. "No. I would rather stay here. I don't want to get too comfortable in case anything happens."

"Ah. Good point."

Something else drew my wandering attention. "Why do all of you speak English? I understand about you and the Cat Clan, since you've been here so long, but the Centaur and Dragon spoke the language as well. I even hear English in my dreams."

"Magic and language are related. A great deal of magic is wrapped around the power of words and words of power. Magic converts languages for those from fae because there are so many different areas there and we have used the magic for so long the ability has become an innate part of our being. The key is doing the same for you in the dream."

"Gryn didn't speak English --"

"He had to think about the other language, and he was being deliberately rude."

I grinned, finding Gryn's actions juvenile enough to be amusing. I slipped away into sleep; not a profound, lost in the darkness sleep, and not one lost in nightmare, either. I knew Tessa moved around, pacing sometimes I thought. I woke long enough to point him to the guest room. He thanked me and I think he went there for several hours, though I had the feeling he didn't sleep. I think I heard him speaking to others.

I awoke once, twice, checked the time, and found the night inching closer to dawn. I awoke the next time to find daylight streaming into the room and Tessa in the kitchen making tea. I felt the weight of the key which must have just returned.

"Would you like some tea?" Tessa asked.

"You aren't my servant."

"No, but I am in the kitchen."

"Good point." I stood. My legs felt weak. "I'm going to go take a quick shower. Bagels would be good in about ten minutes if you want to throw a couple in the toaster." I waved to the cabinet as I went past.

I snagged clothing from my room and wondered why I hadn't I crawled into the nice comfortable bed last night. The shower felt great. I dressed and headed to the kitchen.

And I heard the cell phone where I'd left it on the kitchen counter as usual.

The theme to 2001.

I sprinted down the hall, but Tessa grabbed the phone before I got there.

"Hello," he said.

I came around the corner, waving my hands frantically. I could hear the voice on the other end and Tessa looked at me, startled --

"I can't believe I reached you, Mr. Summerfield!" The man sounded ecstatic. I silently cursed Aster for giving these people my number. "My name is David Ettner. I'm the head of a new Cal-Tech job placement board, and I've found you the perfect position in the top level of a new team working on fusion power --"

Tessa stared at me as though I had grown wings. I took the phone from his hand.

"I'm sorry, Mr. Ettner, but I'm not interested," I said. "Thank you for calling."

"But -- but --"

I hung up and pushed the phone into the charger. "Are the bagels done?"

"A team working on fusion power?" he said. He stared.

"I have a degree in nuclear physics from Cal-Tech. I graduated near the top of my class."

"I don't understand." Tessa shook his head. The bagels popped up from the toaster, startling him.

"I have interests." I took over preparing the bagels since he appeared rather too startled to do anything. "I wanted to understand nuclear power: everything, including the dangers and the potentials. So I went to school. I did well. But this is not the work I want to do with my life."

Tessa nodded as though I spoke some other language he barely understood. I found the reaction rather funny, really. Made the morning brighter, at least.

"What are we doing today?"

Tessa focused on me. He didn't speak for a moment. "We need to check on a few things. I must talk with the Cat Clan and see what I can get out of them. I may have to send them away rather than risk the kind of help they're willing to give."

"You can get them to leave?" I asked broaching what I thought must be a difficult subject.

"I can try." He flashed his Cheshire Cat smile again. I think he did it on purpose. "As you can tell, we have a strained relationship. But I give you my word, Summerfield: I will not allow them to be more of a problem if I can stop them."

I had to wonder how the two of us were going to deal with three angry fae clans.

# CHAPTER 17

We ate our bagels. Tessa made a magic cup of tea for me. Afterwards, we headed out. I thought the morning didn't seem as hot and humid as the last few days though something in the air made me uncomfortable. I could tell this would not be a good day.

As we walked down the street, I thought about my poor Subaru. I'd have to call around and see where they'd towed the car and find out what I needed to do. Simple, human matters to deal with on a day when I knew things wouldn't stay simple or human for long.

We'd gone just past the cobblestone streets of Old Market when a man and woman stepped from between two buildings in front of us. The hair on the back of my neck and arms rose straight up. Tessa lifted a hand and their hands moved as well. I took a little step backwards.

"Centaur Clan," Tessa said for my benefit, I think. He bowed his head to them, but not with any real politeness. They returned the bow, eyes narrowed.

"And you two are from Cat Clan," the woman replied. Her dark blue eyes would have been unnatural in a human. "We have come to discuss an alliance, Centaur and Cat against the Dragon Clan."

Tessa stared back at her. "It's not going to happen."

The answer startled the two who must have expected a member of the Cat Clan to leap at the chance to side with them against their old enemies.

"We have heard what Dragon Clan did to you," the man said, meeting Tessa's look. "And you're saying you won't strike back?"

"Who are your allies?" Tessa asked. "What took down the dragon?"

They both blinked and showed surprise that he knew enough to ask the question. I was learning to read fae emotions far too easily.

"Allies?" the man asked, a moment too late.

"The ones from the Other Side, which you brought into the fae lands to help you."

"Does it matter?" The woman smiled, her eyes brightening with so obvious a lust for power I thought I could feel it. "They took down the Dragon. If you ally with us, you'll be on the winning side, and we shall treat our allies better than the Dragon Clan ever treated their enemies."

"Will you, really?"

"You would be wise to join us," the man replied, as smug as his partner.

"Do you think so?" Tessa stepped forward. "Give me your hand."

He held out his own hand in a gesture I would have thought friendly if the other two hadn't reacted the way they did. Eyes went wide and faces paled. They backed up too quickly, drawing stares from people who had ignored us before this. The woman touched the man on the arm, drawing his attention and shaking her head. They spun and hurried away.

"Well," I said, glancing at Tessa's hand, half expecting to see claws.

He seemed more amused than worried. "That was not their wisest move. They expected anyone from Cat Clan to leap at the chance to take revenge. I suspect someone from Cat Clan must have already been in touch with them or they wouldn't know the history of how we came to be trapped here. I suspect Gryn since he's trying to stir up trouble. We've not seen another fae traveling to this side since the Industrial Revolution."

"Too crass for them," I said with understanding as a bus labored past us, belching out black smoke. "Gryn is the leader of the clan?"

"Our warlord," Tessa corrected. "And some think this is a time of war."

We walked on. I checked over my shoulder, but the Centaur people had disappeared. Everything else seemed so normal I found myself twitchy. No feel of Dragon Clan people nearby, no sign of the Centaurs and I didn't see any of the Cat Clan, either.

I glanced upward but saw nothing flying in the sky except a lone robin, looking as hot and bothered as the rest of us.

"I'm going to talk to my people," Tessa said as we neared his building. "And, in case you missed this point, they kind of hate humans."

"Why?"

"Because they're stuck here, which means they can't be themselves and live with magic. They've become hermits, surviving out in the wilds in small groups or burying what they are and living among the humans."

"Like you," I said.

"I skirt the edge, you know, with the astrology. I can feel some of the major movements open to people. If I had done this kind of thing four hundred years ago, they would have burned me for a witch. Or at least tried."

I glanced at him, almost asking the question this time.

He paused by his shop door and must have seen the question in my stare. "Yes, I was here four hundred years ago."

"I'm not sure I wanted to know the answer." I saw a face

at the window and gave Tessa a quick good-bye nod before I walked up the block. I found myself trying to contemplate age along with a new world view already overcrowded with magic. When I glanced back, Tessa still stood outside the shop and I knew he would remain watching until I safely entered the Woo Woo News building. I didn't linger.

Julia had donuts in her office, which meant she had already been out this morning. She waved me in and pointed to a chair while she finished typing. I sipped coffee and nibbled at a donut with chocolate and nuts on top, trying to reconcile my already odd life with all the changes I'd been forced to accept in the last couple days.

"There's something going on, isn't there?" Julia asked.

I wouldn't lie to her. "Yes. But I doubt this is anything you can use for the newspaper."

"And you won't tell me about it."

"Not without permission."

"Whose?"

"Tessa's."

The answer startled her. We dropped the conversation when Jacobs slouched in, looking even worse than the last couple days. I ignored him and went back to my desk to get to work.

The morning continued at a routine pace . . . so normal and calm my skin crawled. I researched a story about a meteorite strike in Uzbekistan. I tried calling a couple places and ended up emailing various officials instead. My mind had trouble focusing on the story, let alone the language I had to type for the requests. I knew nothing much would come of this, though. No flying saucers today.

At least I hoped not. I had enough trouble with the elves at the moment.

I remembered to check on my car and tracked it down at a lot in Bellevue. The man confirmed the car suffered extensive damage. I got in touch with my insurance people and started them moving. All normal, mundane and strange work. None of this fit into my life.

Jacobs stayed at his desk, pounding out emails of his own. He'd always been a bad typist and I found it oddly soothing to watch him from the corner of my eye: type, erase, erase, type, type, erase, erase, erase and curse. The pattern soothed me. Normality.

However, by midmorning I began to sense something else. Magic built in waves through the air and a check of the weather sites confirmed a major storm settling over the city. I felt something far more powerful and dangerous than a normal storm, of course. This didn't have the feel of Dragon Clan magic; I suspected Centaur Clan, though I couldn't be certain.

"I'm going out for a while," Julia said, startling us both. "Will you sit in the office for me, Summerfield?"

"Sure." I sent off my latest email and grabbed the laptop to take with me. Jacobs didn't complain. I could see his hand already hovering over the phone and I figured he wanted some privacy. After a while, I couldn't care if he worked or not. He was Julia's problem, and I knew she would handle everything in her own way. I followed Julia to her office.

"I won't be gone for long. I want to get some supplies laid in before this next storm hits. I should be back about noon."

"No worry. Take your time. I can handle things here."

She smiled and glanced at the hall. Her voice lowered. "If Jacobs wants to go early, let him leave. I don't want to find myself trapped here with him during some storm. I fear this could be a bad one and it could be a day or more before he got out of here."

"I'll let him go," I promised. I sat at her desk and put my laptop into place. "I'll even encourage him to go if I get a chance."

"Good. Thanks." She laughed. "Don't work too hard. The boss is going to be gone for a while. Have fun."

I laughed and waved her out the door.

I saw her pull away as her phone rang. I spoke with a salesman and went back to work on my laptop. Still no UFOs in Uzbekistan, but I found a few other things to catch my interest and took notes for future articles.

A few minutes later I glanced out the window and saw a small group of people outside. Not uncommon, this close to the Old Market. Then I recognized the two faces of the Centaur Clan people who had talked to Tessa and me earlier. Damn.

I grabbed the phone, wondering how to reach Tessa. I knew he carried a cell phone and would likely have a business phone as well. Tech, crass, human: if I called, the Cat Clan people would make some trouble about it. However, if the Centaurs had sensed the key and came for me, I could do nothing to stop them, and I had the feeling they could do something unpleasant if they wanted to.

I pulled out the phone book and hunted for Tessa's shop. My fingers trembled, so I paused and took several deep breaths, forcing calm. I found the number and checked outside the window. The people had gone. I expected them to step into the building and held my breath with my fingers ready to dial. I repeated the number in my mind like a litany, memorizing it.

They must have moved on. Chance alone must have stopped them outside the window. They hadn't glanced my way. I finally moved my hand away from the phone and forced myself back to work. I typed a little, glanced out the window, typed some more. Thunder shook the building a moment later, and right on cue, Jacobs showed up at the door.

"Go," I said before he started. I could see he wanted an argument. I didn't want to take the time or expend the energy.

"Take the rest of the afternoon off."

He grunted some curse, stood there for a long moment --

"Go before the storm hits," I said. Had he shaved today? Thunder rolled and the first splattering of rain hit the window. The wind picked up. "Have you checked the weather sites and seen what's going to hit about an hour from now? Unless you want to be stuck here, I think you should head out. Julia will be back soon. I'm sure she'll find some work for you if you do stay --"

He grumbled some more and stomped out of the building. By the time Jacobs pulled away, the weather had already gotten worse. I suspected I might be the one trapped here, though I wouldn't want to give Jacobs a reason to believe his imaginings about Julia and me.

Did it matter? Did I care what Jacobs thought? Of course not. But he might say things to others. He would if he thought he had the least ability to cause us some problems as long as it wouldn't give him grief, too. What he said wouldn't bother me, but Julia ran a business with an odd reputation already. And if our names started circulating, the rest of my *family* would hear. That could be trouble.

I went to work on my article. The storm rushed through with a new fall of rain and some wind. I checked the weather sites and found a massive spot of red heading our way, and moving far too quickly. WeatherBug sent out alerts every couple minutes, my computer cheerfully chirping away each time they came in.

Lightning struck and struck again, and the power even flickered for a moment. Things steadied and I went back to searching for odd things to write about.

A police car swept by, sirens blaring, startling me -- and startled me more when the car stopped not far away. A fire engine arrived a moment later and I rushed to the door.

Tessa's place was in flames.

# CHAPTER 18

I didn't think to lock the door or shout down to anyone who might be with the press, though I suspected they weren't in today. I charged forward into the lessening rain. The police wouldn't let me get close, but I saw one of the Cat Clan in the crowd; the woman stared at the building with horror.

"Where is Tessa!" I demanded, grabbing her arm.

"I don't know!" She didn't complain or try to pull free of me. "He sent us off to lunch!"

"I saw some of the Centaur Clan nearby not long ago," I said softly. "I thought all of you were still there with him, and there wouldn't be a problem."

Her eyes narrowed in anger, but she didn't direct the rage at me. I made a quick search, but I didn't see any of the Centaur Clan around now. I did spot something worse: A group from the Dragon Clan arrived, their bard with them. The Cat Clan woman spun around in shock, sensing what I saw. More of the Cat Clan arrived and I still saw no sign of Tessa.

Flames leapt out of the second story window as the glass shattered, the fire climbing the outside of the building. I had slept on the futon beneath a window now crawling with flames. I feared Tessa hadn't gotten out and the thought left me ill.

York crossed to me with his hand held in a gesture indicating he intended no trouble. The Cat Clan woman beside me glared, but I saw more fear than antagonism in her eyes. I believed, despite her argument with Tessa, she still cared about what happened to him.

"We did not do this," York said. He glanced around, not used to human crowds or human authority. "We felt the magic and came as quickly as we dared. Centaur is to blame. But we will do what we can to help. There are more of us behind the building, where the locals can't see them. We think we have found someone inside --"

"Tessa," I said.

"The one who came and rescued us both from Centaur." York gave a nod. "We repay debts."

"Do you," the woman replied, a snarl in her voice this time.

A lift of my hand kept her from going on. I had half expected her to bite my fingers off, but saving Tessa came first. If the Dragon Clan could help, even the Cat Clan wouldn't turn them aside. We could see the police and fire department weren't having much luck in controlling the fire. Most of the building already stood in flames.

"Struck by lightning," I heard someone say. "I was walking across the street --"

York touched my arm and indicated we should follow him. A couple of the Cat Clan people came with us. I hadn't thought much about the key until then. I wanted to save Tessa and I was the only one who had no ability to help.

Part of the roof caved in. York glanced up with a start and turned to Brandis. "We need to protect the other buildings. Do they have him?" he asked softly.

"Out back," Brandis replied. He relayed orders through magic, which swam out around us, almost visible as the power moved through the smoke. "He's hurt but --"

The Cat Clan people didn't wait to hear more. I didn't see what happened, but magic spread around us and we moved through the lines without the police noticing. I went with them. I wasn't safe if the Centaur people arrived. I wasn't safe with them either, but at least we were going to Tessa.

The back of the building had become a wall of devouring flame, but magic trapped it in place. Firemen battled the blaze along the edges of the building, but smoke obscured most of the scene. I couldn't see much until we arrived at a spot where Tessa lay on the cement, two people kneeling beside him and magic playing over his body. The woman I had been with made a startled sound of fear and charged forward to help.

I could do nothing. I stood back, letting the others move in and holding my breath. I could see worry everywhere, which meant they feared their magic would fail. If we lost Tessa --

I didn't want to think about what would happen if Tessa died. I shied away from my personal problems. I imagined the larger trouble left behind: angry Cat Clan, worried Dragon Clan, untrustworthy Centaur Clan. They would fight here in my world -- in my city where no human would have a chance of stopping the battle. As far as I could tell, Tessa alone worried about the humans.

*We needed Tessa.*

Tessa moved, coughed and whispered something which made even the Dragon Clan people grin, though they backed up in haste and let the half dozen Cat Clan people in to take care of their own. Tessa glanced frantically around, spotted me, and relaxed. I kept my distance from either group because we didn't need my troubles adding to this mess. Before long, Tessa stood, cradling his arm, and watching Brandis who had stepped in front of his own people.

"And now we are even for you saving our Bard," Brandis said with a bow of his head.

"And how will you pay us back for trapping us here for all these centuries?" the woman demanded, anger in her voice.

"Trapping you?" Brandis asked startled. "We never --"

"You left us here, closed the gate and took our key. We had no way back!" someone else said, the anger there as well. Magic swirled and came under control once more, but I could see this was about to get out of hand.

Except. . . .

Except Brandis still seemed confused and the reaction drew Tessa's attention. The other Dragon Clan people grew angry, though, and I heard whispers about their honor. Honor meant a great deal to the fae. Perhaps my odd connection to the Dragon Clan blinded me in some ways, but I didn't feel they lacked honor.

"In the last battle, when we faced each other here on this side, you took the key," Tessa said softly. No one looked to the fire nor seemed to care that he blaze grew wild behind us. "And you went across and closed the door behind you."

"We gave the key back to your warlord," Brandis answered. He lifted a hand, silencing the anger in his people. He must have understood the implications. His eyes narrowed as addressed Tessa. "We gave it back and said we would have a truce at least long enough for you to return to fae. We wouldn't leave any fae trapped here! Later, Gryn said you would have nothing of our truce."

"This can't be true!" The anger and loss in the voices rose in protest and power. Betrayal . . . but perhaps not the betrayal they had always believed? Betrayed by one of their own? I glanced around. Gryn was not here.

I felt and saw magic start to falter all around in the wave of emotional distress from both sides. Tessa glanced at the burning building, but even he didn't watch for long.

"We need the truth," Tessa said. He held out the arm he had been cradling a moment before. "Give me your hand."

Brandis took one step backwards in shock. All of the Dragon Clan had gone still.

"You aren't the leader of the Cat Clan," Brandis said, his voice trembling. "You're their totem."

The truth fell into place: Tessa was a shapeshifter, just as the dragon had been, and he had wanted the ability kept a secret when centaur captured me.

"Yes, I am the Cat Clan Totem. I have been known by many names in my past, but I'm Dion Tessa in this incarnation. For centuries I have thought Dragon Clan trapped us here, and there would be an accounting someday. I would *very much like* to know the truth, Brandis of Dragon Clan. I want to put this anger where it belongs."

Brandis held out his hand. His people protested, though not much. I thought they all wanted their honor cleared of this charge.

I believed the truth already, but I had a personal reason to dislike Gryn who had been so rude towards me. I watched as magic lights played around their hands, and darted up Brandis's arm and to his head, where they danced in a lovely array of blues and greens. Pretty things, but I thought this must be something dangerous from the way everyone held their breath. The show went quickly, and Tessa released the man's hand and lowered his arm, grimacing a little at the pain.

"He took what related to the matter of the key," Brandis said aloud. "He asked for nothing more."

I saw relief in the eyes of the Dragon Clan and suspected Tessa could have learned any number of clan secrets. Tessa had his head bowed and his own people appeared worried.

Tessa focused on the others of his clan. I don't think he even noticed me. I'd never seen such anger in someone's face before. He didn't need to say the truth of what he'd learned.

"Find Gryn," he said softly. "Find him *now.*"

Two of the Cat Clan spun and rushed off in a swirl of smoke and magic. Tessa gave a bow of his head to the Dragon Clan people and he might have started to say something, but we heard more of the roof collapse and moving away from this spot seemed wise.

When we reached the front of the building, the fire department had the blaze under control, though Tessa had lost everything. I suspected he didn't care about the *things* though.

"Why?" one of the Cat Clan asked. "Why did Gryn do this to us? Why didn't he give us the key?"

"Because we gave him power he wouldn't have held if we returned home." The woman who had been beside me shook her head as she spoke, as though awakening from a long sleep. "We even allowed him to turn us against Tessa -- against our own totem -- because he convinced us Tessa's involvement with humans weakened him, which was why he couldn't create the key."

"He told me Tessa didn't create a new key because he didn't want to. He said Tessa wanted to stay here with the humans and we'd force him to return to fae," another said.

"He made us mistrust Tessa and the humans as well," a third added. "He kept us tied to him and a battle he had created. The others of our clan in the fae lands --"

"They have held on, against the odds," Brandis answered, though he seemed to be trying to keep his distance from the Cat Clan. They looked angry enough to go to battle with anyone who crossed their path. "Without the key, though, they could not come to find their totem. The other clans knew you were not around, but we thought . . . we thought this was an internal struggle within the cats since we saw how Gryn grew in power."

"And the Gods know what he told the others of our clan," Tessa added. "Since he obviously has been using the key to go home."

We came around the side of the building. Tessa stared at the fire and shook his head with the first sign of dismay. "I need to make an appearance here, or else they'll think I'm trapped in the fire, and risk their lives for nothing."

"You don't have to explain to us," the Cat Clan woman said. "We've been fools, Tessa. Blind fools. I'm sorry. I think we all are."

"Thank you, Kala," he said. His shoulders seemed to relax a bit, as though some heavy weight had lifted for the first time in a long while.

More magic swirled around and over us. We moved among the crowd and the magic dissipated in a quick wave and a little sparkle of light which went unnoticed against the backdrop of the flames. A couple people glanced our way as though they thought they should have seen us before. Tessa and Kala made their way to one of the men in charge. With a little magic, no one seemed to have any problem believing Tessa had escaped through a non-existent side door. An ambulance arrived and treated a few people for smoke inhalation. They wrapped Tessa's wounded arm in bandages as well. By then the Dragon Clan had left and with their honor well intact.

"Find Gryn if you can," Tessa told his own people as we backed away from the scene. "I suspect, though, that he's already gone over to the fae side. He's crossed often without our knowledge."

"And he's the one who set the fire. He must have pulled the lightning down through your shields," Kala added. "He was inside still when the rest of us left. This wasn't an accident, and we all know it. If the Dragon Clan hadn't helped, we would have lost you."

I could see they all believed Gryn had worked against them. They left, mostly in pairs, hands on knives no one else seemed to see. Magic again. The police might have been a bit wary otherwise.

Tessa came over by me, shaking his head. "He was never

one of my favorite warlords, but I never expected such treachery as this from him. This makes me wonder what else he's been involved in."

"The stuff with Centaur Clan?" I dared ask.

Tessa nodded. If he had intended to say anything else, he stopped at the sight of Julia leaping from her car and rushing to us. She grabbed Tessa in a hug which shocked him. None of the Cat Clan remained close by, which I thought probably good. The sight of a distraught human grabbing their totem might have been too much.

"You've lost everything," Julia said, dabbing at her eyes after she let go. "What happened?"

"Someone saw lightning strike the building," I supplied.

"Come with me," she said, and took his arm. "We'll go to my place and I'll fix you some tea."

"That would be very nice," he agreed.

The rain fell harder, and we found ourselves in a downpour by the time we reached the door to Woo Woo News. I thought I felt a little bit of Dragon Clan in the storm, and suspected they tried to help to kill the fire and keep the other buildings and humans safe. I thought I should like the Dragon Clan more and so should the Cat Clan, though I also suspected nothing worked so easily.

We escorted Tessa inside the building, and I told Julia she should go move her car out of the middle of the street so the fire trucks could get out. She glanced back and gave a little curse and started away.

"You two go in and get cleaned and dry. I'll be right back."

I went into the bathroom down the hall from the offices and washed up. I came back to find Tessa staring out the window of Julia's office.

"Trouble?" I asked.

"Not yet." He shrugged and started past me. "This is far

from over."

"I know."

Julia wasn't back yet and I tried not to fret. With all the cars out there, both public and city, she would have trouble getting around and to our little parking lot.

Tessa came out and stood by the window with me. "She'll be fine. I have a little link on her. I placed it when this mess began. I try to make certain my friends are safe. And yes, I have one to you as well, though the key fights it."

"Oh. Good." I felt relieved. When had I started trusting magic so much?

Kenwood strolled past across the street, camera in hand. I never thought to get a picture, let alone do a story. I wondered what he would make of the occult shop catching fire. He glanced towards our building and shook his head, no doubt thinking what a shame it hadn't burned down instead.

I wondered what would keep Gryn from trying to do so. I glanced at Tessa, worried he -- and I -- had become magnets for more trouble than maybe we should inflict on anyone else. I said nothing. Tessa would have thought of this already. I suspect he stood there waiting for trouble, in fact. None came before Julia returned with packages in hand and pushed them over to Tessa. "Clothes, so you can get changed. I guessed at some of the sizes, but they're from the shop where you buy, and the clerks helped out."

"How could you know?" Tessa asked startled.

"You always shop in the Old Market, Tessa. You rarely go farther for anything. I noticed the shop where you buy clothing months ago. How's your arm? Do you need to get to a doctor?"

I had forgotten Tessa had injured his arm and wished the clan had done something more to help him, though maybe keeping him alive at all ought to be enough. I think he had forgotten the wound too, because he grimaced, but shook his head. "No, I'm fine. The medics already took care of the burn."

"Good. I'll go make some tea."

"Thank you," he said and meant the words on many levels.

Julia smiled and went past him and upstairs to her apartment.

Tessa stood there for a moment longer before he shook his head. "We're not safe, staying here. I can put a small ward around this building, but it took me years to build the one Gryn so easily got through."

"Is there some place safe?"

"For the two of us? No. The Centaur Clan has our scent, or at least mine. I think you are confusing them, though. I don't know what to do next, Summerfield, except we need to deal with Dragon Clan. Since I know I have no battle with them, I think the time has come to see if I can do something to help them though this trouble. They need to move on and this mess needs to be cleared up before something worse happens." His eyes narrowed for a moment and his hand moved shifting a little magic in the air. "I don't know where we should go."

"Nowhere for the moment," I replied. I nudged him towards the bathroom. "Get changed. You'll make Julia happy."

He looked at the bag in his hand and nodded, accepting this as the first step.

Police arrived to talk to Tessa as Julia came down with tea and cookies. They had every reason to believe the lightning started the fire since several people had seen the strike. They asked a few questions and didn't stay long. However, by the time they left I could feel magic building out there along with the power of the storm.

"You can stay here with me Tessa," Julia said. She shook

her head when he started to protest. "No. I have room."

"Or he can stay at my place," I offered. Julia accepted the compromise and Tessa started to argue. I shook my head and he fell silent, though he must have wondered when humans took over his life.

We talked for a little while and Julia went upstairs to start dinner for her and Tessa. I had been invited, too.

"What do we do?" I asked after Julia was out of hearing range.

Tessa glanced around, as though he could find answers in the walls. Maybe he could because he nodded. "I'm going to speak with my people tonight. I'll keep a magical link on you, but this is going to be Clan work, and they won't want any outsider around. Besides, I don't want them to know about the Dragon Clan key yet. They're volatile."

"Will there be more trouble tonight?" I asked.

"I don't know. I get the feeling Gryn, and maybe Roan with him, played their hand when they went for me, and didn't expect the Dragon Clan to come to my aid. They wasted power and they have to worry about the two clans joining against them."

"Since I won't be with you, I'll head for home after dinner. You can come there later. You and your friends if you need a place to gather."

"Thank you." He reached over and laid fingers on my shoulder. Magic surged before I could protest, giving me more strength once more.

"You should ask first," I said with a shake of my head.

"So, we could argue?" He laughed a little and sounded more himself. "I've given you some strength and blocked as much of the key as I can. I don't want it attracting others to you. You shouldn't be drawn to them if you sleep, either."

"Do you think the others will find Gryn?"

"Not if he is at all wise."

I said no more when Julia arrived. We had dinner in her apartment, and I said goodbye to both of them and headed home.

As I left the building, I saw Kala, the Cat Clan woman who had been so worried about Tessa. She stepped from the shadows about halfway between the burnt out shell of his former home and the Wolton World News building, startling me. Good thing I didn't have magic.

"Guard him," I said softly. She gave a quick nod of her head and I hurried on to home, feeling better knowing someone watched over Tessa, though a bit unsettled to be out on my own.

When I reached my apartment, I watched the news, trying to ground myself into the mundane, real world once more. It might have worked, if I hadn't feared I knew more about what was going than anyone else did. There had been more gang trouble. They reported the fire, and other weather-related problems. Oh yes, I knew far too much about all of the troubles in the city.

I wanted more answers, so I played my Summerfield card for the first time in years and called a few places to get names and numbers. I called more people and gathered the kind of information they weren't giving out on the news. Within an hour, I suspected I had an idea of where we would be going tomorrow.

The sun had set by the time I stepped out onto the balcony. I stared off towards the park where I could hear distant music. A slight breeze made the night a pleasure after the days of stifling weather or drenching downpours. The storm I had feared for most of the day still held off to the south. I enjoyed this moment, knowing it wouldn't last.

The calm before the storm. . . .

# CHAPTER 19

I arrived at work in the Mercedes the next morning. Jacobs got out of his battered pickup and stared. He grew sullen and annoyed when I got out.

"Where'd you steal the car?" he asked with a smirk.

I shook my head, not ready for any of his usual bad manners. "You saw the bumper sticker on the Subaru," I reminded him.

"Yeah, right. Like this is really your other car."

I smiled and walked past, though I waited at the corner of the building where I could keep him and the car in sight. He had grabbed a key out of his pocket and moved closer to the Mercedes.

"Do it and I'll sue you for repairs. You don't want to know the cost to repaint a Mercedes Benz."

He snarled and cursed. I waited until he had gone past me and into the building.

Tessa stood inside Julia's office. He seemed worn, and I didn't doubt he'd had a long, hard night since he hadn't come back to the apartment. Finding him here eased one huge worry. Julia handed me a cup of coffee and he surreptitiously added a jolt of magic while she gave one to Jacobs, who didn't mind not having to go straight to work.

I could hear the press running in the basement. Good. The current print issue would make the mail in time despite all the weather problems. I appreciated having a nice, ordinary thought on such a crazy day.

"Saw about your place on the news last night," Jacobs said. "Tough luck."

It would have been better if he hadn't been smirking, but Tessa gave him a polite nod. Julia handed Jacobs a couple rolls and somehow got him off to work. Good. I didn't want him around when Tessa and I headed out. I wasn't quite sure how to handle Julia, though.

Tessa had managed the problem already.

"Tessa needs to take care of some things today, Summerfield," she said softly, glancing at the doorway to make certain Jacobs didn't hear. "I can't leave, not on a printing day. Do you mind taking him?"

"No problem. Not much for me to do today anyway. And I don't want to risk having me help with the press."

"Oh Goddess, no!" she exclaimed and laughed. "Not again."

"You had a problem?" Tessa asked amused.

"Not one of my best moments. But the press survived, and the repairs weren't very expensive," I said. "Ready to go? I'd as soon not have to deal with Jacobs on this."

Julia came with us outside, frowning up at the sky between the buildings. Clouds had already begun to form into towering monsters and humidity had been rising steadily since dawn. The feel of magic had gotten so heavy it made my skin tingle. I suspected even Julia sensed something wrong. I could tell by the way she glanced around as though expecting trouble, which was uncommon for her.

When we came around the corner, she turned to me, startled. "Where's the Subaru?"

"Got wiped out in one of the storms," I said. "Good thing I had a second car, or I'd be out shopping today."

"This isn't the kind of weather to be out in this kind of car, Summerfield," she said. Her hand touched the sleek surface.

"It's just a car. Sure, a nice one, but not irreplaceable. "

Tessa paused before he slid in when I opened the door. I think the luxury of the interior took him by surprise, too. He relaxed a little, though the storm had started to pick up already. We watched, making certain Julia got back into the building without a problem. Nothing came from the alley, either.

"I made calls last night," I said as I pulled out to the street, this time heading away from Old Market.

"Calls?"

"Yes. You know, on the telephone."

"I know what a phone is," Tessa answered with a shake of his head.

"I'm never certain with you fae types." I laughed at the joke, knowing full well he used a cell phone quite often.

Tessa made an amused sound as we pulled away into the light traffic. "What did you find out?"

"The police have had trouble with gangs in town the last couple days. People saw the fighting out in the streets. I talked to members of both Rojos and Black Knights and it wasn't either of them or any other gang they know."

"This sounds promising."

"Most of the trouble happened out by Fontenelle Forrest."

"Ah. And now the question is which group is holding up in the Forest."

"I figure we're going to find out."

"This could be dangerous."

"Doing nothing at all is dangerous. Do you think the Dragon Clan is your enemy?"

"Not in this," he admitted. "But clan relationships are not easy to define. However, in this case, I believe Dragon Clan is the closest to an ally we're going to find."

"Your own people?"

"They're rather fixated on getting Gryn. I'm going to leave them to the work for the moment."

He began to show a little more interest in the world around him. I saw him lift his hand and test for magic. He leaned forward and stared up at the sky.

"I think we're in for a rough day," Tessa said.

"Storm clouds?"

"Oh yes, those too. But I just saw about a dozen horses heading the same direction we are."

"Great." I slowed and glanced up, catching just a glimpse of the unusual group. "Others don't see them, right? And they don't show up on radar?"

"Most of the time they stay within shields which makes it impossible for anyone -- or anything -- without magic to see them. You can because of the key, of course."

"Which explains why they appeared on Doppler the first morning, and why no one has said anything about odd shapes in the sky since then. The Dragon Clan lost their shields when they hit the wall created by the Centaur Clan."

"Right."

Yeah, it worried me that I understood all of this stuff.

We ran into other problems before we reached the forest area, though. Bellevue had been hit hard by the storm in which I lost my Subaru. Add the trouble with the gangs in the area, and the officials had taken action. We found National Guard, along with a few patrols from Offut Air Force Base, and dozens of local police guarding the area. I had to head all the way to Cornhusker Road to get off the Kennedy Freeway, and Tessa had to use a little magic to mask us as we headed down Ft. Crook Road, which they had already blocked off.

I thought we could drive straight to the old South Roads Mall. The place had long ago been converted to offices and anything else they could lure in to take over the space. I had intended to park there. However, trucks and equipment had taken over the lot and I didn't think the Mercedes would fit in. I went on to Chandler, but a layer of mud and debris had flowed down from the hills and no one would be driving up that street for a while.

"We'll have to leave the car and hike in," I said, pulling into a convenience store parking lot amid other cars apparently abandoned during the storm. The place was closed and the street abandoned when we got out, so no one noticed. I keyed on the locks and anti-theft protection as we stepped away.

Tessa frowned. "This is an expensive car?" he asked.

"Yes. So? The car is like the rest of the stuff in my life. I don't make those kinds of attachments."

"You don't make attachments at all," Tessa said. He looked startled. "I wonder if that's good."

"Do you think this is the time to analyze my life?" I asked with a little laugh.

"Probably not. I find humans fascinating some days, though. Even after all this time." He glanced at the car and gave a little wave of his hand. "People won't notice it."

I couldn't find the car for a moment, even knowing where I had parked. Good. Lightning flickered across the sky and thunder shook drops of water from the trees. Tessa started away and I jogged to catch him.

"You got me here, Summerfield, but I think maybe you should --"

"Not sit around in the car and hope another person from the Centaur Clan doesn't come along and attack me? Oh hell. The guy we faced here in Bellevue was their totem, right? The big guy with the hooves?"

"Yes, Roan is their totem," he said and started to climb an embankment. "I can't remember the last time he took full human form. I think he feels stronger as he is. And yes, you're right about sticking with me, though you won't be safe."

"I don't expect to be safe," I said as we reached the first

corner. "I do, however, expect to have someone I can trust at my side."

He gave me a smile of agreement and appreciation.

"How is your arm?" I asked, noting that he still wore bandages. "Can't you heal that?"

"The others used a great deal of magic to save me," he said. "I have done what I can not to feel it, and that's enough for now. Besides, humans saw the burn. It cannot suddenly disappear."

We hiked up the road, having little trouble getting past a few guards. Magic does have its uses. We headed into the bluffs moving into a quiet, sparsely populated street with turns and trees so we remained hidden from the houses. The area didn't look as though it belonged in Omaha, nestled on the hills without a view of the larger city. This wasn't the usual tract style housing and strip malls of so many other locations.

Tessa pointed at the street sign and gave a little laugh. I shook my head, chagrined at the sight: *Summerfield Place.*

"You'll find those in Omaha," I said with a shrug. "Summerfield Drive, Summerfield Blvd., Summerfield Estates, Summerfield Plaza."

"And this, finally, makes you nervous."

"Yes, I guess so. I don't belong in their world. We're not going to get into more of the analysis stuff, are we?"

"Fascinating though the conversation would be . . . no. I feel far too much latent magic in this area. Something is going on, but I can't sort out what, or who, is involved. I'm going to go prowl for a while. I won't go far, and I won't be gone for long, but I can cover considerable ground as a cat. Do you have a problem if I change?"

I waved to a grassy area with a fallen branch off to the right. "I'll be over there contemplating how odd my life has become. And you know, that's got to be really strange, considering how I grew up with my parents."

Tessa grinned and closed his eyes for a moment. He changed. I'd only seen the transformation happen once before when he went from cat to fae when we first met. Despite knowing everything I did now, the transition still gave me a very odd feeling. Tessa melted away into the shape of a huge cat, and yes, he had glowing green eyes. He gave his head a little shake.

"Nice kitty," I said.

His tail twitched and his ears went back.

I laughed and went over to the log. Unfortunately, the place was mad with mosquitoes and I spent the next several minutes trying to commit genocide and destroy every one of the little bloodsuckers. This would have been a lovely spot without them.

Well, at least they kept me so busy I didn't have time to think about all the oddness I'd mentioned to Tessa. I swatted at bugs and didn't think much about the key around my neck, flying on horses, and fighting creatures from the Other Side which I didn't, under any circumstances, want on this world where we hadn't the magic to deal with them.

Lucky for me, Tessa soon returned. He changed, and settled on the log, winded and silent.

"You don't do the change often because it's not easy for you, right?"

"It's not easy in this reality." I think the admission helped, because he slumped a little. So, machismo is alive and well in the fae lands.

"Now the others know who you are and that puts you in danger, like the Dragon Clan's totem."

"Yes," he admitted. "But I needed to know the truth from Dragon Clan about Gryn, so I had to reveal I was the totem."

I nodded, as though I understood far more than I did. "What did you find?"

"Magical paths leading into the forest. I can't tell one group from another, but I'm betting on Dragon Clan. The magic has an old, solid feel. Centaur Clan is too wild . . . but I could be wrong. After all, I haven't had much contact with either clan for quite a while."

"What do we do?"

Tessa glanced around and up at the sky. Trees obscured most of the view, but I could see bits of clouds moving too quickly and the sound of distant thunder grew more ominous. We were in for a bad storm of one sort or another.

"As much as I would prefer to return to Julia's office and have more tea, I think we haven't a choice but to go on into Fontenelle Forest and see if we can find whoever is hiding there. If they're Dragon Clan, we have a slightly better chance of surviving than if they're Centaur Clan."

I didn't argue. I think Tessa expected me to, but I had the key to worry about. And I realized if anything happened to Tessa, I would be in a worse position, since he kept me strong and kept the key's nightmares at bay. Without him, I didn't think I would survive for long. So I figured I might as well go with him into danger.

I've never sought out thrills to make myself feel more alive. I have liked my life, both the oddity of moving from shrine-to shrine with my parents, as well as my later life, learning everything I could, even if I didn't adapt the knowledge in ways Cal-Tech expected me to.

Maybe, in some strange way, those odd backgrounds had prepared me for this. I didn't find anything strange about heading into the woods with a man who could change into a cat as we searched for people who routinely flew on horses. Or maybe that said more about my sanity than I wanted to admit. I had steered Tessa away from analysis and I did the same for myself.

We began jogging along the edge of the road skirting the

nature reserve. Bushes and trees grew thick here, and we startled birds and rabbits. The wind grew in spurts and I could see clouds moving in ways I didn't think they should -- up and down, back and forth. I thought about Rich Anderson at WOWT and wondered if he was hyperventilating yet.

"There's an official entrance to the place ahead with a big building off the road," I said.

"Yes, I saw it when I came this way. They closed the place because of the storms so we're safe. Easy access to the trails from there." Tessa made a swipe at a mosquito and whispered a few words.

The mosquitoes disappeared.

"Damn. I want that spell," I said and meant it.

He laughed a little. "Maybe I can bottle the magic in a drink. We'd make a fortune if I could keep up with the production without it killing me."

I had, for some odd reason, stopped walking. He turned, curious, and I shook my head. "Sorry. That was the Summerfield 'make a fortune' gene kicking in on me. I was trying to figure out if we could do it."

He laughed but signaled me to come on. "I think we better wait and see if we survive this first."

The wind howled around us. I heard a branch break and fall not far away.

"Yeah, probably a good idea."

# CHAPTER 20

The rain began falling before we reached the parking lot. I had gotten far too used to being wet and it didn't even warrant a curse this time. When the hail began, though, we jogged a bit and took cover at the edge of the building.

"This means trouble," Tessa said with a hand feeling out things I could barely sense. "There's more magic coming into the world. I suspect Centaur Clan is pulling in more forces. Unfortunately, we have no way to do the same. From what you told me of the dreams, even if you gave them the key, the Dragon Clan couldn't call up many more people. If they had more forces, they would have remained and fought at their keep."

"What if you stepped aside and let the Dragons and Centaurs fight?"

"I don't trust the Centaurs, and I especially don't trust Roan, who has always sought-after personal glory unbecoming in a totem. Knowing Dragon Clan acted nobly towards us, I can't step aside and hope they'll win this battle. Besides, Centaur is showing so little concern for the locals caught up in their war."

"I had noticed." The hail ended, but the wind grew worse. "They're making the storms, aren't they?"

"Some of the storms, yes. They're fueling the weather with magic to make things chaotic, because nature hides them and what they're doing both from the locals and from the rest of us. The first time, when they stopped the Dragon Clan at the river, I believe they learned the trick by chance. But they saw what the weather did, and now they're using the power for their own purposes. It's dangerous. They can't control what they create."

Tree limbs began moving like wild live things, and leaves flew as though autumn had arrived months early. I hoped the area didn't suffer too much damage. Few enough wild places remained in the world.

I didn't appreciate hiking in this wet, windy weather. I slogged along behind Tessa, who I thought would use some magic to help get through. He didn't. I suppose he didn't want to draw attention. We skirted the building and *slipped* down to the forest floor, and headed into the woods, though we didn't follow a trail. The trees provided a little more protection from the storm raging above, at least if we avoided falling branches. We stayed in the hollows when we could, though those spots got noticeably soggy before too long.

I tried to get some idea of our location. I'd hiked these trails for most of a spring and summer a couple years ago, and I thought we had moved close to Childs Hollow. We sometimes followed a trail through the steeper parts of the terrain where the mud made moving up and down the hollows problem enough.

We startled deer, raccoons, birds, and a badger who thought he might hold his ground. Tessa waved him away, giving me a moment to catch my breath.

We left the trail once more. The storm raged and ebbed, and I lost track of our location in my attempt to keep pace with Tessa. I didn't know if he had any idea where he was going, but at least we kept moving, which had to be better than waiting for the enemy to come to us.

We scrambled to another rise and Tessa waited there, hand on a tree, catching his breath this time. The rain had stopped, the wind died, and the weather dial spun to hot and muggy almost immediately. Damn. I leaned over and put hands on my knees, gasping --

And we both stood straighter as we felt the arrival of others. The key tried to pull me towards them, and I took a step forward. Dragon Clan. Tessa put a hand on my shoulder and his magic surged through me, so I regained control.

"You shouldn't be here," Brandis said, stepping around a tree. He had a bandage on his arm covering a recent wound. I saw more wounds on the others who appeared from somewhere behind him. "This is no place for Cat Clan and especially not for their totem. The woods are not safe."

"Recent events have made me all too aware how little safety there is anywhere in this world," Tessa replied. Brandis agreed with a quick nod, though he appeared nervous, and I don't think their reactions came from meeting the two of us. How far away was the battle? Tessa stared beyond him into the woods for a heartbeat and focused on the Dragon Clan. "I have come to offer my help."

Brandis, and the others, stared at him with such shock I think everyone forgot the other danger.

"Even without the misunderstanding perpetuated by your warlord --"

"*Former* warlord," Tessa corrected.

His answer won a quick, feral grin from Brandis. The others grew nervous, though. And I saw how some had moved out along the edges in guard positions. Tessa watched them go and turned to Brandis.

"I did tell you this place wasn't safe," Brandis reminded him. "We have been hunting a few members of Centaur Clan after they attacked our camp. I don't think they're in the immediate area, but we shouldn't take a chance. Besides, I think they might have brought a few friends with them."

"We've had trouble with the trolls in the city," Tessa said.

"Oh yes, the trolls. Those aren't a problem. We can track them. I think there might be something more here. Something from the Other Side."

"Oh damn." Tessa shook his head, dismay showing in his face. I remembered the swarm of black creatures which had killed the dragon and I felt a clammy chill of my own. "What the hell are they up to?" Tessa asked.

"Taking over, of course. They must wipe out Dragon Clan in order to do so. That's what Centaur wants, at least. I don't know what things from the Other Side want, and I'm sure Centaur doesn't either. However, they somehow made common cause, at least for this long." Brandis swatted at bugs and grimaced. "I hate this weather. How do the humans survive in this heat and humidity?"

"I'd like to say this has been worse because of the magic and storms -- but I won't lie," Tessa admitted.

I grinned but said nothing. There had been summers as humid and miserable, though not with as many dangerous storms. If I hadn't known about the invasion of magic into the area, I would have thought we suffered from one of those bad summers where the jet stream doesn't move.

"Why are you here?" Tessa asked.

Brandis paused for a moment but gave a little shrug and put a hand to his wounded arm. He seemed resigned to the trouble.

"We had a battle with Centaur Clan in the fae lands and we didn't do well. They pushed us, and we had to run," Brandis replied.

"I need to know the entire story. I have the feeling my *former* warlord is involved in ways I need to understand, but I can't begin to search answers out if I have no idea what's happening. Why have you remained here?"

Tessa knew much of the story. I wondered if he asked to confirm or as a way to test what they would be willing to tell him. I kept quiet, of course.

"We lost the dragon. Something from the Other Side killed it. We ran, and in the first battle here, we lost things we needed in order to go back to fae. One was our bard, but you and your companion returned him to us, for which we owe you. However, we also lost our key. I fear Centaur Clan may have found a way to hide it, and as long as it survives, we cannot create a new one."

"They don't have the key." Tessa put a hand on my shoulder and nodded.

I pulled open my shirt. I heard Brandis give an almost silent gasp as he stepped forward and his hand reached out. I felt the key more surely then and saw the shape resting on my chest.

"Praise the Goddess," Brandis whispered, and sounded shaken. "But how can a Cat Clan wear -- you aren't. You're human."

The others stared, so shocked I hoped no Centaur Clan -- or anything else dangerous -- came our way. Brandis laid his hand on the key and drew back.

"You did well, keeping the key hidden." Brandis put a hand on my shoulder. "You and Tessa have done us a service and neither of you had reason to help."

"I had no choice," I admitted. "Though I would have gone along with Tessa anyway, once I understood the problem."

"Yes, I know," Brandis replied. "The key wouldn't have stayed if it didn't trust you. If Centaur had somehow hidden the key as we feared, they would have done to us in truth what Cat Clan thought we did to them. You and the Cat Clan totem have done us a favor we can't repay."

"But now you can take the key and open the way home," Tessa replied.

Brandis shook his head and seemed so bleak, I thought I

didn't want to hear the next part of his tale. "We can't return. When the Centaurs attacked, we lost the dragon egg."

I heard Tessa's breath catch in a ragged gasp. I'd never seen him so worried and so surprised before. I thought this must be a disaster transcending all the other disasters, which had already looked damned bad before this revelation.

"The egg?" I asked. I had a dream memory of getting the egg --

"Our dragon -- our totem -- died in the battle. The power and memories of the creature returned to the egg. We grabbed it and moved as fast as we could. However, when we arrived, the Centaur Clan pulled magic from the water in the river and threw it at us. Many of the clan who had travelled with us leapt to somewhere else, and since they haven't returned, I assume they're lost. We hope to find them, later. However, we lost our leader, our warlord, and many members. We tried desperately to control the flux they let loose before the storm destroyed part of the city. The egg fell, caught in the storm. We don't know where it went, but we are certain Centaur doesn't have it. Not yet."

"Oh hell." Tessa ran a hand through his hair. "Damn. The egg will hatch soon?"

"No later than dawn, the day after tomorrow. Perhaps sooner."

Lightning rent the sky. The wind viciously attacked the trees around us. I saw the others guarding us, staying clear of the conversation. I think we embarrassed them, in fact. I think losing the egg was the final blow to their clan.

"You saved the city from massive damage." Tessa laid a hand on Brandis's shoulder. "And this is why you have allies here and Centaur does not. They approached me and the Cat Clan. I can't say the others of my clan will come to your aid, but to be honest, we're too few to make much difference anyway. But I am the totem, which does give me some powers the others don't have. I am your ally. I'll help you find the egg, and I'll help you win against Centaur Clan, because they care for nothing but themselves."

"We accept your aid," Brandis replied with a true bow and quite formal, reminding me I didn't know the laws and etiquette of the clans. "We accept this aide most gratefully because we don't know this world and nothing we've done so far has helped. These groups of people we have encountered, the fighters --"

"Gangs," I supplied. "The Black Knights and the Rojos. They're worried another gang is moving into their territory."

"No such groups existed when last I came this way," Brandis said with a shake of his head. The wind blew back his hair. The temperature continued to drop, and I started thinking of Mr. Dorey and the fear of snow again. "There were armies, yes -- and much else that was dangerous. But even so, much has changed."

"Yes," Tessa agreed. "It's been difficult to watch, in some ways, but the people are the same."

"We were always this obnoxious?" I asked.

Tessa laughed first and Brandis grinned. But one of his people gave a little whistle, and I saw hands go to weapons. Both Tessa and Brandis moved to stand by me as guards. I'm not sure I liked the feeling because it emphasized how much danger I faced.

I saw hand signals passed, and more people came out of the woods, which set my heart pounding until I realized they were Dragon Clan in their brown and green clothing. I remembered the Rojos calling Centaur Clan people the Browns. The Centaurs I had seen dressed in dull brown clothing, which might help me identify enemies in the future.

"We don't have much time here," Brandis said, waving most of the others off into the woods. I thought I could hear yells not far away, and perhaps the clash of metal against metal. Brandis put a hand on my shoulder. "Keep the key, if you would. I think it safer with you than with us. Tessa, can you keep him safe, both from the Centaurs and from the key?"

"For a while longer," he agreed. "But you need to reclaim it soon."

"We should find the egg first," Brandis replied with a quick glance around. The sound of trouble grew louder. "Until then it's better if the three pieces we need are scattered, don't you think?"

Tessa agreed. To give Brandis credit, he also turned to me, waiting for my opinion. I gave a nod. What else could I do at this point? Maybe, if I had said I wanted out, they would have taken the key. But if they took the key . . . then I wouldn't know what was going on.

Curiosity killed the cat, only this time, I feared it would kill the cat's companion.

"You have a hard time finding the egg?" I asked.

"An egg, out in the wild, takes on camouflage to hides its true nature," Brandis explained. He glanced at Tessa. Maybe this was something the totem of another clan shouldn't know, but Brandis gave another little shrug and continued. "All the magical energies are trapped within the shell, feeding the dragon. The exterior takes on a shape, but usually chooses a large, misshapen rock --"

"Oh hell!" I grinned and grabbed out my cell phone. I prayed to whatever powers might be watching over us that the storm hadn't knocked out all service, as I dialed Julia. I hoped she could answer something I barely remembered.

"It's Summerfield," I said after she answered. "You were listening to things the morning of the first storm. I heard something on the radio about it raining huge rocks. Did you catch anything about the person or their location?"

Both Tessa and Brandis stared at me with eyes gone wide.

"I remember something," she said and paused. I could

barely hear her, and the connection wouldn't last for long. She didn't find the question strange at all. Years at Woo Woo News must have warped us both. "I can't quite recall. I'm sorry. You aren't outside, are you?"

"Do I look like the kind of idiot who would stand around in a storm this serious?" I didn't give her a chance to answer. Tessa grinned. "Thanks. I'll check with the station. I might be able to get an answer there."

I hung up and tried a couple other numbers, but I couldn't get through. "I'll keep trying once the storm is past, though it might be tomorrow before I can reach anyone with answers. If we're lucky, I can at least get us into the right area. What happens if you don't find the egg before the dragon hatches?"

"Oh, a number of things," Brandis replied, but appeared hopeful for the first time. He glanced into the woods, but the sound of battle had died away and a few of his people appeared, giving nods. "First, a wild magical creature hatches in a world where almost no one believes in magic. This, alone, is a big problem which could cause the kind of disruption and scare which might create massive strain on human culture and civilization. Second, the dragon is going to be very hungry and lost. Former memories will remain muddled at best. The dragon could turn wild and attack anything at all, including humans."

"This doesn't sound good," I admitted.

"And, if the egg hatches without the Dragon Clan being there in a square around it, to help contain and control the new dragon, we may lose the totem and never get him back." Brandis ran fingers through his hair. "We think Centaur Clan is aware we lost the egg. We need to find it before they do."

"I can contact people at the radio station, and if they don't talk to me, they will talk to one of my sisters."

"Sisters?" Brandis asked, uncertain.

"One of his *five* very powerful sisters," Tessa said with a grin. "He's right. Praise the Goddess we found you people. I think our friend can help you get to the dragon egg. Let's hope we do so in time."

# CHAPTER 21

We left the area, Brandis moving along with us and guards ranging out on all sides. Tessa said we would be back the moment we learned anything about the egg, but it might require we deal with humans, so we had best go on our own.

We had gone a few yards before I heard yells quite close. Brandis cursed and sent orders flying with magic and with hand signals.

"Time to get away from here," Brandis said, this time more forcefully than before.

Neither of us argued. I did my best to keep pace with them and I think the key might have helped in this case, knowing it didn't want to fall to the enemy.

We went down another ravine and up a slick incline. The storm came with us, growing stronger. I could feel magic in the air and lightning flashed too often. Once, when we paused on a rise, I saw a line of battle behind us. Tessa grabbed my arm and dragged me on.

We came, at last, to the road at the edge of the forest. Brandis had kept with us along with a couple others whom I recognized through the dreams; a surreal moment for me, since I felt as though I had fought with them many times before.

"I have accepted your help. Will you accept a pact with us, Tessa of Cat Clan?" Brandis asked at the edge of the road. "Will you help us, not only to recover the egg, but also to hold back the forces of the Centaurs and whatever other beings they have allied with?"

"I will," Tessa replied and held out his hand. Brandis grinned and took it, and with a quick flash of magic I assumed they sealed the pact. "I can't promise any others of the Cat Clan will join us, though."

"If we are able, we'll help you deal with your *former* warlord," Brandis replied, which seemed to surprise Tessa. "And any members of your clan who would wish to join us in fighting this trouble would be most welcome."

Another shout echoed from the woods. Brandis put a hand to his injured arm and started to turn away.

Tessa laid a hand on his shoulder. I could see the flow of magic through Brandis and I knew Tessa healed the wound beneath the cloth. Other scratches and bruises disappeared as well.

Brandis stared at him, shocked.

"They need you to be strong. And now you have strength to lend to others. Use it well, my friend."

Brandis gave a bow of thanks and moved into the trees. Tessa tapped me on the shoulder, and we headed away, down a short incline and to the muddy road. I felt a wave of relief. I didn't want to be part of this battle, even though we were bound to find trouble.

The trouble came sooner than I expected. We had begun to jog down the road, avoiding the worst of the mud while the storm ebbed and rose as though powered by the breathing of some huge creature. I suspected Centaur Clan felt the strain of trying to control this weather and once they lost their hold, I feared what the storm would do.

The dirt road had been carved into the hills, leaving naked dirt embankments on both sides of us, and trees towering overhead. Two deer darted from one side to the other a few yards ahead, plainly trying to escape the storm. I felt sorry for them. I felt sorry for Tessa and me, since we didn't have much more of a chance at escaping the weather than they did. The storm already began to get worse.

We needed to get to better cover.

Something moved in the shadows to our right and I spun even before Tessa did. For a moment I saw nothing until then the movement began again. Not something in the shadows; the shadows themselves moved. I faced what I had seen in my dream as a mass of black flowed down the hillside and straight towards us.

"Back!" Tessa shouted. He lifted his hands as I did my best to get behind him before he let loose what was bound to be a spectacular show.

Like lightning going off in a small room: the brightness blinded me, and the power sent me flying backwards until I landed in the mud on the other side of the road. Tessa stood his ground and sent another blast of magic against the black. I stood in haste, uncertain what I could do.

"Go!" Tessa shouted.

I'm an idiot. "No! There has to be some way I can help!"

"Summerfield!" He sounded breathless and annoyed at the same time, but the wall of black tried to make another attack.

I got my first true look at this thing -- *things* -- from the Other Side. They slithered forward over the mud. What I had thought was a homogenous single mass showed rills and bumps which sometimes rose a couple inches as though small heads peeked out of the whole.

The black rolled on towards us and Tessa took a step backwards, worried. His magic kept the creatures from surging forward, but if we tried to run, these things would catch us before we could get far. Nothing stopped them.

I wondered if Tessa had enough power left to lift us. I considered running to give Tessa a chance to escape himself.

However, I could see more of the black had already moved in the road ahead of us. I wouldn't have survived even this long if I had chosen to run when Tessa had ordered me.

"We better hope . . . hope the Dragon Clan figures this out," Tessa said, breathless though he sent a spray of magic plowing into the creatures and divided the mass. Some of the edges swept in so fast they formed a ridge where they hit each other. A few hand sized spherical blobs didn't reach the others. Three of them tumbled forward into a pond.

They disappeared in a little puff of steam.

The rest formed a narrow wall, rising higher as they came forward and curving around --

"They avoid standing water!" I shouted.

Tessa didn't take the time to check my observation. He reached out and grabbed rain and pond water, forming it into a huge wall, which slid in front of us. I could already see the things backing away in haste. Tessa made a grunting sound of pleasure and pushed the wall forward and it hit the creatures like a speeding car might hit a building. I saw many of them flatten before they disappeared in puffs of grey, while others flew backwards.

I realized Tessa hadn't seen the other blob coming our way yet. I started to yell a warning--

Water rose in another wall. It took me a moment to realize the magic hadn't come from Tessa, who spun startled at the sight. A number of Dragon Clan people called out from the hillside above us and I could hear shouts of triumph along the ridge. Brandis came at a run to join us on the road.

The fae literally boxed the creatures in with water and contracted the squares until the mass of black within dissolved into a grey dust. The fae swept the dust into tiny boxes of water and those disappeared with flashes of light, as though cameras took pictures in a dozen places at once.

Tessa went straight to his knees.

I reached him first and sat in the mud by him since there wasn't much else, I could do. He gasped and I put a hand on his shoulder to steady him while the others scoured the area around us, making certain we had no more unwanted company. A moment later I heard the clash of bladed weapons and saw the kind of fight on the hillside which might have been staged in a movie. Swords clashed against each other as a dozen people fought.

"It's all right," Brandis said. He didn't sit down to play in the mud as well. "We have them."

The battle disappeared back into the woods.

"Thank you," Tessa said, giving a little bow of his head.

"That was too damned close." Brandis put both hands on his knees, bent over as though he had run a marathon. No one else appeared any better. "How in the name of the Gods did you figure out about the water?"

Tessa, still gasping, waved a hand towards me.

"I couldn't do much else but watch," I replied. "I noticed they avoided standing water. Tessa trusted me when I told him. I suspect he didn't have anything to lose by then."

"You . . . you should have . . . run," Tessa said with a gasp.

"I wouldn't have gotten far. I saw more ahead of us on the road." I sounded unreasonably calm, I think. The rest of these people still appeared panicked and several of them moved off to hunt for the black things. "I was, as always, safer with you."

"Maybe --"

Whatever he had begun to say never went any farther. From the corner of my sight, I saw something small, black and fast launching straight at Tessa. I yelled and Tessa started to lift his hands. Magic would take too long.

I threw myself at the little ball of black and knocked it aside with my right arm.

I had fallen face down in the mud before I realized the depth of the pain. I thought the creature had seared off my arm, or it might still be on fire. I couldn't move or breathe, and when someone lifted me out of the mud, it wasn't any better. Fire had rushed up into my head, and I saw red and shadows. . . .

And then blessed emptiness.

I couldn't have been unconscious for long, but when I opened my eyes, the pain was already a fading memory. Brandis sat in the mud as well. Others had ranged out around us forming a square within a square. I felt oddly protected.

"Better?" Tessa asked.

"Fine." I sat up. My arm ached but nothing worse. I could see a discolored spot just below the elbow.

"Damn good thing you're so fast," Tessa admitted. "Thank you."

"Nice to know I can do something. I don't enjoy being helpless."

They both understood. Brandis stood first and offered me a hand to get to my feet. I accepted and did the same for Tessa. He stood more slowly, but he appeared steady.

"Time to go. Thank you for your help, Brandis. We would not have survived."

"We're allies," he said and smiled. "This is going to be an interesting association."

Even I recognized an understatement and a joke. We laughed and parted company. Brandis offered to send scouts with us, but Tessa shook his head.

"We're almost out of the area. You need your people. If you need us --"

"We can find you," Brandis replied and lifted his hand towards my chest.

"You should take the key," I said, despite not wanting to let it go. I must have been crazy. "The key isn't safe with me."

"The key feels differently. I would know otherwise," Brandis replied. "We're the ones in the greater danger. Go."

I had never thought about the Dragon Clan losing this war. And if they did, what would happen to me and the key? I wanted to ask, but instead I walked away with Tessa. I watched the shadows more carefully than I had before. I suspected a long time would pass before I trusted them again.

We walked down the road and back around to the front of the nature preserve. I glanced into the parking lot by Fontenelle Forest's main entrance, but nothing moved there.

"What do you want to do, Sunflower Breeze Summerfield?" Tessa asked a little later. We rested with our backs against someone's privacy fence. "So far, you've been dragged along against your will. Maybe the time has come for you to make a choice. I can get you out of this."

I thought about suggesting he get us out of the storm, but he appeared very serious about his question. If I had said I wanted out, he would have drawn someone from Dragon Clan to take the key.

I shook my head.

"I can help," I said. I touched the place where the key hung around my neck.

"You could help without the key."

"Maybe. But I have to trust Brandis wouldn't let me out of his sight if he didn't think this was the right thing to do. But on other things -- I think I can help find out where the egg fell, Tessa. My family owns the station I was listening to that morning. If I want the answer, they're going to do their best to get it for me."

He grinned and gave a little snarl towards the sky. "I'm tired of being wet."

We started away. A dog barked once and fell silent at a wave of Tessa's hand. Now there might be another good bit of magic to know. I got tired of taking walks and listening to dogs instead of birds.

We worked our way to the old mall, neither of us in any hurry. The rain had made small streams through the sloping yards, turning the landscape treacherous, even for Tessa. He slipped twice and I refused to think it cold enough to turn water to ice. The clouds over head seemed less chaotic, though and the wind had died down.

Tessa slipped, landing on his knees.

"Go as a cat if it helps," I said. "I've gotten kind of used to the idea."

"I want to check things out ahead of us anyway," he admitted. "We'd be fools to walk into some other trouble just because we were in a hurry."

"Go carefully. They're hunting for you in cat form, you know. They think you're the one who did the killings, not the trolls."

"Good reminder. Centaur Clan has many things to answer for when this is done."

"Which will happen if we win, and from where I stand, that doesn't look certain."

"I wondered if you had noticed." He rested against a tree, glancing around to see if someone might spot us. Unlikely. Only idiots would be out in this storm. "I wish I could give you more hope, Summerfield. I don't want to see your world irrevocably changed."

"You think knowing about magic would change everything?"

"Oh yes. Once the humans know something is real, they want it. Unfortunately, very few humans have the ability to use magic. The change would be disastrous when those few gained the power to control the forces of nature and to affect the actions of others around them. You do *not* want magic to come into your world this way."

"I wonder what's going on in your own lands," I said. He

glanced my way and his eyes narrowed. "If the Centaur Clan and their allies are here, have they won the battle in the fae lands and don't have to worry?"

"I wouldn't like to think so." I could see in his face that he did, and the idea worried him.

I didn't ask more. We had enough to worry about with my world.

"I'm tired," he said. He sounded wearier than he ever had. "And shifting takes power. Still, the sooner we get out of this area, the better. Stay here while I check. I won't be long."

He shifted to a cat and moved away before I could say more. I wondered about Tessa and the Cat Clan. Would they get their own key returned to them? Would he go home to his clan? He had nothing left here to tie him to this world, as far as I could tell. They'd destroyed his home and business.

I waited by the fence, feeling cold and miserable. Tessa radiated magic which felt warm to me these days and had kept me going through this storm. I wanted to get to my car, go home and get dry.

I heard the sound of trucks and made quick work of finding better cover. Several loads of National Guard headed up the incline, moving laboriously against the flowing water and mud. They must have heard about the battle in the forest. I hoped the Dragon Clan people got clear fast enough.

Tessa arrived a couple minutes later, in human form, looking drenched and unhappy.

"I saw them loading and had to wait until they got out of the way. The path is clear, though."

With the guard and the police searching for gangs fighting, I decided clearing out would be a good idea. I didn't want to have another discussion with the police about my involvement. I followed Tessa along a torturous route which had no doubt been easier for a big, four-footed cat. We both slid down several embankments before we reached the lot and my car.

"I used to enjoy rainstorms," I complained. "I used to think they were wonderful and rejuvenating. I'm moving to the desert."

"Sounds like an excellent idea."

Somewhere, far up in the hills, we heard gunfire. Oh damn, damn. Tessa lifted his hand. He held his breath and gave a nod.

"Magic, I think. Sending the guards chasing phantoms. Time to go, Summerfield. Time to go and prepare for more trouble."

And find an answer, I hoped.

# CHAPTER 22

We had no trouble driving out the same way we got in. Tessa eased us into the area where other cars still moved along the road and no one took notice. He let go of the magic, though maybe too soon since we found ourselves in a traffic jam as people came to sightsee the area.

"Where have I seen the guy who just pulled up over there?" Tessa asked with a wave of his hand.

I squinted through the falling rain and spotted a small black car on the grass. Someone got out. "Kenwood. He's the reporter who gave the pictures to the police."

"Is he?" Tessa's hand moved a little.

Kenwood bent to lock his car, somehow lost his balance, and slid about two feet down the street on his ass.

"A shame about that," Tessa said.

I hadn't expected it. I glanced his way, and he didn't appear in the least bit contrite. Karma, I reminded myself, but still grinned.

Kenwood caught sight of me in the car and glared as he stood. I don't think he even noticed I drove a Mercedes Benz. I grinned and drove away as the cars started to move. There would probably be hell to pay with Karma later, but sometimes you have to enjoy the moment.

I began shivering and cranked the heat up in the car. Tessa gave an appreciative sigh and leaned forward, his fingers against the vent. I had the feeling maybe technology didn't seem quite so crass to him these days.

"This is supposed to be summer." We had stopped two blocks later while unhappy people honked as though they hadn't gotten themselves into this mess. I squeezed water from the front of my shirt. "You aren't supposed to have to run the car heater in the summer."

"Oh, I'm sure real summer will return soon enough," he said.

I agreed, knowing the weather wouldn't be any more pleasant for the change. I made a call to the station while we dried out and waited for the traffic to move. I couldn't get through to anyone important, despite giving my name. I wasn't on 'the list' and they suspected a crank call.

So, I called Rose.

"Sunflower?" The use of my name was a clear sign of her worry. She hated the name and every year on my birthday she sends me possible alternatives for a legal change and offers to do all the work *pro bono*.

"Hi. I need a favor." I tried to keep my voice light, because I didn't want Rose worrying that I had some serious problem.

"What do you need?"

"I need some information from the radio station about a call they had on the morning of the big storm."

"You mean the *first* big storm," she replied with a snort of amusement.

"Yeah. *That* one."

"What kind of information?"

I winced, knowing the kind of reaction my request would win. I couldn't think of any way around this one, though. "Someone called in about it raining huge rocks in her area."

Rose made the sound she always did whenever I stepped outside the norms of her world. "Sunflower --"

"You can lecture me at the birthday party, as usual, okay?"

I said. "But right now, the information would help me out and I don't have the clout to get anyone to check for me. I really need the info tonight."

She paused. I thought she might be counting to ten. Then came the inevitable sigh. "I'll see what I can do," she promised. "I'll get back to you as soon as I can."

"Thanks Rose."

I hung up before she could pester me about anything else. The conversation had gone better than most and I wanted it to end on a high note.

"I will need to talk to my people." Tessa lifted his hand and sent a bit of magic out. I almost heard the words buried in the power. The car missed a beat, but since we were virtually sitting still, it didn't matter. "They're going to wonder what the hell was going on out there in Fontenelle. They may even have felt my involvement. I don't want them to get the wrong idea of who the enemy might be. We'll meet at Mount Vernon Gardens."

Tessa leaned back and relaxed, though I didn't know why. As far as I could tell, we'd learned far too many bad things in our meeting with Brandis. Maybe knowing everything gave Tessa directions in which to move. I suppose I felt a little better since I had some idea of how to find the dragon egg.

Knowing this dragon egg could hatch any moment in Omaha worried me. Nothing else had gone especially right since the Dragon Clan arrived and I feared we wouldn't find the egg in time. I thought about how Tessa said magic would change my world. There is a lot of my reality I don't like, but I could see how giving a few people the power wouldn't make things better. We live in dangerous times. We didn't need to add something so volatile as magic to the mix. As the lone human involved in this mess, I took it upon myself do what I could to protect our world.

The idea of such responsibility scared the hell out of me,

but I couldn't see any way to back out.

I let Tessa out by the Mount Vernon Gardens. He walked away, steady, and straight backed. Machismo, I thought. Or maybe he knew better how to take on the role of leader. I could see a couple of his people already there, so I didn't worry about him running into trouble -- as though he couldn't take care of himself.

By the time I reached the office, a new round of storms had hit. Julia shook her head as I paused at her office door. "What are you doing here?"

"The office is on the way home," I pointed out, and won a little smile. The power flickered but held.

"I'm glad we got the last edition printed and out before this shit hit again. What a horrible week this has been. How is Tessa doing?"

"He's fine," I said. Small hail pelted her window and rain blurred the view of the street. "You know, I don't think he's upset about the loss of all those material things."

"Oh. You're probably right. He always said the shop was just a place he had lighted for a while, and he'd move on when the time came. But he's been a good friend, and a steadying influence on me."

Wind shook the window in her office. I headed to my desk, glad to find Jacobs had already left. I needed to get some stuff written for the next on-line edition.

As I sat there, I realized I hadn't anything I could write about. Though involved in something which made any of our most outrageous stories look tame, I couldn't report any of it. I traced all the steps back, trying to find a story. Finally, I thought about the first storm and what I had heard on the radio. Valkyries, angels . . . yes, I could write something about the day when everything changed, even if I didn't tell the rest of the story. And I thought this would make an interesting article.

I had written over 500 words when Julia came to the office door.

"Someone's outside who wants to see you," she said. "He doesn't want to come in."

One of Tessa's people? I shut down the computer out of habit, even without Jacobs nearby, and headed out with Julia behind me. The storm had passed. I hadn't noticed. I hurried around the corner of the hall and to the steps by the door. I could see the movement of someone --

Brian Kenwood.

"Well, hell. Not the person I expected to see, but I'm curious why he's here."

"Go."

I went down the steps and opened the door. The day had become windy, but the rain had stopped. Kenwood frowned when he saw me.

"What the hell do you want?" I asked.

"I need to ask you about something." He seemed annoyed and embarrassed at the same time. The comb-over of his bald spot flapped back and forth in the wind, like a signal flag to the birds.

"So, ask."

"Not here. I can't be seen outside the Woo Woo newspaper talking to their reporter! I have a reputation to protect."

"Then you should have come inside."

"Oh, right. And be seen entering or leaving the place? No thanks. Come on. I have a proposition for you. I'll buy you a beer."

I wanted to tell him to go to hell. He headed down the sidewalk as though he expected me to follow. I glanced to the door to the building, but I didn't go in. Hell. He had my curiosity. What could Kenwood have he thought would appeal to me? In a week like this, anything was possible.

So I gave a wave to Julia at her office window, and caught up with Kenwood a yard later. He smirked, as though I had already agreed to his proposition. We walked in silence to an Old Market pub. I settled into the leather chair, relaxing as I waited for his great revelation. Not many people around this time of the day. He ordered a beer. I ordered a tea, which amused him. We got the order quickly and I sipped while he stared at his beer.

"So, what do you want, Kenwood?" After all, being seen with him wasn't going to help my reputation, either.

He pushed the beer half across the table and stared at me, his eyes narrowed. "You know more about what's going on out there then you've let on." His voice dropped and he leaned forward with an intensity which still couldn't hide his anger. "I don't know how you talked your way past the police, but you did. You keep showing up at all the right places and far ahead of anyone else, so I know you have inside information. And what are you going to do with it? The Woo Woo newspaper can't handle any *real* news. So, here's the deal: I'm going to let you share a byline with me and get you into a real newspaper. It'll be the start of a good career. This is a big break for you. All you have to do is tell me everything you know about what's going on."

I put my hands around my glass. I hadn't expected him to ask for my help. And hell, since he'd been so nice about it and all. . . .

I nodded. He leaned forward a little more and I dropped my voice.

"There are exiled elves living in Fontenelle Forest and we're caught up in the middle of a war between two clans."

He blinked.

And then his face turned a color red I don't think I've ever seen before.

"Son of a bitch!" He shoved his chair back so hard it hit

the wall and drew everyone's attention. His voice started getting louder. "You bastard. I offered you a way out. I offered to mentor you --"

"Maybe I don't need a way out. And from where I stand -- well, sit -- you're the one who came asking for help."

"Is there a problem, Mr. Summerfield?"

I glanced over my shoulder to find the pub's owner standing behind my chair. Craig out bulked both Kenwood and me, and none of it came from fat. Kenwood took a quick step backwards, and paused, turning from the owner to me.

Maybe the name finally clicked in.

"Everything is fine, Craig. I think Mr. Kenwood is finished. Do you have any roast beef left for a sandwich?"

"Oh yes, sir. I'll have one sent out, right after I escort Mr. Kenwood to the door."

"Son of a bitch," Kenwood said, but softer this time. He gave me one last glare mingling disbelief and hatred in equal measures and headed for the door without Craig's help.

I grinned after he'd left. Some people don't appreciate the truth when they hear it. And hell, I hadn't even had a chance to mention the dragon.

# CHAPTER 23

Wasn't that Kenwood?" Julia asked when I came back. "He walked by a few minutes ago and seemed really, really pissed. I made certain he didn't stop by the Mercedes."

"Thanks. Yes, it was Kenwood. He isn't a happy man. He thought I would help him on an article if he let me share his byline."

Julia found even the shortened version of the story amusing. It brightened my day. "Where's Jacobs?"

"Didn't come in today."

The day just got better and better. I went back to the blessedly quiet and empty office and went to work. For a few hours, I even pretended my writing was all that mattered. I wrote articles and did research and even finished my term paper and emailed it off for Glynis to go over.

Quiet, peaceful normality.

It wouldn't last.

Tessa arrived about the time I should have been leaving anyway. I was in Julia's office when he came in. He appeared weary.

"Whenever you're done with work, there's some stuff I need to do, if you have the time," Tessa said. His eyes flickered a little, which I assumed meant we had problems and needed to get to them *right now.*

Julia gave us both odd glances. I suppose, considering we'd just met, we were spending a lot of time together. I wasn't certain what to say.

"Go and do whatever you need to do." She put a hand on my arm and frowned. "Will I get a good story out of all of this?"

The woman was no fool. I smiled. "The best I can tell," I promised. I would find some story I could sort out from the rest.

She smiled and waved us away. Tessa watched her, but Julia had gone back to work and didn't notice. I nudged him forward and we headed out of the building.

"I didn't give her credit for figuring out something is going on, you know," Tessa said with a shake of his head as we crossed to my car. "But you weren't surprised."

"I work with her. Oh, and Kenwood and I met for a quiet talk this afternoon."

"What did he want?"

I paused before I unlocked the doors to the car. "He wanted to offer me a byline in a newspaper if I told him everything I knew about what's going on."

"Ah. And what did you say?"

"I told him the truth, of course. I said there are exiled elves living in Fontenelle Forest."

Tessa laughed so hard he was still gasping by the time I started the engine and pulled up to the edge of the street. "Where are we going?"

"To -- to a meeting out by Fontenelle. My people will join us along the way. They have made decisions. I am getting a feel that we are running out of time."

As I headed south, I could see clouds gathering along the edge of the city: Prophetic, probably, or perhaps just inevitable when it came to the fae and their battles.

"I think we're being followed," Tessa said a few blocks later.

I saw the car I expected to spot. Kenwood's black

Eclipse trailed us about two cars behind.

"Kenwood." I took a few random streets just to make certain. He wasn't particularly good at the work and I almost lost him once. If we hadn't stopped for a light, he might not have found us. "What do you want to do about him?"

"Well, we could take him with us," Tessa suggested. "I wonder how he'd react to finding out you told him the truth."

"I don't think I want to know. With my luck, he'd come to work for Woo Woo News and life there is already bad enough with Jacobs."

"And if he knew the truth we'd be stuck with him as well. Not a good plan. I guess we'll have to go for something blunt."

He leaned out the window and waved towards Kenwood. The light changed. I glanced back to see steam escaping from under Kenwood's hood. He'd already jumped out from the car.

Poor guy.

When we got back to Bellevue, I parked the car in the same spot by the convenience store. Tessa waved his hand and magic hid it. The late afternoon sun slanted through the ubiquitous layers of clouds but the wind was almost still. Tessa didn't have to tell me we were in for a hellish night of storms. More people were out on the streets, but Tessa cast a little more magic and we walked away unnoticed. We moved along the edges of shadows and sometimes out into the light. I saw one man glance our way, rub his eyes, and shake his head before he went back to work on the engine of a truck.

A few yards later we slipped into the protective shadows of trees. Tessa didn't drop the shield for another block. There we found the rest of his people, none of whom appeared any happier than they had the first time I had met them. Learning the Dragon Clan hadn't trapped them here didn't improve their attitudes. I stayed near Tessa, and said nothing at all.

We scrambled over retaining walls and raced along the edges of privacy fences. Sometimes the group used magic to get past areas where people had gathered. I could hear worried talk about the weather and the gangs and I tried not to feel responsible for either.

We skirted the nature preserve and moved onto the narrow path of Camp Gifford Road, not far from where we had fought the black creatures from the Other Side. I hadn't hiked so much in years. Soon the embankments rose and trees lined the tops. Broken branches littered the road. I also saw the prints of horse hooves and wondered if fae or the locals had passed this way, since a horse ranch sat at the end of the road. I'd rented horses there a couple times.

"Where do we meet them?" one of the young men asked.

"There's a railroad crossing somewhere along this road," Tessa said. "They'll meet us there and we'll make our formal pact with them."

"You've already made the decision for us," Kala replied with a snort of derision.

"If this were so, I'd tell you where to go to fight for them. I am not Gryn. I'm not going to make decisions which affect all of you. But consider the current situation, my friends, rather than our old wars."

I saw reluctant nods. I had thought, since they came to meet the Dragon Clan, they had already made the choice. I didn't want to find myself caught in the midst of yet more trouble.

The day grew oppressively hot and I felt as though I breathed in as much water and bugs as air. Tessa did a little magic and banished the bugs. Everyone seemed better as the swarms of mosquitoes and gnats parted for us like fish in the ocean.

I still wanted to know how to bottle the stuff.

We reached the railroad crossing with the sun half down

the horizon and the shadows long around us. The clouds built overhead into huge threatening cumulonimbus masses, but something held them at bay for a little longer. Cicadas and crickets sang out and fell silent at intervals. We waited as the minutes passed and I could see Tessa's people growing uneasy.

About twenty of the Dragon Clan scrambled down the hillside, hands on their weapons. The Cat Clan people held their ground, until Brandis bowed in a way which seemed to indicate politeness and set the others at ease.

"Thank you for coming," he said and sounded sincere. "You people know more about this world than we do, and we need such help. So, I propose a pact to band together to fight Centaur Clan to whatever end may come to this mess. If we're trapped here afterwards, to work together to survive -- but if we win, Dragon Clan will help reestablish Cat Clan to their full power in the fae lands."

Kala made the first sound of surprise while the others stared in shock and disbelief. "You would do this for an enemy?" she asked.

"We are not enemies, not here and now. Nor have we been in the fae lands for a long time. The Cat Clan has held on there, though not strong after the loss of their totem. I don't know if they've done well since the current problem, though. It is only here, through the deceit of your *former* warlord, that our old war held on so long. Everything has changed."

"You have my agreement to the pact already," Tessa said. He gave a little bow to the others of his clan. "Make up your minds but do so quickly. We've little time left."

"Why?" Kala asked. I suspected I saw the new leader emerging in the void Gryn had left behind. "There's something happening. We can feel the power growing and we can tell Centaur Clan is going to make their move soon, but I think there must be more happening. There's a reason why the Dragon Clan is hiding here in this bug-infested forest and not taking the offensive."

Brandis glanced at Tessa who gave a little wave of his hand, leaving everything to the Dragon Clan leader's discretion.

"When we came here, we lost our bard, our key and the dragon egg." Cat Clan people fell silent in shock as they weighed the full implication of the trouble. I didn't know how they might decide. "We have the bard back. We know where the key is, but we're still hunting the egg. This is our priority, and far more important than fighting the Centaurs. We're running out of time. The egg will hatch soon and we haven't a clue where to search in this damned huge city."

The Cat Clan people made sounds of surprise and Brandis glanced my way, hoping for some better news.

"I haven't heard yet, but I will soon," I said. "Really."

"Good. Thank you for your help."

I gave a bow of my own head, trying to be polite in ways they would understand. I went and sat down on the control box by the railroad crossing and let the two groups work out their problems.

I heard the promise to help them with Gryn, if the chance came, which seemed to please the Cat Clan. Obviously, at this point, they didn't care who got hold of him.

I watched the clouds and waited. Rose wouldn't fail. I seldom asked help from any of my sisters. She knew, despite the oddity of the question, that this had to be important. Patience. I knew patience would get me the answer faster than calling and bothering her.

Sunflowers grew along the edge of the tracks. I walked over and stared at one as though I expected to read my future in the pattern of seeds. I glanced at the clouds suspecting I would find the more immediate future there.

Tessa came to stand with me. Both clans appeared to have

relaxed. They had come to terms with one another, which gave me a little more hope, despite the clouds.

"Things are bound to get bad tonight," Tessa said. "Bad for us and bad for the locals. We can feel magic building out there along the edge of the storm. Centaur Clan knows we're running out of time to find the egg. They know the dragon will hatch soon and we think they're preparing to send more trolls and a good many of their own people into the city."

"I had the feeling this might get worse."

"You are getting far too good at picking up magic in the air," Tessa said with a shake of his head. "As long as you have held the key already, this might be something which stays with you afterwards."

"That wouldn't be all bad," I said with an odd welling of relief, because I didn't want to find myself cut off from all of these odd new things. Tessa didn't appear assured. "I know all this magic exists, Tessa. Not having any of the feel for it would be hell in some ways. It might even be dangerous if I thought I could see things going on, but couldn't tell for certain. I know the fae exist. I know what's going on. I will find myself back in this trouble, especially given the kind of work I do."

"Yes, maybe," Tessa agreed and grinned. "Humans with any kind of magic make me nervous."

"I kind of thought so. You can trust me."

Tessa blinked, his eyes gone off kilter with another vision. I held my breath. But he focused on me and smiled. "Yes, I can trust you."

He turned and walked back to the others.

Damned fae were going to drive me crazy.

# CHAPTER 24

Thunder rolled in the distance and a breeze blew over us, so heavy with magic I felt as though the power tried to suffocate me. The others watched the distant storm, and I saw heads shake with growing despair. I didn't ask what they felt out there.

I pulled out my phone, as though I could have somehow missed the call. Nothing. But I thought of something else. I hit speed dial and waited a moment.

"Hello?" Glynis said.

"Hello! It's Summerfield."

"Well, there you are! Are you all right?" she asked, and sounded so worried I felt guilty about not talking to her before now.

"I'm doing better," I said. "I sent you my term paper if you don't mind checking it out. How are you?"

"Oh, fine!" She laughed and sounded so happy I wished I could be there with her. "The classes are killing me as usual, and I have a monstrous assignment from Brockworth. I'm heading to the library and do some research. Any hope you might join me?"

I glanced at the clouds and the crowd of my companions. "No, I'm afraid not. Glynis, the weather looks even worse tonight. Maybe you should stay in."

"Really?" she asked, startled. "I heard the weather this morning and they said maybe some brief thunderstorms, but we should be fine."

I felt the wind pick up. "I think they're going to be wrong again. I know this sounds odd --"

"Odd, from you? Who would have expected such a thing?"

She made me smile, despite the situation. "Okay, you have me there. But even so, I think you should stay in and remain safe. This is going to be a rough night."

I heard her make an exasperated sound. "I'm looking out my dorm window -- and maybe you're right. Okay, I'll stay here and do some reading instead of research."

"Thank you," I replied and with such heartfelt sincerity I heard her breath catch a little. "I'll see you soon, Glynis. We'll do something fun for a change, rather than tie ourselves to the books and class."

"I think that would be nice," she replied, sighing as though the idea of fun was something she hadn't experienced in a while. I'd make it up to her.

"I'll talk to you later, Glynis."

"Later, Summerfield," she said and laughed as she hung up.

I called Julia and suggested she should stay in tonight. She had no problem with the idea.

"You and Tessa stay safe," she replied and sounded worried about us.

"We will. We'll see you as soon as we can."

I hung up and held the phone. Tessa and Brandis moved to stand by me, both worried.

"I've never had to depend so much on technology," Tessa said. Brandis needlessly nodded agreement. "If I had not met your sisters in passing, I'd be worried. But just the three of them radiated enough power to make me nervous."

"You're joking," Brandis replied.

"No. There are five of them. They've happened upon the power of the number and even three of them are remarkable to deal with. They're all lawyers?"

"The three you met are lawyers. One is the CEO of a hospital and the other is head of a non-profit organization."

"The world is lucky they're not all in the same business together. It wouldn't be safe."

Tessa sounded far too serious. I wanted to laugh until I thought of the few times I had lived with two or three of my sisters in the same house for any amount of time.

"You're right. I guess I've been too close to them to see realize the implications."

The wind blew harder, and splats of rain hit the ground around us. The rain felt too hot against my arm and I brushed the drops off. Magic, I thought.

The sun drifted downward in a blaze of fiery reds as the shadows grew. The coming night worried me.

The phone rang out with Straus's *Roses from the South*. I nodded and answered as quickly as possible.

"Rose?"

"I got what I could for you, Sunflower," she said. She had rarely used my name so often in one day, even when we were younger. "The Station didn't log the calls because they came in too fast, and the power kept going down. However, the guy at the boards at the time remembers something about the Adam's Park area."

"Is Adam's Park out by Florence?" I asked. The trouble had started out there, so the Dragon Clan must have been flying in the area when they lost the egg.

"Yes. Does the information help?"

"A great deal. Thank you, Rose. Really."

"Mom and dad called a few minutes ago," she said before I could hang up. The news caught me by surprise.

"Really? Are they all right?"

"Yes, they sounded fine. They had to hike ten miles to the nearest phone to call . . . but mom said they picked up some bad vibes about you and the rest of our town." She started to laugh, but thunder rumbled through the air, loud where I stood and echoing at her end. "Sunflower . . . whatever you're into, please be careful, okay?"

"I will, Rose. Stay in tonight. Can you call the others and ask them to do the same?"

"Yes, I will," she said and without a sound of disbelief or disgust. Sometimes we are plainly from the same family. Rose and my other sisters may have more ties to the real world, but they'd seen some odd things of their own in those early years before my parents and I left the US.

"Thanks Rose." I hung up as I stood and nodded to Tessa. "I have something which should get us close to where the egg fell. We're going to be heading into a gang area, though, which means we'll risk having trouble from the gangs, police and National Guard as well."

"This can't be helped," Brandis replied and I could see hope and worry war in his face. "What do you have?"

"Someone who lives by a park in the north of the city called into a local radio station during the first storm and said it was raining huge rocks where she lives. I'm betting she lives somewhere within view of the park, so my suggestion is to search around all the houses facing onto Adam's Park. Tessa and I can get you into the area. We know the town."

Brandis grinned and began ordering people to prepare. I hoped I had the right information. I closed my eyes while the others began getting ready, trying to remember sitting in the car and listening to the crackle of noise on the radio along with the panicked calls. Adam's Park sounded right in my mind, an echo of the radio report --

I heard horses. Here.

I opened my eyes, startled to see everyone mounting horses which had not been there a moment before. I gave a startled yelp and stepped back. Tessa had two horses by the reins and looked worried.

"You're afraid of horses?" he asked softly.

"Hell, no. I'm just not used to them appearing out of nowhere."

"Ah. Can you ride?"

I took the reins of one of the horses and vaulted on to the saddle, smiling. "I grew up with horses rather than cars. I can ride quite well."

"Good." Tessa mounted, though with far less grace as the horse fidgeted. He patted the animal and I saw a glitter of magic pass from his fingers before the horse calmed. "The animal senses there is a big cat sitting atop him and he's uneasy. I don't usually ride, but I want to stay with all of you. Fae horses have the ability to fly so we'll use less magic than if we had to move on our own. "

"This is going to be dangerous." Brandis said, drawing the attention of everyone. "The Centaur Clan will have no trouble noticing us as we head into this area, but we haven't any choice at this point. So everyone be ready for them." He turned my way, embarrassed. "You -- human -- you have a name?"

I grinned.

"Sunflower Breeze Summerfield."

Brandis blinked several times. I saw people turn, heads tilted in comical surprise.

"This is truly your name," Brandis said.

"Yes, really."

"Such a name would be odd even for one of us, you know."

"I'll mention that to my parents."

I had apparently lightened the mood and proven I could ride a horse, both of which helped. We headed along the road at a canter while magic shimmered around us, keeping the group hidden behind a shield. The others had placed hands on weapons. Cat Clan and Dragon Clan mingled as though they had not been blood enemies so short a time before. Tessa rode at my side and seemed more perplexed rather than worried. I thought we might share a lot of the same feeling as we tried to decide how we found ourselves in this situation.

And so we headed for battle.

# CHAPTER 25

The storm grew in intensity before we'd reached the end of the road and the houses scattered throughout the area. Magic did double duty as it hid the group from sight and protected us from the storm. Tree branches broke and tattered leaves plastered themselves on the shield. The dirt road became a river of mud, but we moved on a layer of magic without a problem. Sometimes I could see clouds swirling in ways which would have had me running for a basement if I hadn't been on this horse.

As though this was some logical excuse to stay out in the weather. I needed to examine my entire thought process at some point in the future.

A moment later sirens went off in town, which spooked the horses and the Dragon Clan people.

"Tornado warning," I said, waving my hand toward the clouds. "It's a warning for everyone to get to cover."

"Wise," Brandis said, glancing upward.

"Only for those smart enough to do it. Many people will come out hoping to spot the storm."

"Humans." Brandis shook his head as though he didn't dare say anything more, though in this case I would have agreed with him.

We didn't slow as we neared the convenience store parking lot and Fort Crook Road. I thought we would dash straight forward, despite the occasional traffic, but the horses took to the air a few yards short of the first cars. I grabbed tighter to the saddle this time.

"A little warning," I said softly, though I doubted anyone heard me.

We flew into the night sky and the clouds. Lightning played along the layers of white but the fae kept the power away from us. Pouring rain sometimes pressed through our shield in spurts of cold and ice, and winds tried to push us off course until we reached a calmer spot within the clouds.

I wondered if many other humans had ever experienced this. Having lived through such a journey in the dreams helped and I didn't fear the way a sane man might have. Being here made me want to have powers and be part of these people in a way I had never quite felt before. Considering the number of changes in my life, and the places I'd lived as a child, this seemed an odd time to want to fit in.

And to the one place I never could.

I didn't have time to evaluate the feeling. We'd gone a good distance already and we'd be over Florence soon. We'd have to go lower before I could get any idea of our exact location. I wished I had a map.

A shape moved in the clouds off to the left where nothing should be. My first, heart-pounding fear was a plane.

"I think we have trouble!" I shouted, and waved towards the shape, as much as I hated letting go with even one hand.

Brandis pulled his horse aside, lifted a hand and cursed.

"Down!" he shouted.

The horses began to descend far faster than they had taken to the air. I felt my ears pop and my eyes blurred with tears from the wind and cold as the others dropped the shield and prepared to do battle -- something I *did not* want to see here in the air as I recalled the moment of death for the last person holding the key.

We reached the ground in a bone-jarring landing. I squinted through the rain and dark and saw the trouble following us into the parking lot of some huge old, half-fallen warehouse. A single streetlight cast a faint yellowish glow over us. I had no idea of our location.

"To your weapons!" Brandis shouted. He leapt from his horse and the animal disappeared as soon as he let go.

When I saw the horses disappearing, I grabbed tighter hold of mine. I didn't want to lose the only quick way out of this trouble. The others had gotten down and prepared to fight, though. I saw the creatures descending towards us. Trolls and I couldn't count how many, seeing glimpses of shapes lost in the haze of the storm.

If I wanted to run, this was the time.

I let go of the horse and I found myself within a circle of fae, with Tessa close by my side. Trolls arrived with grunts, growls and what sounded like curses. I hadn't realized they could speak and had considered them nothing more than intelligent animals. I stared into the red glowing eyes of an enemy during a moment of surreal peace before the battle began.

The first line of a dozen trolls took a single step forward like a well-trained army brigade. Thin, dark lips curled up to show their dagger teeth before they all bellowed, creating the sound of a huge truck moving past. I had heard the sound before from one troll, but this time the ground shook at the shout.

With a flash of sliver and light, swords appeared in the hands of the Dragon and Cat Clan people. Brandis stepped closer to the trolls and their misshapen heads turned to watch him. Rain ran along the blade of his sword as he lifted the weapon. The closest troll moved with a fast swipe with his long, clawed hand --

And the sword darted in through the creature's chest. The troll bellowed at the wound, stumbling aside as the sword came free. He went to his knees . . . and to his stomach. Red flowed out from under him.

The silence held for a heartbeat before the trolls yowled in anger and attacked.

Swords flashed in the dull light of the storm and blood mingled with rain. The trolls were big and powerful but the fae were smart and faster. Trolls swarmed in and attacked *en masse*, and the fae fought and killed them, one after another, the bodies falling and forcing us all to change position.

The sheer mass of the enemy began to count against the fae. I saw one of the Dragon Clan take a bad cut across his face. The troll, seeing him falter, leapt in with mouth wide and prepared to make the kill, but the two fae beside their friend killed the beast. They both took wounds as well, but they had saved the other.

Trolls growled and howled, and though their number had dropped by at least half, they didn't seem any more inclined to give up. The storm grew fierce, and I felt helpless in the center of this maelstrom. I didn't enjoy the feeling. I didn't want to kill anything, but I didn't want the trolls to win either.

I heard sirens and saw the flash of red lights in the rain. The police couldn't be more than three blocks away, and this wasn't the battle we wanted them to find. Even the trolls glanced over their shoulders. They howled, grabbed their dead, and leapt upward into the sky, disappearing so fast they must have used a shield.

They left us in the middle of a bloody battle field with police cars racing our way.

"Close in!" Brandis shouted. He had a cut from his shoulder to his waist but waved frantically to everyone else. "Close!"

Everyone crowded around him. Tessa put a hand on my arm. The others created a shield and I saw the same rippling effect which I knew kept others from spotting us. I hoped this worked because we didn't have time for anything else. The first police car came sliding to a stop so close I feared we'd go tumbling. I saw cops jumping out and heard a round of curses as more police joined them.

"Damn those bastards are fast!" someone said. "I know I caught sight of people as we reached the parking lot!"

"Something big happened here. Look at all this blood!" Another knelt and frowned.

If one of them took three steps forward he would run into a wall he'd never be able to explain. We held our breath. Someone, already wounded, started to fall. Another caught hold of her. We kept silent.

"No one in the building," a cop reported, jogging over to join them. He wiped rain from his face. "Nothing here at all. I'm not standing out in this damned weather any longer."

The others agreed. I felt the relief of everyone around me as police piled into their cars. Brandis signaled us all to the right and the police car pulled past us, brushing far too close to where we stood.

But in another moment, they disappeared into the rain and dark. We remained there, silent until Brandis waved a hand and the shield around us dissolved. Wind and rain returned in force while lightning and thunder filled the air. A few of the fae went to their knees, and others bent to help them. I watched the sky, expecting the trolls to return.

"We need to get away from here," Kala said with a nod to me. "The trolls shouldn't have been able to fly. They haven't that kind of power which means someone sent them to slow us. Centaur Clan can't be far away."

"They'll track us too easily." Tessa focused on Brandis. "We need to split up. Summerfield can get some of us to the right area while the rest --"

"Lead the Centaur Clan away," Brandis agreed with his own worried glance at the sky. "The majority will have to take on the clan, while the rest of us must find the egg."

No one argued, though Kala came to Tessa. She looked worried and confused.

"Go with them, my friends. Help them. We'll do our best to find the egg."

"Horses coming!" someone shouted.

"No time!" Brandis signaled a couple of the injured. They hadn't used magic except on the worst wounds. "Come with us. The rest of you lead the enemy away. Join us when you can. Take care. We still need you!"

Most had called their horses and mounted but I could hear other horses, too. Our companions began to move away, though at a slow pace so Centaur Clan would spot them.

"Get back to the building," Tessa said, waving toward the decaying hulk behind us. "We need cover."

The others began limping towards the building. I glanced at Tessa and shook my head with worry. Trouble couldn't be far away and we wouldn't do well in a fight.

Part of the wall had been torn out, and haphazardly covered with some old crates, which meant vagrants used the place. I worried about what we might find. However, I decided on possible vagrants as the better choice rather than a definite encounter with Centaur Clan. We moved past the outer wall into an area with a broken floor. The place stank of things I didn't want to consider. Walls had holes and graffiti everywhere, little of it readable to someone who didn't know the gang signs. I crouched with Tessa and felt a little tingle and the brush of fur against my arm. A very large cat sat beside me, which still gave me a start. I suspect the Dragon Clan people had the same reaction since I heard a little gasp.

"No magic," Brandis said softly. "Use no magic at all."

A hell of a lot of Centaur Clan arrived so close their shadows moved against the walls as they passed by the various holes.

"Roan," Brandis whispered. "They're too close. Back."

We cautiously retreated into the stinking building. I feared we'd run into crack addicts and meth labs but I only heard rats and mice. Since I had a huge damned cat for a companion, I didn't worry too much about either of those.

Brandis signaled us to stop, though we could still hear the shouts of people and the squeals of horses. I wondered what would happen if the police returned. Who had spotted us fighting with the trolls and called it in? Would they see the people on horseback? I could almost feel sorry for them and the police dealing with this insanity.

The Centaur Clan stayed for a long time. They shouted and I heard dissention in their voices before they rode away. The night grew silent, except for the inevitable thunder and wind. Brandis signaled us to follow and I moved with one hand on a large furry shoulder I couldn't mentally connect with Tessa.

"Clear," Brandis said as he stepped outside. I gave a little jump. I think the others did, too.

I hurried out of the building and into the storm, glad to have the rain washing over me, letting the stink of the place drain away. Tessa remained a cat and lifted his head into the rain as well.

Someone came from the shadows to the right of the building, and swords appeared in hands.

"York," Brandis said with a little hiss of anger. "That was a stupid thing to do!"

"I need to be with you if you find the egg," he replied with a wave of his hand, and appeared far more self-assured than the last time I'd met him. "There was no point in me remaining at the camp. You need me."

Brandis started to berate him but stopped when York's head came up. "All or nothing. You're right."

"I need to find out where we are," I said, trying to get an idea of our location. "We need to find Adams Park. I think we're in Florence, so we should be close."

Tessa darted away. He would be able to get our bearings fast enough.

"Be careful! Remember they think you're the one doing the killings!"

I saw a lift of his head and what might have been a cat equivalent of a nod as he disappeared into the rain, wind, and darkness. I hoped he could find the park quickly, and we could find the egg before someone else found us.

# CHAPTER 26

B randis, York and I headed out on the streets, along with two of the Dragon Clan (Steen and Caris, my mind supplied, via the key). I could hear sirens, though they didn't come closer.

Walking city streets made my companions nervous. They lifted swords at the sounds of cars coming too closely, and shied from the noise of people gathered at a house watching the storm. Lucky for us the storm kept almost everyone inside. We did startle a raccoon -- though, to give the guy credit, he scared the hell out of us, too.

Tessa came at a run, spotted us, and spun, heading away once more. We ran as fast as we could as he led us to the park. There he changed to human form, gasping and unsteady.

"I'll prowl the yards!" Tessa waved towards the shadowed houses nearby. Power out, but I could see the moving arcs of flashlights and the flickering of candles in some windows. "I have the feeling the egg is close, but I can't locate much through this storm. Too much magic in the air."

"We'll try along the edges of the park," Brandis added. "I'm putting up a shield and we'll use magic to try and feel the area out. We need to make better time, and there's so much magic in the air a little bit will go unnoticed unless the Centaur Clan searches in this direction. And if so, they'll find us anyway."

The others gave reluctant nods of agreement. Tessa

changed. I worried he'd be worn out, but he rushed away into the night. We moved along the front yards of houses and the edge of the park. I remembered the woman saying she lived near Adam's Park, and I hoped she hadn't seen the stone fall into the huge park rather than into her own yard.

Close at least. Closer than we had been.

I watched through the sheet of rain and wind held at bay about a foot out in front of me. Something seemed to be changing in the air and magic brushed over us. I think everyone in the city had to be feeling the oddness by now. I had never seen the streets so abandoned, even in the worst of the previous storms. Everyone knew this wasn't a normal storm in any sense, and instinct drove them inside to cover.

All except for the fools like us, of course.

We had come full circle on the park when the clouds let loose with a new fury. I saw Tessa, in human form, and running towards us.

"He's found something!" I said grabbing hold of Brandis before he started another round of the park.

Tessa raced through the rain and slowed as he passed through the shield. He caught his breath before he spoke. "This way! The egg is already cracked on one side."

"Oh hell." Brandis said and the shield disappeared, probably out of shock.

We ran as best we could down a slick sidewalk, through a narrow alley, and at last to an open gate into a yard behind a huge white house. The windows all appeared dark. Did someone inside watch us? Had the place been converted into apartments? How many --

"I set up a mirror shield," Tessa said, waving at the house. "No one will spot us from there and they won't hear anything, either. But --"

"But we're drawing other attention," Brandis warned.

Four trolls dropped into the yard with grunts and wide,

feral grins. I backed away as my companions drew weapons. I thought I could hear horses, too. Damn!

Then I spotted the egg. I could have been living in the house and never would have thought much about it, except to wonder how something so large suddenly appeared in the yard. The egg looked like one of those huge red boulders people set up as lawn ornaments -- waist high and bit elongated. I could see where it had impacted with the ground and rolled a short distance, taking out part of a flower garden.

I could also see a crack from which came a glow of unnatural green light, already growing bright enough to illuminate the night around us. As I watched, the tip of a black claw emerged, pulling at the rock shell and a little more gave way. I wanted to watch --

But I wasn't suicidal. Brandis, crazed with worry, threw himself straight at one of the trolls. Tessa fought another. He slipped from human to cat in a quick surge, and startled the creature long enough to launch himself at the thing's neck and sink teeth into the thick skin.

I had to remember not to annoy Tessa any time in the future.

Kala appeared at the gate along with some of the others. Brandis gave a shout relief and worry in the same sound.

"The Centaurs are close behind," Kala warned. "Once the trolls found you, they had a clear link. We'll hold them off as long as we can!"

She glanced at the egg, shook her head, and rushed back into battle. I could hear the sounds not far away, and saw people fighting in the alley. The police would arrive soon, hunting for gangs and they would find themselves caught in something they couldn't begin to understand.

The four trolls died quickly, at least. Tessa, Brandis, and I moved closer to the egg, though I had no idea what I could do. I saw three claws followed by a second set of claws prying at the broken edges of the shell. Magical green light flared around us, and I thought I could hear a soft growl of sound from within.

"The Centaurs are going to break through," Tessa warned, waving towards the alley. He had turned human. I saw him reach down to the shell and pull a strand of the green light out. The magic settled into him, though he did seem to shiver at the feel of the power.

People fought, sword against sword, in a scene which should have had a castle as a backdrop rather than trashcans and an old pickup on blocks. I could see our forces pushed to the gate with the Centaur clan filling the alley. Kala held the enemy for the moment, with both Cat Clan and Dragon Clan fighting at her command. I suspected she would make a good new Warlord for the Cat Clan, if any of us survived.

Brandis rushed forward and grabbed the arms of a couple of the wounded people. One went to her knees, and Brandis pulled her to the side. Tessa and I went to help as well, and I took hold of another one, helping him to some cover by the side of a huge old maple tree. Tessa healed those whom he could. I feared such work must be dangerous, expending so much power -- but everything was dangerous, and at least with the fighters back on their feet, we had a better chance of surviving.

I brought the wounded to Tessa and neither Cat nor Dragon Clan people argued.

I could see the shadowy shape of Roan in the crowd towards the rear of his people. The narrow area of the alley helped us, along with the privacy fences opposite the yard where we fought. Together, they created a narrow funnel, rather than a wide long line we could not have held.

Kala or Brandis had already set people to hold the area around the front yard as well, so no one could come through.

Brandis grabbed York, who had started towards the

battle.

"Let me go! I can sing --"

"There's no time. I need you for control! We need to form the square around the egg! The rest of you keep us safe!"

He pulled York into the square around the egg along with another two. I could see almost all of a green-scaled and clawed leg emerge from the shell opening, and for a moment, I glimpsed a huge emerald eye. I felt chilled at the alien-ness of this thing . . . but I remembered how Vane had sacrificed himself for his people. I gave the dragon a bow and looked back to the battle as a group of the enemy broke through the lines. A half dozen Centaur Clan and four more trolls charged straight at us.

"We have to keep them back," Tessa yelled. "Damn!"

I hadn't thought the battle would come down to the last moment and I refused to believe we couldn't win. So when I saw one of the Dragon Clan fall, I grabbed the sword, half expecting the weapon to disappear. The key, though, grabbed hold of the magic as I brought the blade around blocking a blow which would have killed the already downed man. I'd had some training with a sword, though I wasn't an expert with the weapon. I did have righteous anger, fear and adrenaline on my side.

I would be no match for a troll, so I did my best to fight the Centaur people instead. Another surge of the enemy came through the gate along with two more of the damned trolls. I tried to fight one of the ugly beasts, but it grabbed me by the shoulder and tossed me aside in its haste to get to the egg.

I hit the maple tree and fell, my head ringing, blood running from my shoulder and across my chest. I couldn't breathe for a moment. Fire raced from my chest through my body as the key healed what it could and gave me new energy. I struggled to my feet feeling woozy and not navigating well in the mud. But I could fight --

Two trolls reached the square. The first grabbed Caris and killed her before I could even cry out a warning. Tessa leapt at the creature and took a bad wound across his chest and collapsed, almost trampled beneath the trolls' feet, before Brandis yelled and leapt from his own place by the egg, attacking trolls and Centaur Clan with new ferocity.

I rushed forward. Someone tried to stop me. I swung, the key helping, and the blade cut deep into the neck of one of the Centaur Clan. I didn't watch after I severed the artery.

I reached Tessa, frightened by the amount of blood I found as I knelt beside him. Tessa, however, got to his knees, frantic.

"There! Stand there!"

He shoved me into the corner where Brandis had been. He took the other abandoned corner after gently pushing aside the body of Caris.

The dragon had two clawed legs out of the shell. A nose appeared followed by a long head with wide emerald eyes blinking as he looked around.

"What the hell am I supposed to do?" I asked, panicked more than I had been during the battle. Probably because now I had time to think.

"Just stand there," Tessa ordered with an arm tight to his bleeding chest. With the other, he spread magic in lines along the sides of the square we made. "We'll do the rest. Don't break the square!"

The chaos of the battle closed in, moving within two yards of us. "It won't be my choice."

Tessa swayed a little and I feared he would be the one who went down. I heard Kala and Brandis both shout orders to the others. I wanted to join the battle and help where I could, rather than standing here, feeling useless and helpless.

The dragon pulled itself up, kicked the egg into pieces, and rose on his back legs, screaming.

All hell broke loose. The dragon's first yell seemed to swallow everything around it: sound, colors, scents -- the battle froze, or the world did. I don't know which, but I understood why this creature should never have been hatched in my world. It did not belong. Not in anyway.

The dragon stood about six feet on the back legs and three feet high at the shoulders when on all fours. The scales shimmered with greens and blues, and he licked rain from the corner of his mouth. He dashed towards me. My body wanted to leap backwards, but I held my place, and without the help of the key. I knew if I broke the square, all would be lost.

I would hold. I stared into the face of the creature, and I suspected he searched for a flaw in the square and knew I was the weak link. I could see wildness in the bright eyes and tried to remember the man I had seen in my dreams.

The dragon slashed at me and a claw caught my arm.

I looked into his face and felt an echo of another's words, a whisper from the nightmares which first led me to this trouble.

"We won't let you go," I said softly.

I think he remembered those words from Karolan, back in another life, whispered over the egg. He backed away.

The familiar warmth of Tessa's magic pushed over us with a blanket of calm. I saw the dragon's head lift and his eyes focus on the world for the first time. He headed for Tessa at a more deliberate pace. I could hear York singing as well. Calm. Peace in the world. . . .

The battle still raged. I dared a glance towards the gate and found the enemy retreating into the alley. I saw Brandis break free, pat Kala on the shoulder, and sprint back to the square, almost slipping in the mud-covered yard. He came to a breathless stop, glanced from me to Tessa and to the dragon pacing relentlessly back and forth between us.

"Oh, this can't be good," he said with a stunned shake of his head.

The dragon heard him, walked toward the edge of the square, and stood on his back legs. I could already see more reasoning in him. York sang a soft song in words I didn't understand, but I felt purpose in them. I felt contentment, and knowledge . . . and I thought even I understood better for it.

"Can you take my spot?" I asked, frantic with fear I would do something wrong.

"Not wise to break the square until he does it himself," Brandis replied. He shook his head. "But Gods of all creations! A human and the totem of the Cat Clan, bonded with our dragon?"

"Bonded?" I didn't know what the word entailed, but Brandis didn't have time to explain. The dragon dropped onto all fours and walked towards me once more, his head tilted, the eyes showing more reasoning, and perhaps a little too much cunning.

"Be wise," I said softly.

And he stopped.

"They're rallying!" Kala shouted from the gate.

Brandis cursed, took stock of his own people with a quick glance around the area. Then he gave the dragon a deep bow. "Do well, my friend Vane. Grow strong."

He spun and headed towards the gate like a man who knew he wasn't coming back.

The dragon roared and crashed against the edge of the square -- once, twice. York sang louder and the Dragon backed away, panting. I saw wildness take the creature once more and the storm blew in a chaotic maelstrom bringing down tree branches, parts of roofs, and knocking people aside on all sides. Not far away, I could hear the sound of sirens once more.

"How long?" I shouted to Tessa.

"Longer than we have, I'm sure," he answered, holding to his wounded chest. I feared he would fall.

I looked to the Dragon Clan woman who stood opposite me.

"I don't know, friend," she said softly. She had a bleeding shoulder as well but stood her place steadier than Tessa or me. "I've never been part of a hatching. No one has for thousands of years. And even so, this one isn't normal."

I saw Tessa start to fall and barely catch himself --

"We need help!" I shouted.

Kala came at a run, with three Cat Clan members who ranged themselves around us so that they formed a square outside the square. Power rose in waves. Kala put a hand to Tessa's shoulder, and I saw the flicker of magic from her to him. She almost went to her knees afterwards, but he stood straighter.

The dragon paced, paced, and twice howled, throwing itself at the side of the square. The last time I saw a flicker of magic where he hit. He stood, almost man-like. I saw the creature shimmer a little, as though he started to change. Not yet, I thought. Too soon.

The Centaur Clan broke through, fully into the yard now. I saw our side surge backwards, splinter, and everyone throw himself into the battle, one against one.

Roan pranced forward, his mouth wide in a feral grin. Long hair grew into a mane at the back of the head and neck, all of it snarled and hanging with leaves and twigs, giving him an air of wildness. Roan plowed through the gate, knocking down part of the fence with a shout of triumph, as thought he had succeeded in some great battle. Brandis charged straight at him and cut him along his side. Roan screamed and retreated, but I didn't think the wound would keep him away for long.

"We can't stop them," Kala shouted, a hand on Tessa's shoulder. "Damn, we can't hold them!"

Centaur Clan people yelled and sprang forward even while Roan backed up, howling with a hand to his wounded side. They rushed in a line and two got past the outer square, but not the inner one. I had the sword in my hand, but I didn't dare turn to use the weapon. I stared at the dragon. He stood on his back legs and watched the chaos of battle coming at him.

Larger. I realized he had grown much larger already.

"Kill them!" Roan shouted from the far edge of the yard.

Kala leapt away from Tessa and the others moved to reform a line, but they couldn't hold the enemy. I shifted the sword in my hand. We would fail --

Kala gave a shout of dismay and anger as she went down, though not dead yet. She crawled to the side as Roan charged in behind his people. They massed, moving forward, and pressing both Dragon Clan and Cat Clan backwards, though neither group gave up the fight.

They couldn't win, not with the numbers against them and the damned trolls lining up as well.

I felt calm come over me again. I had the sword in hand and if -- when -- they came this far, I would use it. I had never wondered how I would die, but even so, I don't think I could have come up with this scenario . . . though in an odd way, it suited me.

The Centaurs shouted and formed a line, Roan moving to the middle, prancing with his head high. I thought I spotted Gryn back farther in the group, but I didn't point him out to Tessa. He didn't need to see the man win the battle.

They started forward again, swords up and ready --

And the dragon stepped to the edge of the square, stood on his back legs and parted his hands . . . and stepped through the magical boundary.

He had broken the power of the square! I watched elated and exhausted at the same time, though I feared he had found his power too late. The others rushed to attack him, and Tessa moved to protect the young dragon. I did as well.

"Nooooo!"

The dragon shifted and became a young man clothed in green and blue.

*Vane!* His hands rose, and magic spun through him, forming circles of rainbow colors so bright and beautiful I stared, mesmerized and blind to any danger. Tessa moved to his side, magic of his own in hand and growing so the powers circled and twined together, spreading outward.

Everyone had stopped moving.

"Two totems!" Roan retreated in haste, all the way to the fallen gate. I saw fear in his face. I thought about all the battles and how he had sent his people in ahead of him. Not a brave totem, I suspected.

The Dragon and Cat Clans formed into a line, the totem magic circling around them and giving power to each of their own spells as they shoved the enemy away. York stepped forward to the middle of the line and began to chant a new song, calling the fury of the storm. Lighting struck the ground to the left, to the right --

Roan ran and his people followed. Gryn disappeared again. Kala and Brandis led the charge after them despite their wounds. A few others followed with shouts of pleasure.

We had won? The dragon survived, and Dragon and Cat Clan still held the battlefield. Bodies littered the ground, though not as many as I expected, and some disappeared as I watched. Tessa's work. He had his hand up still, chanting his own magic, though he swayed with every line.

York's song settled to a calm, quiet melody and drifted away on the dying winds of the storm. Vane glanced at me, smiling before he shimmered back into dragon form and set about sniffing at the ground like a puppy let loose in the yard for the first time.

"Gods, I didn't think he'd be able to change so soon," Brandis said as he returned and sat in the mud, muck, and trampled flowers.

Tessa went to his knees. I rushed to his side, despite being the last person who could help. He needed magic. "I need someone!"

York limped to us and settled in the mud, pushing Tessa into my arms while magic flickered from his own fingers and across the bleeding wound on Tessa's chest. He healed some at least. The dragon moved to Brandis and nuzzled in by him until Brandis petted the scaled head and the dragon's eyes closed.

"Better," Tessa said, his voice shaky. "Save your power. Others will need you."

I could hear sirens which came far too close for a moment before they changed direction and went away. Kala came back through the fallen gate to where the rest of us still sat while both clans worked at helping each other. I had the feeling there would be more than a normal alliance between Cat and Dragon Clans in the future. Odd to think such things.

"We diverted the local authorities to follow some stragglers from Centaur Clan," Kala reported, and appeared quite smug. She stared at the dragon and shook her head as though to draw herself back to the problems at hand. "But we have to go. Someone is bound to come back this way."

I stood and helped Tessa to his feet. I had no idea what would happen next.

And my cell phone rang, startling us all. Weapons appeared and people shouted in worry.

*Age of Aquarius*, of course. Julia. I pulled the phone out --

And the dragon came over, took the phone from my hand with a quick swipe of his front leg . . . and ate it.

We stared in silence for a moment.

"Well. I guess I won't have to worry about calls for a while," I said.

"I think we better get him somewhere and feed him," York suggested, patting the dragon on the head. "Proper food, before he acquires a taste for things we'd really rather not be feeding him."

I swear the dragon smiled.

"Sunflower Breeze Summerfield." Brandis crossed to me and put a hand on my shoulder. "You have helped us in many ways we can never repay. And now, I think, the time has come to give back that which you have kept safe."

I pulled aside the front of my shirt and saw the key when Brandis lifted the dragon amulet over my head. Kala stared in shock which meant the Cat Clan hadn't figured out the real reason I was around.

The chain untangled from my hair and I felt odd. Weightless . . . and as though I could breathe for the first time in days. I hadn't realized how much the key had affected me.

My work, and with it my link to the fae, was over.

# CHAPTER 27

I awoke to a bright, clear morning . . . or rather nearly afternoon according to the clock by the bed. I crawled out from under the covers and took a long, relaxing shower. I had bruises and cuts, and more bruises, but the wound in my shoulder had healed. I suspected Tessa's work, though I didn't remember. I recalled how he got us back to the Mercedes and me driving home.

I'd had no dreams or nightmares last night. With the key gone, I was free of the mess I had gotten myself into by being far too curious. If I hadn't decided to search for what the big cat had been hunting. . . .

Damn. The loss of the key left an odd void in my life.

Tessa wasn't around my place. I ate bagels, glanced over the newspaper, and thought about things I might never have settled if I hadn't survived last night. I decided I had put off one personal problem for far too long. . . .

I found Glynis at her favorite little café. She sat in a booth by the windows reading her textbook as she nibbled on a salad. I watched for a moment, the little turmoil in my mind settling as I took the last steps and sat across the table from her.

"Summerfield!" She dropped the book and smiled before her expression turned to worry. "You look like you've been through hell!"

"The storm caught me last night," I said.

"You went out, even after you told me to stay in? Are

you crazy?"

"Yes, sometimes I am," I said with a nod of agreement.

She laughed and reached over to pat my hand. "I kind of thought that might be the case."

I ordered an iced tea and salad of my own, asked her about classes, and mainly skirted around what I'd come to tell her. She laughed, happy to see me. I watched her sipping her tea --

"My name is Sunflower Breeze Summerfield."

She coughed and sputtered tea everywhere as the woman arrived with my order.

"Good God!" She dabbed napkins on the table and stared at me, wide-eyed and face flushed. "You could have waited until I wasn't drinking tea to tell me!"

"Oh no," I replied, shaking my head. "This is the sort of thing which has to be told at *exactly* the right moment."

The waitress laughed. After she left, I found Glynis still staring at me.

"Sunflower," Glynis said the name for the first time. "Sunflower Breeze Summerfield. Well, at least I know why you go by your last name."

I nodded, and leaned forward, smiling as I took her hand. "My family owns more land and businesses in Nebraska than any other single family. My parents are the odd balls of the group. They're hippies and New Agers, and they travel the world visiting various shrines, living in villages far from civilization, and helping wherever they can. That's how I grew up, Glynis. I take classes at Creighton because they interest me. But I already have two degrees: Cultural Anthropology and Nuclear Physics. And I work for Wolton World News."

Her mouth opened, closed, opened. She shook her head, as though the facts I had told her wouldn't quite settle into place.

"You work for Woo Woo News?" she finally asked.

"Woo Woo News," I agreed. "And I work there because my parents asked me to help Julia Wolton out and because it's an interesting job."

"This is going to take some getting used to," she admitted.

"I know. But I thought --" I settled all the doubts in my mind and smiled. "Friday is one of my sister's birthdays, and I want you to come with me to the gathering. Afterwards, I thought we might drive down to Kansas City and spend a couple days enjoying ourselves."

"I can't afford --"

"I *can*. I don't do it often enough, and I don't want to go *alone*."

Her eyes blinked and her fingers tightened around mine. A smile. "I'd like to spend some time with you, Summerfield. Or should I call you Sunflower?"

"Summerfield," I said with an emphatic nod of my head.

And we both laughed.

I drove her to her dorm in the Mercedes. I think the car finally convinced her of the truth in what I'd said. I saw her watching and shaking her head as I drove away, but I felt better for having told her everything. Another weight had been lifted from me.

The day seemed normal, with a few scattered clouds in the sky as I drove to the office. City crews had carted away more fallen branches and I saw one glass truck outside a shop where men replaced the shattered window. I felt badly about the damage, knowing the weather had been part of the battle. I thought about what could have happened if we hadn't, somehow won. The paper hadn't reported any deaths and property could be repaired.

I parked in the lot and cast a nervous look towards the alley. How long until I quit worrying about trolls leaping out to attack me?

As though my life hadn't been odd enough already.

Julia smiled when I waved at her from the door to her office.

"Sorry I'm so late," I said.

"You work too hard anyway," she replied and sat some papers aside. "Besides, Tessa told me you both had a rough night with the storm."

"You've seen him today?"

"He's upstairs getting some cookies. He'll be down soon."

So, he hadn't gone back to the fae lands yet. What should I feel? Relief came first because I wanted to know what happened next. I wanted more answers. Worry grew in the next breath as I wondered what had gone wrong.

Jacobs sat at his desk, pounding away at the keyboard and muttering in anger. I didn't try to see what he wrote. I dropped into my chair and pulled out the laptop without greeting him. I had far too much on my mind already.

"Son of a bitch!" he shouted. "She can't do that to me!"

I glanced his way but said nothing. I didn't care about his tawdry little problems. Besides, something in my own email caught my attention. Julia had forwarded a note about someone spotting a huge lizard in Fontenelle Forest this morning.

Hell. What were they still doing there? Why hadn't the Dragon Clan gone back to the fae lands yet?

"Jacobs," Tessa said from the doorway. "There are sandwiches in Julia's office."

"Huh." Jacobs stood, shoving his chair back and stalked out of the room.

Tessa crossed to me and set a cup of tea by my computer. I nodded thanks and tapped the email on the screen.

"It's not safe for them to take Vane across yet," he explained softly as he leaned closer. "There's too much chaos on the other side and he's too young and weak. So, they'll remain here for a while."

"How long?"

"I don't know. I think part of the problem is also the dragon's ties to you and me. There's no way to break those bonds, by the way. We stood as part of the square at his hatching and that can't be undone. I talked to Brandis this morning and he's considering adoption into Dragon Clan."

"Me?"

"Both of us." He gave a sudden, bright laugh. "Oh and won't this cause a stir back home!"

"It's crazy!"

"Of course, it is."

The news made me happy, though. Crazy and happy. Even without the key, I still had links back to the fae.

"Any word on Gryn?" I dared ask.

"No," Tessa answered, his eyes narrowed. "But he can't hide forever."

I said nothing more as Jacobs returned with his sandwich, crossing to his desk, and glaring at both of us. He gobbled the food and went back to answering emails. Tessa pulled a chair over by me but didn't interfere in my work. I suspected he didn't have anywhere else to go.

Julia came in a little later, standing at the doorway.

"I have an announcement to make," Julia said. She glanced at Tessa who gave a quick nod. What the hell was this all about? She smiled. "Jacobs, you're fired."

Jacobs wasn't the only one shocked by the news.

"You can't --" he began, his face gone red and then white.

"Last I saw, I was the *Bossy*, wasn't I?" she asked and faced him down without any help from Tessa or me. "You are fired. I'd warned you more than once about your work ethics and manufacturing stories. The one you gave me yesterday was the last straw. Besides, the writing was crap."

"Shit. This paper wouldn't have anything if we didn't

make up the stories."

She lifted a hand, silencing him. "You're fired. Pack your personal belongings and leave."

"Son of a bitch!" He stood, and for a moment he looked frantic. "You can't do this. I need the money for my lawyer!"

"You'll have to find it somewhere else."

"I'm in the middle of a divorce!"

"I know. I talked to Pam yesterday. She's going to start working for me in a couple weeks."

"You can't give her my job!"

"No, not your job. She's actually going to *work* for her check. And she's going to take a job as a receptionist and clerk."

"You can't. I'll make you sorry you ever --"

Tessa stood and crossed the room to stand by Jacobs' desk. Jacobs cursed and began grabbing things. Julia went out and got him a box. I sat and watched in amazement. This was *Karma* at its full power: job lost, wife divorcing him. A lesson for us all, I thought, and began to think of some of the things for which I should make amends. I had already worked on my relationship with Glynis. I suspected my sisters would be next on the list. I tried not to wince.

"You can't run Woo Woo News with one local reporter to deal with all the material coming in," Jacobs said, standing with his box in hand. "And you're never going to get someone else to work for this joke of a newspaper."

"I already have someone new," Julia said with a bright smile.

I felt a new twinge of worry. Jacobs had been bad enough, but I hadn't thought about having to work with someone new. I tried not to think bad thoughts before the person started. Karma, karma, karma.

"You'll get some jerk off the street who doesn't know a thing," Jacobs predicted. He stalked to Julia, glaring at her, but he wouldn't do anything. I could see it in his stance. Jacobs had started his downward spiral, and he would hit rock bottom before too long. "You'll never get anyone as good as me."

"I don't know much about newspapers," Tessa replied, leaning on the desk which had been Jacobs' a moment before. "But I'm sure I'll learn quickly."

"You?" I asked, relief making me giddy. "You work here?"

"Yes." He grinned. Cheshire Cat, of course.

Well hell. I got the feeling things could get interesting.


THE END

# PREVIEW: SUMMERFIELD 2 -- AUTUMN WINDS

## CHAPTER 1

The email alert pinged, and I glanced at the inbox with a mixture of dread and disgust, seeing another note from a local. I sighed before I clicked open the message. Then I sighed again.

"Problems, Summerfield?" Tessa asked from the desk where he scribbled away on paper. Tessa and computers did not get along very well, which left me to deal with all the crazies who frequented the Weird World Web.

"Annoying stuff," I grumbled as I opened the note and read the first few lines. "More vampires spotted down in La Vista. I don't know why people think this is funny. I'd like to know who is behind this email campaign. I have enough real work to do."

I heard Tessa shift in his chair, and I glanced his way see him staring blankly at me. I knew that look: He had connected with something that wasn't part of the world as I knew it. Being fae, and the shape-shifting totem of the exiled Cat Clan, gave him certain powers I would never understand. However, I did appreciate them. I watched for a moment, waiting for what he had to say.

He shook his head and focused on me. "Things are weird out there."

"It's four days until Halloween. It always gets weird this time of year and I don't need you to tell me about it."

"You humans have strange customs."

"I won't argue with that one. Glynis and I are going to a costume party on Halloween. That should be fun," I said with obvious misgivings.

Tessa grinned and went back to his work. I glanced at the note about vampires. I couldn't just wave it off. I wrote a polite thank you and then turned my attention to the report of a lizard man living somewhere along the Amazon River. Oh yes, far more believable than vampires on Omaha's south side.

"I'm going to go upstairs for a while," Julia said from the doorway. "Let me know if anything interesting happens."

"I have another vampire report. You want to go check this one out?"

"Ha. If the weather didn't look so bad, I might be tempted. There's something in the air--" She stopped and frowned.

I nodded and glanced at Tessa who frowned again. I had the feeling there might really be something in the air. Well, maybe it meant things would get interesting --

*Hell.*

I tried to take that thought back. Never -- *NEVER* -- tempt fate and karma with a line like that one. I knew better! Now it was just a matter of before my unwise thought came and bit me in the ass. I even began to work a little faster at getting my article done so when trouble did hit, I'd be ready.

It's not that I think the universe pays an inordinate amount of attention to me. I'm just paranoid. However, because of my recent connection with the fae, I am also too well aware that things did happen around me. I had become a sort of godfather to a young dragon, having stood the square that kept him safe while he hatched. My friend and co-worker is the Cat Clan totem. We attracted oddness.

Karma didn't make me wait long today. I had just saved and started editing the Lizard Man article when the power flickered. In the next breath, magic surged through the building, the power so strong I felt it and got to my feet in a rush of panic. There should never have been that much magic in this world.

I had been tied to the Dragon Clan Key too long before I gave it back to them. The contact left me with a legacy to feel things most humans couldn't. Oddly, I'm glad; I don't mind knowing what's going on.

Tessa hadn't stood. He sat stone still, his eyes staring at the wall and his face pale. "Trouble," Tessa whispered. He looked at me and blinked several times. I didn't know if he really saw me or not, though.

"What's going on?" I finally asked, trying to keep my voice steady.

"Nothing good." He stood, but I could see he looked shaken. "Something is going on out there. It's disrupted magic everywhere. I can't find any of the others in this mess. I'm going to go out and look."

He hurried out of the room, moving so quickly that I feared he would change to his cat form before he even got to the door. I heard him say something to Pam Jacobs on his way past her little office and a moment later the door to the outside opened.

This couldn't be good. I wanted to be with Tessa and find out what had happened -- and part of me felt really annoyed that he'd run off and left me like this.

*Childish.* And stupid. I knew from Tessa's reaction this meant a hell of a lot of trouble, and something a powerless human should avoid. Maybe this time the problem would stay fully in the hands of the fae and not involve me --

The power flickered and went out. A heartbeat later, I heard the wind. I headed out to the front of the office as Julia came rushing downstairs. The storm had hit fast and strong: Wind blew rain almost horizontally up the street with a chaos of debris mixed in.

"They said we might have rain, but I didn't expect anything like this!" Julia exclaimed in shocked dismay. Pam joined us at the door, and we watched in silent awe until the front passed and the wind died back.

"The temperature has dropped." I put my hand to the glass of the door and felt the sting of cold and a frosty pattern formed around my fingers. I pulled away in haste. "A lot. I think the rain is going to turn to ice before long. This could be bad."

"You two need to go home," Julia said. "Lucky the printing crew isn't here today. It would be a waste with the power out anyway. Tessa --"

"He went out a couple minutes ago," I said. "He'll be fine."

Julia nodded. She never worried over Tessa. Without even knowing his secrets, she seemed to realize he could take care of himself.

"I'm going to wait and see if the weather clears a little." Pam stared out at the storm with worry, and I thought about her little rundown Toyota, parked in the lot beside my much-coveted (and hard to get since they went out of business) Hummer. I remembered feeling rather sorry for her car when I had pulled in this morning, as though the car could have feelings.

Maybe my thoughts had just been misplaced and it was Pam I felt sorry for, though I knew she did far better now than she had before she started the divorce against her husband, and my former fellow reporter, Ted Jacobs.

I looked at her worried face and smiled. "I'll drive you

home, Pam. No, don't argue. The Hummer can take on this weather without a problem."

"Oh no. It's not necessary --"

"It will make me feel better," I said and with enough sincerity that she looked startled. "Let me take you. You'll want to get to the day care in case the power is out there, too."

"Yes, that's true," she said and looked worried again. "I don't want to be a bother -- but thank you. Let me get my coat."

Julia patted me on the arm after Pam had left. Maybe I was reversing some of that bad Karma I had accidently pulled up earlier. I hoped so. As I looked out at the storm, I had the feeling I was going to need it.

"You're a good person, Summerfield," Julia said softly. "Thank you for taking care of Pam. She's been really worried lately. Jacobs is giving her grief over the divorce and the children. It's not right that he can cause her such trouble. She needs less stress over the things we can fix for her."

I nodded, but my attention turned back to the storm as the winds kicked up once more. This wasn't natural. Tessa had already known something was going wrong. While Julia looked out at the street, I peered up through the buildings to watch the sky. I thought I saw things moving there that had nothing to do with weather.

This was going to be a rough night.

# ABOUT THE AUTHOR:

Hello!

I am an eclectic and prolific author who publishes in many genres, including Contemporary Fantasy, Epic Fantasy, Science Fiction, Mystery and Young Adult adventures. While I started on the outer edges of traditional publication with sales to small press and magazine publishers, I have since moved most of my work to the Indie world, and I am madly in love with the new era of publishing and the direct contact with readers. Feel free to write me!

I live in Nebraska with my husband, my cats, and a small but entirely useless dog.

Connect with Zette:

Web Site: http://lazette.net

Facebook: http://www.facebook.com/lazette.gifford

Joyously Prolific Blog: http://zette.blogspot.com/